A Lady of Secret Devotion

LADIES *of* LIBERTY

A LADY *of* SECRET DEVOTION

TRACIE PETERSON

BETHANY HOUSE PUBLISHERS
Minneapolis, Minnesota

Cover design by Brand Navigation/Deanna Pierce
Author photo by Mark Dixon
Cover photography by Steve Gardner, PixelWorks Studios, Inc.

Published by Bethany House Publishers
11400 Hampshire Avenue South
Bloomington, Minnesota 55438

Bethany House Publishers is a division of
Baker Publishing Group, Grand Rapids, Michigan.

Printed in the United States of America

Library of Congress Cataloging-in-Publication Data

Peterson, Tracie.
A lady of secret devotion / Tracie Peterson.
p. cm. — (Ladies of liberty)
ISBN 978-0-7642-0532-3 (alk. paper) — ISBN 978-0-7642-0147-9 (pbk.)
1. Socialites—Fiction. 2. Philadelphia (Pa.)—History—19th century—Fiction.
I. Title.

PS3566.E7717L34 2008
813'.54—dc22

2008014237

To Cathy and Chris
Thanks for the laughter, the love
and the joy of our friendship.

TRACIE PETERSON is the author of over seventy novels, both historical and contemporary. Her avid research resonates in her stories, as seen in her bestselling HEIRS OF MONTANA and ALASKAN QUEST series. Tracie and her family make their home in Montana.

Visit Tracie's Web site at *www.traciepeterson.com*.

Books by Tracie Peterson

www.traciepeterson.com

A Slender Thread • *I Can't Do It All!***
What She Left For Me • *Where My Heart Belongs*

ALASKAN QUEST
Summer of the Midnight Sun
Under the Northern Lights • *Whispers of Winter*

BRIDES OF GALLATIN COUNTY
A Promise to Believe In

BROADMOOR LEGACY*
A Daughter's Inheritance • *An Unexpected Love*

BELLS OF LOWELL*
Daughter of the Loom • *A Fragile Design*
These Tangled Threads

LIGHTS OF LOWELL*
A Tapestry of Hope • *A Love Woven True*
The Pattern of Her Heart

DESERT ROSES
Shadows of the Canyon • *Across the Years*
Beneath a Harvest Sky

HEIRS OF MONTANA
Land of My Heart • *The Coming Storm*
To Dream Anew • *The Hope Within*

LADIES OF LIBERTY
A Lady of High Regard • *A Lady of Hidden Intent*
A Lady of Secret Devotion

WESTWARD CHRONICLES
A Shelter of Hope • *Hidden in a Whisper* • *A Veiled Reflection*

YUKON QUEST
Treasures of the North • *Ashes and Ice* • *Rivers of Gold*

*with Judith Miller   **with Allison Bottke and Dianne O'Brian

CHAPTER I

Philadelphia

April 1857

Cassandra Stover couldn't put the screams and sight of blood from her mind. The sounds and images had haunted her for the last three days, three days of torment and torture as she remembered the ten-year-old boy whose hand had been torn off by the iron teeth of a machine gear.

It had been Cassie's second day of work at the textile factory, but it also proved to be her last. She couldn't bear that such horrific accidents were seen as commonplace, yet most of the workers had continued with their duties. Only a few went to take charge of the child and whisk him away. Injuries were seen as just one more risk of employment.

"Still, I need a job," she told herself as she left the steps of Christ Church, where she'd just spent the last hour praying for guidance. Her mother and little sister, Elida, were depending on her. Now that Elida was nearly ten, she was old enough to help their mother with the family laundry service and Cassie could venture out to find a job that could offer even more money for their living expenses.

"The only problem is," she whispered to herself, "I'm not qualified for much of anything. My sewing is atrocious and my cooking, only fair."

She sighed and looked across the grassy park. The day was proving to be quite pleasant. Flowers bloomed, offering delicate touches of color against the new grass. The budding trees revealed new life, and the world seemed fresh and renewed.

Cassie strolled for some time before deciding to take a seat on one of the park benches. "Father, I don't understand what I am to do," Cassie said with a sigh. She glanced heavenward at the wispy white clouds and tried to imagine she could hear God answering her with some profound wisdom that would change her life.

She smiled to herself. *How silly I can be.* She recalled her childhood games of pretend when she would serve tea to Jesus and His disciples. Except, of course, for Judas. Giggling to herself, she recalled explaining to her mother that Judas didn't deserve tea and cookies. After all, he would betray Jesus. Her mother, however, explained that no one deserved to share tea and cookies with Jesus, but that everyone certainly needed to do so. After that, Cassie had set up another cup and saucer away from the other twelve. Judas could have his tea and cookies, but he would do so at another table.

Make-believe had accompanied Cassie most of her life. She had loved to pretend as a girl that she was a princess from a faraway country. She had dreamed of being rich and not merely the daughter of a modest merchant.

"Papa, if you were here, you would surely know what to suggest." Of course, if Papa were still alive, there would be no dilemma regarding their welfare.

Cassie heard noises behind her and fell silent. No sense in letting people believe her teched in the head. She bowed in prayer, pleading with God to see her need and answer her questions.

Her mother's laundry service had provided well enough since Cassie's father's death, now nearly ten years past. They weren't poverty stricken, yet providing for their needs was a constant concern. Everything good came with effort, her mother would often say, but Cassie worried that such effort was aging her mother before her time. Not only that, but from the moment her father had died, Cassie had longed to ease her mother's burden, to take her turn caring for the family. Finding another job would allow Cassie to do just that.

"Oh my."

Cassie raised her head and opened her eyes to find an elderly woman leaning heavily against the back of the bench. Stylishly dressed in a dark rose walking-out suit, the woman looked oddly familiar. Cassie immediately got to her feet and offered to help her sit.

"Are you all right?" she asked gently.

"Goodness, I believe I've walked too far today." She pulled a fan from her reticule and attempted to open it.

Cassie took the fan in her hand as recognition dawned. "Here, allow me." She opened it and let the air work to revive the woman before adding, "Aren't you Mrs. Jameston? We attend Christ Church, and I'm certain we've met before."

"Oh yes, you're Cassandra Stover. I know your mother, Dora, quite well. She has often helped with various church affairs."

Smiling, Cassie nodded. "That would be my mother. She loves to help others."

Mrs. Jameston smoothed out her jacket and closed her eyes for a moment. "I feel much revived. You are a good nurse, my dear."

"Well, please sit and rest for a while longer. I'll walk home with you when you are ready, but you mustn't press yourself too hard."

The older woman opened her eyes at this. "It seems I've been pressing too hard all of my seventy years. A habit that is difficult to break, for I come from stubborn stock."

Cassie grinned. "My mother says the same of me. I have a tendency to be opinionated, outspoken, and stubborn."

"Well, those traits can also be used for good," Mrs. Jameston replied. "I know that much firsthand, for they are also my own companions." She shifted and seemed to relax a bit more. "So tell me what you're doing here today. You looked as though you were praying."

"I was," Cassie answered. "I desperately need direction."

"God is the best to seek that from. But, pray tell, what would a young woman like you so desperately need at this juncture in her life?"

"I'm hardly that young anymore. I'm four and twenty, soon to be five and twenty. Since you know my mother, you know also that my father is deceased. We have worked to get by without him these last ten years. Everyone does their part, and that is why I was praying. My sister, Elida, is now old enough to help with the laundry service, and with summer approaching, she'll be out of school and able to help full time. I want to figure yet another way to support our household, but to be frank, I'm not good at anything."

Mrs. Jameston chuckled. "I seriously doubt that to be true."

"Well, I tried my hand at serving tables at one of the local eating establishments, but I was rather clumsy. I think all the noise and people caused me to be nervous. Then I tried working at the textile mill, but . . ." She shuddered and tried to block the ugly image from her imagination once again. "A little boy lost his hand. It was horrible."

"Oh, my dear child, I cannot even imagine how terrible that must have been for you." Mrs. Jameston patted Cassie's arm in sympathy.

"I knew I couldn't work there," Cassie said, shaking her head. "Now I'm not sure what to do. You would think that God might have gifted me with more beneficial accomplishments, but perhaps that is my own fault. I never cared much for mending, even though there was always a great deal to do. I can iron well, but there aren't all that many opportunities for such a thing, unless you also make a good cleaning maid."

Cassie looked at the woman and smiled. "Have you ever met anyone quite so hopeless?"

"You are hardly hopeless, child. Besides, I believe I might have a solution."

"I doubt it." She clapped her hand to her mouth, then lowered it gingerly. "I'm so sorry. See what I mean? I tend to speak without thinking."

Mrs. Jameston laughed. "I am not in the leastwise offended. My dear, what I have in mind will benefit us both. I am a lonely old lady. I have one living child who rarely gives me more than a moment of his time, and that is only in order to get money from me. He's a scallywag to be sure. Then, of course, there are the servants. They have been with me for years and are dear folks, but I need a companion. I like you, Cassie Stover, and I believe you could easily be that very person."

"But what would I do as your companion?" All sorts of thoughts danced through Cassie's head. Perhaps a companion was simply a nice way of saying maid or nurse. "I'm hardly trained to care for the sick."

"And I am hardly in need of a nurse," Mrs. Jameston said. "I'm talking about a friend—someone to live in my house and keep me company. Can you read and write?"

"Yes. I read all the time. I had to leave school at sixteen, but I've kept up with my reading by visiting the library every week."

"See there—you could read to me and write my letters. My eyes are failing me, and I cannot do close-up work like I once could."

Cassie smiled. "I think such a situation sounds too good to be true," she said. "You hardly would need to hire me to be your friend. I'd be happy to come visit you on occasion."

"That is kind of you," Mrs. Jameston replied, "but I want someone who would live with me. As I get older, my feet are less steady, and as you have just witnessed, I often overdo. As my companion, you could help to keep me in line." She smiled rather conspiratorially and added, "Or at least enjoy the adventure with me."

Cassie laughed. "I think I would like that very much. I hadn't thought of living elsewhere, but I'm certain my mother would understand."

"It's settled, then. Walk home with me, and let me show you around. You can decide for yourself once you see my house." She got up and immediately Cassie rose as well.

"Let me help you," Cassie said, offering her arm. "I wouldn't want you to overdo again."

Mrs. Jameston allowed Cassie to assist her. They strolled slowly in the opposite direction Cassie would take to go home. No doubt Mrs. Jameston lived in a more elegant part of town.

"I love Philadelphia in the springtime," Mrs. Jameston said as they walked. "My husband, Worther Jameston, God rest his soul, loved to walk with me this time of year. I suppose that is what caused me to cast aside the better sense I usually display and set out by myself."

"It's my favorite time too," Cassie told her. "A time of renewal."

"Indeed. I have seen so many springs," Mrs. Jameston admitted. "I'm not sure to see many more, but with each one, I find that I appreciate the colors and scents more than ever. There is a garden at my house; you'll spend plenty of time there if you decide to work for me. There are wonderful rosebushes and lilacs, and a bevy of other flowering plants. My man Wills is quite expert in keeping the yard in bloom. It looks festive and peaceful but also fills the air with sweet smells."

"I shall look forward to seeing it," Cassie said, trying to picture the variety.

"I have benches and chairs out there and frankly spend far more time outdoors than in, when the weather permits. I seldom leave Philadelphia, even during the heat of summer."

"What of the epidemics?" Cassie wondered aloud.

"Sickness is everywhere. We try to take precautions, but I will not give myself over to worry. We often traveled during the summers when Mr. Jameston was with me. Perhaps, if you agree to be my companion, we can take a few trips as well. I've not traveled in years." Mrs. Jameston gazed ahead. "My house is just up the street. The last one on the right."

Cassie caught a glimpse of the impressive four-story brick structure as they drew near. "It's beautiful," she exclaimed. "The homes on this street are so grand."

Mrs. Jameston paused at the drive. "Sadly, it doesn't feel quite as much like a home anymore as it does a museum. As I mentioned before, my son Sebastian is seldom here, but when he is, he gives no thought to others. I find most days, I simply wander the rooms until I grow bored, then take myself outdoors."

Cassie felt sorry for Mrs. Jameston. Here she was with her money and her beautiful home, yet there was no happiness in her voice. She was lonely and idle—and Cassie wondered if she was merely waiting to die.

The drive stretched alongside a beautifully manicured lawn. The grass had greened in the warmth of early spring, and along the walkway were tulips of various colors. The sight was cheery and bright, yet a palpable sorrow seemed cast over the entire place.

Mrs. Jameston smiled as she opened the front door. "I hope you like it."

Cassie stepped inside the house and stared in wonder. Many times in her life she had walked past the houses of the wealthy and wondered what she might find inside. Now here she was.

The foyer was large with a highly polished tile floor. The walls were covered in a gold-patterned paper that gave the room an air of elegance. There wasn't a hint of dust on any of the paintings or furnishings, and everything smelled of wood oil and lemon.

"Ah, here's Brumley," Mrs. Jameston announced.

Cassie noted the man appeared to be in his late fifties. He was dressed in a dark suit that had been tailored to fit him some twenty pounds ago. Still, he carried a look of refinement as he gave the ladies a curt bow. "Madam," he said, acknowledging Mrs. Jameston.

"Brumley, this is Miss Stover. We attend church together, and I have asked her to become my companion and live here with us. She is considering the idea at present."

Cassie couldn't be sure, but it seemed a look of relief passed over the man's features. He straightened his snug coat.

"I'm pleased to meet you, Miss Stover. Please let me know if I might be of assistance."

Cassie nodded. "Thank you. It's very nice to meet you, Mr. Brumley."

"Brumley has been with me for more years than either of us care to own," Mrs. Jameston said with a smile. "Now come, Cassandra. I will show you around."

Boston

Marcus Langford looked up from the paper gripped tightly in his hand and frowned. "If only Richard would have communicated more often. I have his latest letter, but that's nearly a week old."

"Does it offer anything useful?" Nelson Stafford asked as he took a chair opposite Mark's desk. As head of United American Mariner's Insurance, Nelson had been equally grieved to learn of Richard's death while investigating a case of suspected fraud.

"Time and again the same name is mentioned whenever Richard was able to convince someone to talk." Mark slammed his fist on the desk. "I'm certain the man must be involved in his death. I intend to figure it out for myself and see that he pays for what he's done."

"Are you sure you can be objective about this, Mark?"

"I can," he assured, "but I cannot be without feeling. Richard was a good friend."

"To both of us," Nelson said, leaning forward. The three men had worked hard to help make United American Mariner's Insurance a successful company. Nelson's brown eyes seemed to bore into Mark's soul. "I want to catch the person or persons responsible as much as you do."

Mark leaned back, nodding. "I know that, and I didn't mean to imply otherwise. I'm going to leave for Philadelphia in the morning. I will find Rich's killer. I promise you that much."

CHAPTER 2

Philadelphia

"Mrs. Jameston has hired you?" Dora Stover asked her daughter.

Cassie laughed at her mother's surprise. "Yes. She said she needed a companion—a friend. I told her she needn't hire me to be her friend, as I would happily do that anyway, but she insisted. She wants me to move in immediately."

She pulled a small carpetbag from beneath her bed. "I know it's unexpected, but the pay will be such a help. I can't bear to work in the factories. And with Elida's help with the laundry service, you should be able to get by without me. Since I'll be living with Mrs. Jameston, you will have my portion of food as well."

Her mother sat on the edge of the bed. "We've hardly been starving, Cassie. I knew you were hoping to find a position, but I hadn't expected that finding one would take you from the house. It will be hard to have you gone. I'll worry about you."

Cassie went to her mother and smoothed back an errant strand of graying brown hair. "You mustn't worry over me. I will come home to visit as often as possible. Mrs. Jameston said I may have Saturdays off to be with you. I can also help with the laundry if there is too much for you to handle. And of course we will all be in church together on Sundays."

"Oh, I know all of that," her mother replied, taking hold of her daughter's hand. "I'm just surprised."

Cassie sat down beside her. "I won't take the job if you'd rather I not." It hadn't occurred to Cassie until just that moment that perhaps her mother was afraid to live there without her eldest daughter.

"I wouldn't dream of it. It's definitely an answer to prayer. The extra money will help to make repairs on the house. We've long neglected our sweet refuge."

A quick glance around the room at the sorry state of peeling wallpaper and chipped paint on the window frames proved that much. And that was just at first glance; Cassie knew that the chimneys were in need of repair, as was the roof.

"We shall soon see the house set to rights," Cassie promised. "Not only that, but there should be money enough to buy some new clothes for Elida. She can hardly continue to wear my old rags."

"I know you're right. Mrs. Jameston has a generosity of spirit that is unmatched by any woman I know. She will be good to you, I've no doubt. I suppose I shall have to endure missing your company."

"Why will we miss Cassie's company?" Elida asked as she bounded into the room. She spied the carpetbag. "Where are you going?"

"I have a new job," Cassie replied. She got up and went to the dresser to gather her clothes. "I am moving to Mrs. Jameston's house to become her companion. You will need to come home quickly after school each day and help Mama with the laundry."

Elida frowned. "I don't want you to go. I'll be afraid to sleep here by myself. You know how noises frighten me, and Mama is so delicate. You said so yourself."

Their mother looked at Cassie oddly. "Delicate? You described me as delicate?"

"You are delicate, Mama." Her cheeks flushed. "Father always said so. He said you were like a delicate flower."

Her mother snickered as if it were an old joke. "He also said I was as stubborn as a mule. I hope you won't start calling me one now, however."

Elida put her hand to her forehead as if she were about to swoon. "It will be ever so terrible without you here. Who will read to me?"

"I'm certain that while Cassie is a superior reader," their mother interjected, "I am quite capable of sharing a good book with you, Elida."

"But this room is so big and at night it will be so empty without you." Elida looked at Cassie with her eyes wide. "What if I get sick? What if I have a fit of apoplexy?"

Cassie laughed at her sister's dramatics. "Do you even know what a fit of apoplexy is?"

"Well, it must be truly bad, because Mrs. Radisson has such fits all of the time, and she is often too ill to attend to her family." Elida crossed her arms and shook her head. "I do not think you should go."

"Even if I did not move to Mrs. Jameston's house," Cassie began, "I believe I would move to another room and give you more space."

She and Elida had shared the large bedroom to conserve on heat. They each had their own bed and dresser, with Elida's side of the room also strewn with dolls and mementos that were precious to a young girl. "You're nearly grown and you need a room all to yourself. I was going to suggest as much on your birthday. You needn't be afraid."

"But I will be," Elida insisted. "I don't want you to leave." She came and wrapped her arms around Cassie's waist. "Sometimes I wake in the night and hear creaking upstairs. I start to worry about it, but then I see you sleeping so peacefully that I know everything is all right or you would surely be awake too. Now you'll be gone, and I'll have to face that all alone."

Putting aside her clothes, Cassie sat down with Elida. "I will be back for visits, but you must be brave. The house creaks and groans because it's old. This job will allow us to make proper repairs. It might also allow us to buy you some new clothes." She looked at the pale blue dress Elida wore. It had once belonged to Cassie and had been made over for her little sister. The years had taken their toll on the gown. "You've seldom had a new frock. Just think of it. A dress that no one else has ever worn but you."

"Your sister is right, Elida. You're growing so tall, we definitely need to find you some new clothes. I, too, will miss our Cassie, but I am not so delicate as you girls have portrayed me. Goodness, but you would think I was incapable of getting out of bed on my own in the morning."

"But Papa always told me to watch over you when he had to be away," Cassie said.

"And because of that, you believe yourself responsible for me—for this house—for your sister," her mother said softly. She shook her head and smiled. "I am a grown woman—your mother. It is my duty to see to your needs, not the other way around. Elida and I will be fine here, but we will miss you dearly. The day will not be the same without your chatter and sweet spirit."

Looking at her mother's bittersweet smile was nearly Cassie's undoing. "Both of you must stop!" she said, getting to her feet. "We're all being silly about this. It's not like I'm moving across the sea. Mrs. Jameston lives but two miles away, and she promised that you may visit as often as you like. Now, please bring those shawls over here, Elida." Cassie pointed to two neatly folded wraps on her dresser. Her sister did as directed.

"Does she live in a very fine house?" Elida asked in a pout.

"She does indeed. Her house is very grand, and the servants are quite kind. You will enjoy visiting me there."

"But I won't be able to tell you about my day at school."

"Elida, sometimes these things must happen. Besides, school is nearly complete for the summer," their mother said rather sadly. "One day, none of this will matter. You will both grow up and marry and leave home to make new lives with families of your own. I will not always have my girls with me. I think we should be very happy for Cassie, for it will benefit us as much as it does her." She got to her feet. "I must go now and check on the stew. Elida, you make yourself useful to Cassie."

"I will," the girl promised, still clutching the shawls.

Cassie went to their wardrobe and took out her well-worn gowns. They hardly seemed the quality that a companion to Mrs. Jameston would wear, but they would have to do.

"You won't forget us?" Elida questioned as she toyed with one of the fringed wraps.

"Of course not, you goose. I love you and Mama too much to ever forget you."

Elida sighed and plopped down on the bed. "I wish Father might have lived. I would not be afraid if he were here. You were always so brave."

Cassie looked at her little sister and felt a sorrow she could not put into words. Elida had been born only a few weeks before their father's death. Elida had never known him as Cassie had. Cassie had adored him and told Elida stories of her girlhood when their father would take her on long walks or tell her wonderful tales of when he'd been a boy.

"You must remember, Elida, that while Father cannot be here, Mother is. She is right, you know. She's a strong woman. And not only is she here for you, but Jesus is as well. He is with us every day. He never leaves us. You aren't alone, and if you remember that, you will be so much braver. Now, hand me the shawls."

Elida nodded and walked to where Cassie stood. "Mama says that, too, but sometimes I cannot help it."

Reaching for her wraps, Cassie nodded. "I know. I cannot help it at times, myself."

The servants were hard at work putting the finishing touches on Cassie's room when she returned to the Jameston house. Mrs. Dixon, the housekeeper, led her up the stairs and explained that while rooms for the rest of the staff were on the upper two floors, Cassie's room would be on the second floor, in a room adjoining Mrs. Jameston's.

Cassie stepped inside and gasped, overwhelmed. The room was furnished with a large canopied bed, beautiful damask draperies, and a variety of tables and chairs. In front of an ornately carved fireplace sat a lovely sofa in blue silk upholstery. A large armoire of cherry wood stood at the far end of the room, where a small alcove offered a dressing table and other amenities. "This must be a mistake."

"There's no mistake. I hope you like it," Mrs. Jameston said as she joined them. "It once belonged to my mother. She was only with us a few years before her death, and the room has remained unoccupied until now."

"It's wondrous," Cassie said, still taking in the vision before her. "I have never seen anything so beautiful."

"I'm glad you think so. Since it adjoins my room, I thought it a perfect place for you. That way, should I need you in the night, you will be very close."

"That does sound wise," she agreed. Another woman entered the room and offered Cassie a smile.

"This is Ada," Mrs. Jameston explained. "She is my personal maid and will now work for you as well."

Cassie stammered. "But . . . I . . . ah . . ."

Mrs. Jameston laughed. "You must understand that while you are here, you will be treated as a member of my family. I have instructed my staff to consider you as my granddaughter. Ada is quite talented at dressing hair and preparing clothes."

Cassie touched a hand to her own golden brown hair. The simple bun she'd created by pinning up her long, straight strands was no doubt offering a poor image.

"I'm pleased to meet you, Miss Stover," Ada said. As if reading her thoughts, she added, "We'll soon have everything set right."

"Please call me Cassie. I couldn't bear to be called Miss Stover all the time."

Ada looked to Mrs. Jameston, who smiled and nodded. "I believe that would be acceptable in private. In public, though, you will simply have to get used to the idea. You are, after all, a lady of quality."

"More like a lady of pretense." Cassie slapped her hand to her mouth, knowing she had spoken out of line. Mrs. Jameston, however, only laughed.

"Child, you are a beautiful young woman. No one will mistake you for being anything other than that. There is no pretense in that fact."

"I pray I don't prove to be otherwise—for your sake, Mrs. Jameston." Cassie opened her bag and took out her well-worn gowns. "I wonder if I might have an iron so that I can see to these."

"Give them to Ada. She'll have Essie see to them," Mrs. Jameston said. Then she surprised Cassie by coming closer and fingering the material. "You will need some new clothes.

I often have to attend various social functions and would want you to accompany me. Ada, tomorrow measure Cassie for new gowns."

"Oh, but I couldn't . . ." Cassie paused, trying to think of how she might explain that she couldn't spare the money for such things.

Mrs. Jameston seemed to immediately understand. "I can well afford to dress you in an appropriate manner, fear not." She smiled. "Consider it your uniform, my dear."

Cassie nodded. "I never thought about my appearance. I apologize."

"Nonsense. Trust the matter to me, and we'll soon have you appropriately attired. In fact, Ada, I want you to go to the dressmaker's straightaway tomorrow after you get the measurements. I know it is Saturday, but I believe Sadie can offer us some ready-made things. Have her put it on my account."

"Yes, ma'am," Ada said.

Later that night, Cassie slid between the delicately embroidered sheets of her bed. For the first time in ten years, she slept on sheets she hadn't had to iron for herself. The large down-filled mattress cushioned her weight, and Cassie couldn't help but utter a sigh at the luxury of it all.

All the games of make-believe from her childhood could not begin to equal the reality that she now enjoyed. She truly felt like a queen, and with a yawn, it was only a matter of moments before she drifted into a very pleasant sleep.

The morning came sooner than expected, and Cassie found herself surprised at the sight of Ada pushing open the draperies. Hadn't she just closed her eyes?

"Good morning, Cassie. I hope you slept well."

"I did," Cassie admitted, sitting up.

"I thought you might care for a bath. I've prepared one for you, just in case."

"Oh my! That was so very thoughtful."

Ada brought a lovely velvet dressing gown to Cassie. "Mrs. Jameston said this would serve you until we could arrange for a new one."

Cassie got up and allowed Ada to assist her into the robe. "It's lovely. Much nicer than anything I've ever known."

"It's one of Mrs. Jameston's. She's shorter than you, of course, so the robe is hardly long enough, but it fits well in every other aspect. Now, if you'll follow me, I'll show you to the bath. It's just on the other side of your room."

Cassie followed Ada to the beautifully ordered bathroom. A large tub, already filled with hot water, awaited her attention, while on a stand beside the tub were bath salts, lotions, and oils.

"I wasn't sure what scents you might care for, but I added some rose oil to the water."

"How wonderful." Cassie noted a large stand with a bowl and pitcher, as well as a beautiful oval mirror on the wall.

"If you'd like my assistance in bathing," Ada began, "I can certainly stay."

Cassie laughed. "No. I am quite capable of seeing to my own bath. In fact, I hardly expect you to draw a bath for me each time. This is a definite pleasure, however."

Ada smiled. "Mrs. Jameston wants you to feel like family, and I'm happy to help. She has always treated me well. I have never known her to be anything but kind and considerate." She paused, as if trying to decide whether to continue. "Forgive me for speaking out of line, but lately she has been quite lonely. I think your presence has already helped her."

"I hope so," Cassie said. "I find her easy to be with. Nevertheless, I hope you and I shall also be good friends." Cassie lowered her voice. "I know she wants me treated like a grand lady, but, Ada, I'm just like you. I'm accustomed to working to earn my keep."

Ada nodded. "I understand. And I would very much like for us to be friends."

An hour later, with her hair carefully styled, Cassie joined Mrs. Jameston for breakfast. The older woman looked up as she entered the dining room and smiled.

"You are radiant this morning, Cassandra. I hope you rested well."

"How could I not?" Cassie replied, taking the chair offered her at Mrs. Jameston's right. "The bed was like sleeping on air."

"I'm glad to know it. Are you hungry?"

Cassie looked down at the beautifully set table. The delicate china bore a floral pattern and gold trim around the edges. It seemed quite appropriate for Mrs. Jameston's table. "I am hungry," she finally answered. She fingered the embroidered linen napkin and marveled at the handiwork before placing it on her lap.

Mrs. Jameston motioned and a serving girl poured hot tea. "I wasn't sure," Mrs. Jameston said, "if you took tea or coffee. I, myself, prefer tea."

"As do I. I find coffee a bit strong for my taste."

Just then another servant entered and brought two silver compotes of fresh fruit. One was placed in front of Cassie and the other in front of Mrs. Jameston. Luscious red strawberries swam in a golden syrup alongside yellow pieces of fruit that Cassie didn't recognize.

"I wanted to offer you something very special."

"I recognize the strawberries, although to have them so early is such a treat. But," Cassie looked at the yellow fruit and smiled, "I have no idea about the other pieces."

"That would be pineapple from the West Indies," Mrs. Jameston told her. "I hope you find it to your liking. First, however, I will offer grace." She bowed her head and began to pray before Cassie could even close her eyes.

"Father, we give thee glory and praise for another day of life. We thank thee for thy bounty, and for the gracious mercy thou hast shown us. Amen."

"Amen," Cassie said, looking up. She watched as Mrs. Jameston picked up a small fork and began to sample the fruit. Cassie quickly did likewise.

The flavor was unlike anything she'd ever known. The strange pieces were remarkably chilled, yet tasted as though they'd come straight in from the garden. They were sweet, but tangy, and she found the combination much to her liking. Within moments the fruit was consumed and the servants were bringing new dishes to the table. Pastries were set before her that looked so light and flaky Cassie could only marvel at them for several moments before choosing. She was not disappointed by the buttery richness.

"I must say, my dear, I slept better last night just knowing you were here. I think God has provided for us both."

"I'm glad," Cassie replied. She sampled the sausage on her plate and nodded her approval. "This is quite delicious."

"It seems eating is one of the few pleasures left me." The older woman took up a cinnamon scone, then motioned the servant to pour more tea.

Cassie could scarcely take it all in. "Everything is so good. I'm used to having only oatmeal or toasted bread for breakfast."

"I enjoy oatmeal on occasion. We shall certainly have it from time to time."

"Don't bother on my account," Cassie said without thinking. She smiled in apology. "What else do you enjoy?"

Mrs. Jameston considered her words for a moment. "I love to take walks, but I fear my health is not up to great distances anymore. Carriage rides will perhaps be their replacement. I enjoy my garden, as I mentioned yesterday. I would love to read there but find my eyes grow tired so quickly."

"I shall be happy to read to you there. What kind of books do you enjoy?"

"I find myself capable of enjoying a great variety. Of course, I love the Bible. The stories of history, as well as the guidance I find there, encourage me and keep me directed on the right path. But I also enjoy other works. I have very much enjoyed Nathaniel Hawthorne's stories, as well as Dickens and Cooper. I recently read Thackeray's *Vanity Fair* and was less impressed, but was quite fond of Charlotte Bronte's *Jane Eyre*."

"I've read that one as well. I thought it a compelling story," Cassie admitted. "I was upset by some turn of events, but overall satisfied in the end."

"As was I. It portrayed a definite understanding that often life is not what it should be."

"Have you read Elizabeth Wetherell's *The Wide, Wide World*?" Cassie asked.

"No. Perhaps that can be our first to share."

Cassie nodded. "It's a wonderful story about a young woman named Ellen Montgomery. I think you shall like it very much."

"Then I will give you money to secure us a copy. We will do that right away. Now tell me, did Ada get your measurements this morning?"

"Yes. She took them right after my bath."

"Good." Mrs. Jameston turned her attention back to her plate but continued to speak. "I want you to feel as if this is your home, Cassie. It's important to me. I have instructed the staff to treat you as they would me. In turn, I hope you will not mind if I take to directing you in the ways of my society. I do not mean to imply they are better than yours, nor to belittle what you have known as your own place in the world. However, it is my hope that I might better you in some way."

"Your friendship will surely do that," Cassie replied. "Not to mention that my mother and sister will benefit from your generous pay to me. My mother already spoke highly of you, but now she believes you to be very nearly angelic in nature."

Mrs. Jameston laughed. "It is your mother who would fill that role, for a more patient and loving woman I have never known. She has often helped with tireless efforts whenever there was work to be done at the church. Her compassion never fails to bless me."

"My mother is a good woman," Cassie agreed. "She has suffered much in life, but maintains a cheerful disposition. My sister and I have been quite blessed."

"Well, in turn, I'm convinced that we can bless her. I would like very much to know what her needs are. As I've said before, I have more than I need. It would do me good and please me greatly to bless someone less fortunate."

Cassie reached out and boldly patted Mrs. Jameston's hand. "You have done just that by hiring me here. I see a new hope for my family, and I know that God has brought us together for just such a purpose."

"Family is very important, Cassie. Never forget that. I'm afraid that is an area in which I failed." Her expression grew sober. "I am only now seeing just how many mistakes I have made."

"Mother says we all make mistakes—even when we have the best of intentions. Please share with me about your family. I know that you have a son. Why don't you tell me about him?"

"Because he's a great disappointment to me, and I'd rather not ruin our lovely breakfast." Mrs. Jameston turned her attention back to her plate. "Sebastian has offered me nothing but pain of late, and we'd all be better off to forget him."

CHAPTER 3

Boston

Mark looked at the food on his plate and pushed it back. The lamb was roasted to perfection, but it tasted like sawdust in his mouth. He turned an apologetic gaze to his mother as he threw his napkin on his parents' table.

"I'm afraid I have no appetite."

"Son, you mustn't take Richard's death so hard," his mother said, reaching out to give his arm a sympathetic pat. "He wouldn't want you to grieve so."

"Your mother is right," Mark's father replied.

"I know," Mark said. "I know that very well. That's why I'm going to go to Philadelphia."

His mother gasped and put her hand to her throat. "What? You're going to Philadelphia? Surely you cannot mean it. Look how dangerous it was for Richard!"

"That's exactly why I have to go," Mark said, shaking his head. "Someone has to be willing to fight for what's right. Richard was doing an honorable service. In turn I will do the honorable thing for him. I will see his killer brought to justice."

"Son, this is hardly an appropriate time or place for such a conversation," his father said, frowning. "You're upsetting your mother."

Mark got to his feet. "I'm sorry. I knew coming here would be a bad idea, but I wanted to tell you of my plans and see you before I left. I take the train in the morning."

"This is so abrupt. Are you certain it's wise?" his mother asked. "Richard hasn't even been gone ten days."

"I know, but the longer I delay, the better chance his killer has of getting away with the deed. Worse still, he could take someone else's life."

"But that someone could be you, Marcus." His mother's eyes filled with tears. "I could not bear to lose you."

"I know the risks at hand, Mother. Try not to worry." Mark pushed in his chair. "I have to do this. I have to avenge Richard. He would do the same for me."

His mother sniffed and dabbed at her eyes. "Oh, I do wish your brothers lived closer. They might talk some sense into you."

"This isn't a matter of not being sensible. I have a job to do. It just so happens that job will also see justice done for my friend. Whether Richard had died or not, I'd still be working to figure out the missing cargoes and insurance claims." Mark could see the worry in his parents' expressions and offered them a weak smile. "I promise I will not risk myself in an unwarranted manner. I will be wise."

Mark thought of that promise hours later in his own home as he set aside his packed valise. The entire project would warrant a risk, but there was no sense telling his parents.

The clock struck nine and the echoing of the chimes reinforced Mark's loneliness. At least sleep would hopefully free him from the intense solitude he endured.

He walked to the fireplace and put on another log. Though the days had been quite warm, the night air held a chill. He poked the wood until the fire blazed up. How many fires had he made at this hearth? How many days had passed since he and Ruth had called this house home?

Looking across the room at a small framed painting of his deceased wife, Mark knew a deep, abiding emptiness in his heart. Ruth had been his childhood sweetheart. They had been nearly inseparable until cholera claimed her life. Mark, too, had nearly died from the epidemic. He had thought God rather cruel to take his beloved Ruth, leaving him behind to bear the loss.

Now, seven years after the fact, the pain had eased considerably. He missed her—missed her smiles and her sweet words. Missed the way she looked after him and doted on him. His mother said he needed to marry again, and in truth, Mark was compelled to do just that. But whenever he began to share the company of the local women, he found either haunting reminders of his dead wife or disinterest.

A knock at the front door drew his thoughts from the past. Opening it, he found his father, hat in hand and a look of concern on his face.

"Might I come in?"

"Of course. It's quite late for you to be out and about the town, however," Mark said, ushering his father inside. "I was just about to retire."

"I couldn't sleep. I knew I had to see you before you left for Philadelphia," his father replied.

Mark noted the tired, even worried expression on his father's face. "You sound concerned."

His father took a chair and nodded. "I am exactly that." He raised his hand as Mark started to speak. "Please hear me out. I'm not here to try to talk you out of going, but rather to encourage caution on your part. Whoever killed Richard Adkins obviously has no qualms about breaking the law. I fear this person would not hesitate to do so again, should he feel the threat to his industry."

"I agree. In fact, I've already decided to take an entirely different approach. Richard gave us a name—a single name. I'm going to start by learning all I can about that man. Richard focused on the docks and the cargoes. I plan to focus on Sebastian Jameston."

"I hope, for your sake, you will also focus on God's direction."

Mark frowned. He hadn't meant to. He knew it wouldn't be taken well by his father. Theodore Langford believed strongly that God controlled man's destiny and that man had only to seek Him out to know what direction he should take. Mark had felt the same way at one time. Now, however, he only felt confused.

"Mark, I cannot understand what you are thinking, but I'm convinced it isn't what it should be."

"I'd rather not discuss it, if you don't mind." Mark turned away and pretended to attend to the fire once again.

"I do mind. You know very well that I do."

Mark turned to see his father. By the set of his jaw and the way he had squared his shoulders, Mark knew he intended to speak his mind. With a sigh, Mark sat down and waited for his father to do likewise. There was no telling how long this would take, and Mark had no desire to see it continue even a moment longer than necessary.

"I know you feel that God has somehow betrayed your faith in Him," his father began. "I sympathize and tell you that I do understand. I have walked that road myself. So much in our world—in our lives—seems so senseless. We cannot understand the things we are forced to endure."

"Even when I pretend to understand," Mark said, sending his gaze back to the fire, "I find no relief or comfort."

"God doesn't ask you to merely pretend," his father countered. "He has no need for it. He already knows your heart. He knows all."

"Which makes it particularly hard to understand why He would allow Richard to die. He knew Richard was working for a greater good. God knew the job we had was to overcome the evil plans of someone who obviously had no concern for God or His ways. I grow weary of trusting and having faith when wrong continues to prevail and innocent people are cut down in the prime of their lives."

"This world is a battleground," his father said softly. "The battle is the Lord's."

Mark jumped to his feet in anger. "Then perhaps He should start fighting instead of sitting idly by. Please understand, Father, I have no desire to blaspheme God. I simply do not understand why this has happened or why my best friend lies in a cold grave, three blocks away."

His father seemed to consider his words for several minutes. Mark thought he might find the conversation useless and go, although there was a part of him that hoped his father would continue.

Tell me I'm wrong, Mark whispered in the depths of his heart. *Offer me proof that my thoughts are false. Show me somehow that my faith can be restored when all I feel is loss and grief and pain.*

"Mark, anger is marring your ability to think clearly. I fear it will cause you to act rashly or make improper judgments. Anger is not in and of itself wrong; even the Bible speaks of being angry, but not sinning. Your anger is justified. It speaks to the depth of love you hold for your friend. However, there is such a narrow path, and to step into sin, compelled by that anger, is quite easy. Not only that, but to venture to the other side of that same narrow path is to lose your ability to reason and focus. There you will find a consuming self-pity that will keep you from making any proper and reasonable decision."

The words were driven deep into Mark's conscious mind. He had fully expected his father to chastise his disrespectful comment about God standing idle, but instead, Father, being the wisest man Mark knew, had figured to appeal to another side of the matter. Mark could easily see how all issues tied together.

He blew out a long breath. "I know you are right." He shrugged and offered his father a sheepish grin. "What is the sense of being thirty and two if I still reason and act as one a score of years younger?"

His father chuckled and got to his feet. "Son, I have often asked God that question on my own behalf. I know you feel abandoned by God, and it is that very issue that drives your anger, more than anything. I only ask that you consider the situation for what it is. Richard's death was a tragedy, but there are dark forces at work in this world. We must not leave the authority and protection of God's truth, even if it does cost us our lives, as it sometimes does. Richard felt he was fighting to see good overcome evil. Now you will take up that fight. I simply plead with you to consider what that fight is really about, and who it is that might help you most in winning such a battle."

Mark heard the longing in his father's voice and knew that he desperately needed assurance. Reaching out, Mark hugged his father tightly. "I will be careful. I promise you that I will put my anger aside and do what is necessary to handle the matter with a clear mind."

His father pulled away and met his gaze. "I will pray for you every day. I know that you must go and do this thing, but I wish it were otherwise. Please let us know how things are going. Keep us apprised, or we will worry overmuch."

Mark nodded. "I will. I promise."

He walked his father to the door and bid him farewell. Watching the older man walk down the pathway to his waiting carriage caused Mark a twinge of something akin to regret. He would have loved to have given his father complete peace about the entire situation, but he knew there was no chance of turning back now. They were in too deep. They needed to follow through. Richard's sacrifice would not be in vain.

"So long as there is breath in my body, I will see this through to completion," Mark vowed.

Philadelphia

The pain was more than Sebastian Jameston could bear. He allowed his friend Robbie to treat the wound, but only because going to a doctor would arouse suspicions. Gunshot wounds always did.

"It's actually better," Robbie said as he worked to remove bits of bandage from the oozing flesh. "I think what you need, however, is a great deal of time off your leg and good care."

"Fine." Sebastian spat out the word from between clenched teeth.

"At least you're not as bad off as you could be," Robbie chuckled. "That Boston fellow won't be stirring up any more trouble for you."

"Maybe not, but they will surely send someone else. We'll have to change some of our methods and plans."

"Perhaps," Robbie suggested, "it's time for a new scheme."

Sebastian eased back against the pillow and pulled a bottle of whiskey to his mouth. He took a long drink, letting the liquid course through him before speaking again.

"We'll go to my mother's house for a time. You'll come as my caretaker and stay with us. I cannot allow anyone else to treat me."

"Are you sure she won't put up a fuss?"

Sebastian narrowed his icy blue eyes. "Not if she knows what's good for her."

Robbie laughed. "I swear you have no conscience, Sebbie. What man makes such threatening statements about his mother?" He took the bottle from his friend, then motioned for Sebastian to roll over so he might treat the back of the leg. Thankfully the ball had passed completely through, but in doing so, it had torn muscle and nicked the bone, leaving tiny fragments with which to contend.

Sebastian moaned with each painful movement. If only he had been more cautious. He should have known the insurance man would carry a weapon. But the fellow seemed so naïve and civilized that Sebastian had never figured him for armed. Things definitely were not always what they seemed—especially when it came to people.

"Would you just finish this and be done with it!" Sebastian cried out as Robbie pressed an herbal concoction into the wound.

"I'm nearly done. Keep still or you'll cause it to bleed again."

Sebastian forced his body to still. He thought of what his mother might say when he showed up on her doorstep. She wouldn't be pleased, but neither would she turn him away. Of that he was certain.

Mark stepped from the train and waited for the porter to bring his horse. He had been torn between bringing Portland on the trip and leaving him in the care of his family. The necessity for transportation won over, however, and he paid the extra expense of shipping the sorrel gelding.

Portland seemed completely unimpressed with his experience. He danced nervously as the young black man fought to keep him under control. Mark was glad to see they had already saddled him and took the reins from the nervous teen.

"Here's something for your trouble," he said, tossing the boy a coin. Mark quickly turned his attention back to the horse and reached into his pocket for a couple of sugar lumps. "And here's something for your trouble, Portland. I know that was not to your liking and I do apologize."

The horse nuzzled his hand for the sweets and then bobbed his head up and down as if agreeing with Mark's comment. Mark laughed and walked his mount from the station. He felt confident that if he allowed Portland to get away from the noise and rush of the trains, he would soon calm and be willing to let Mark ride.

They strolled only a short distance before Mark saw the situation was going to be quite impossible. Like Boston, Philadelphia was a bustling town, and quiet and calm seemed far away.

Mark climbed onto Portland's back with only minor protest from the gelding. The horse sidestepped several times before allowing Mark to guide him forward. "There you go, boy. See? It's not so unnerving as you thought," Mark said, patting the steed's neck.

They joined the traffic of wagons and carriages as Mark moved deeper into the heart of town. The day had grown humid, and given the heavy look of the clouds, Mark guessed they were soon to experience a rain.

He pressed on, knowing the address and basic directions for getting to the boardinghouse where he would stay. He'd arranged for his trunk to be delivered later that day. The proprietor, Mr. Westmoreland, was expecting him. Westmoreland, a former police officer who'd been injured in the line of duty, was said to be a valuable aid to those who needed private investigation. Mark hoped he might prove to be useful.

A few sprinkles of rain were just starting to fall when Mark found the house. It was small, only two stories, but it looked sufficient. Not far from the house, on Front Street, were businesses and plenty of activity. One such place was a livery. Perhaps he would be able to board Portland there while he conducted business in Philadelphia.

He dismounted, tied the gelding to the small hitching post, and gave another glance at the house. This was to become his home—for how long, he had no idea. Mark drew a deep breath and squared his shoulders.

CHAPTER 4

Life at the Jameston house seemed idyllic to Cassie. They had fallen into a companionable schedule as easily as if they had known each other all of their days. Mrs. Jameston found Cassie's sense of humor and manner of speaking her mind to be refreshing, and Cassie appreciated the older woman's candor in return. The servants were personable and seemed to enjoy the fact that Cassie had come to keep their mistress company.

Silas, a white-haired man of sixty, ran the Jameston kitchen in perfect order. He had spent a lifetime working in some capacity for the Jamestons. His mother and father had gone to work for Mr. Jameston's family when Silas had barely reached the age of ten. He learned early on how to work in the kitchen and loved cooking so much that Mr. Jameston's mother arranged for him to go to Paris and take formal training.

Essie, the only servant of color, often helped in the kitchen. She preferred working with the meals, but also did laundry and ironing. She was as loyal to Mrs. Jameston as any person could ever be. Having been a slave in Virginia until the age of thirteen, Essie was rescued from her miserable fate when Mrs. Jameston spied her being whipped. As the story went, Mrs. Jameston was visiting friends when Essie was punished for having broken a vase. Horrified at this treatment, Louise Jameston immediately offered her friends twice what the girl would have sold for on the block and whisked her away to Philadelphia, a city quite sympathetic to seeing slaves set free. Once safely in the Jameston house, Essie was given her papers and offered a proper job in the household.

Wills and Miriam were a husband and wife who, although young, were very hard-working. Wills cared for the grounds and horses, while Miriam helped Mrs. Dixon keep the house and helped her husband on occasion with the garden. Then, of course, there was Ada, who acted as personal maid to Mrs. Jameston, and now Cassie.

Brumley was the butler and household manager of funds, and Mrs. Dixon ran everything else. She and Brumley together handled all matters regarding the other servants, but in truth, Cassie thought they all seemed more like family than employees. They loved Mrs. Jameston and would have done anything for her, though they despised her son.

All except Silas. The aged cook seemed to tolerate him with a gruff affection Cassie learned had been born over the years. Apparently, Silas had married a lovely French girl while abroad.

She returned with him and went to work in the Jamestons' household, taking over the position of nanny when Sebastian had come along. Jeannette had been unable to have children, and she and Silas doted on Sebastian, even nicknaming him Sebbie. During Mrs. Jameston's darkest days of sorrow over the death of her older sons, Silas and Jeannette had shown Sebastian the attention and love that he lacked.

"When Jeannette died," Mrs. Jameston had told Cassie, "Sebastian was devastated. She was as much a mother to him then as I—maybe more, for I was often lost in my grief, while she spent every waking moment with him."

Cassie thought it very sad. She tried to imagine Mrs. Jameston's son as a little boy. An oil painting of him hung upon the wall in the formal sitting room, and Cassie thought him a very distinguished-looking young man. His eyes were of the palest ice blue, however, and seemed void of feeling. Given the other things Cassie had heard in passing about the man, she thought him a definite enigma. It wasn't long before Cassie was given the opportunity to form her own opinions.

Sebastian Jameston appeared in the foyer of his mother's house one Friday in April. He hadn't bothered to knock and was supported on one side by a tawny-haired man and by a crutch on the other.

Cassie stared at him from the doorway of the sitting room. He was glassy-eyed and flushed, swaying as if drunk or perhaps sick.

"Where's my mother?" he asked as Brumley took their hats.

"I believe Mrs. Jameston is lying down," the butler replied.

"Then wake her and tell her that I'm here," he said.

"That can wait," his companion interjected. "Mr. Jameston is injured and needs to go to bed. We'll need hot water and clean bandages."

Cassie continued to watch as the man pushed past Mr. Brumley, taking Sebastian with him. She worried about Mrs. Jameston and the shock of having her son come home in such a state. Slipping up the back stairs, Cassie made her way to her own bedroom and knocked lightly on the door that adjoined Mrs. Jameston's room before entering.

Mrs. Jameston was already awake. She smiled at Cassie and beckoned her in. "Come, child. Come and read to me."

"I would love to, but I'm afraid you will be much occupied in a few moments. Your son has returned, and he's in a sorry state."

Mrs. Jameston's face lost its joyful expression. "What kind of sorry state?"

"Well, there is another man with him, and he says that your son has been injured. He called for hot water and bandages. From the looks of it, I believe Mr. Jameston might well be feverish."

Mrs. Jameston got to her feet with a sigh. "Help me change from this dressing gown." She undid the hooks and shrugged out of the gown.

Cassie assisted Mrs. Jameston, tightening the woman's corset before depositing the dress over her head.

"That boy always manages to get himself in one kind of mess or another. He has been strong-willed since the day he was born. It could have served him well—had it been tempered. Instead, I can't even tell you the sorrow he has caused me."

It felt strange to hear a mother speak thusly of her child. "I'm sorry to hear that," Cassie remarked as she did up the back buttons. Just then Ada appeared. The worried expression on her face said it all.

"Mrs. Jameston, Sebastian is home, and he's asking for you. Well, in truth, he's demanding you come to him." Her tone made her disgust quite clear.

"Cassie mentioned his return. I was just having her assist me in dressing. Tell him I will be right there."

Ada nodded and hurried from the room. Cassie turned to Mrs. Jameston and offered a weak smile. "Even Ada despises him, I see." She grimaced as the words left her mouth. "Sorry. I suppose that was a bit bold."

Mrs. Jameston shook her head. "Sebastian has done much to alienate most of the staff. They all share their own histories with him—all but you." With that, she opened her bedroom door and disappeared into the hallway. Cassie followed quickly.

At the opposite end of the second floor, Sebastian Jameston had already taken residence in a decidedly masculine room. Cassie stepped inside the bedroom after Mrs. Jameston and marveled at the bustle of people already in place.

"Mother, I have need of you," Sebastian called from the four-poster bed.

Mrs. Jameston took in the scene and moved slowly toward him. "They told me you were injured. What seems to be the problem?" Cassie heard guarded concern in the woman's voice. She had only seen Mrs. Jameston as the warmest and kindest of people, yet here, with her own son, she seemed almost afraid of what might be revealed.

"It's really nothing. I had some overexuberant entertainment and was accidentally shot in the leg. It became infected."

"Shot? Brumley, send for the doctor."

"No," Sebastian said sternly. "Robbie is good at the healing arts. He'll take care of me. I just needed a dry, clean place where we could have access to all the supplies we'd need. It's actually much better." He motioned to the stranger. "This is Robert McLaughlin. He'll stay with me while I recover. I've already told Mrs. Dixon to have the adjoining room made up for him."

Cassie remained back by the door. She could see that Mrs. Jameston was far from pleased with the situation.

"When did this happen? How bad is it?" his mother asked. Cassie recognized the motherly alarm in her voice and felt pity for the older woman. *How torn she must feel,* Cassie thought. *She loves him . . . but fears him at the same time. Fears the pain he might cause her, as well as the pain she might experience in losing him completely.*

"It's been a couple of weeks and it was very bad," Sebastian said as he sank back against the pillows. "Robbie has kept me just this side of becoming a one-legged beggar."

Robbie glanced up. His dark eyes met Mrs. Jameston's, then quickly turned back to the work at hand. "He's not a good patient at times, but the best thing he can do for himself is rest."

Cassie thought the man's voice held a hint of a Scottish accent, but it was evident he'd worked to disguise that. He was a nice enough looking man. In fact, both of them were, but there was something sinister about them that she couldn't quite put her finger on.

"Well, he can certainly have plenty of that here," Mrs. Jameston said. "If your man has this under control, I shall dismiss the servants. There is no need for them to remain here." She looked at her son as if considering what more she could do and added, "If you change your mind about the doctor, please let me know."

"I can handle this on my own, ma'am," Robbie said without looking up.

Brumley, Ada, and Mrs. Dixon left the room quickly, and Cassie couldn't be certain, but it almost seemed they gave a collective sigh as they moved down the corridor.

"Who is this beauty?" Sebastian asked his mother.

Cassie realized Sebastian was speaking about her, and she felt her face grow hot under his leering gaze. His eyes were glassy and his expression pained, but it didn't stop him from fixing her with a most disturbing stare. He seemed to have no shame in ogling her as though she were a commodity for sale.

"This is Cassandra Stover. She is my companion, and as such, I expect you to treat her with the utmost respect. She is not a servant but rather a friend."

"I'd like to be her friend," Sebastian said with a wicked grin. "I'd like to be her very good friend."

"Sebastian, you are completely out of line. You have scared half of the young women in my employ. I won't have you offending Cassie."

He winked at Cassie and patted the side of the bed. "I promise not to scare you, and I'm not at all interested in offending you. Quite the contrary. Come sit by me and tell me about yourself."

"Nonsense," Mrs. Jameston replied before Cassie could speak. "She's my companion, not yours. Come, Cassie."

Cassie followed Mrs. Jameston back to her room. It was clear that Sebastian's appearance had upset the older woman.

"I want you to be careful," Mrs. Jameston told her. "My son is quite devious and corrupt. He will stop at nothing to pester you and impose himself upon you. He's scared poor Essie practically to the point of quitting me. I always try to see her tucked away somewhere else when he's around."

"He doesn't worry me," Cassie said boldly. But in truth, she did feel rather uncomfortable.

"My dear, I don't want you worried; I just want you cautious. Sebastian cares for no one but himself. He's actually taken . . . liberties with women in the past. I would not want to see you harmed in such a way."

Cassie nodded. "I promise I'll give him a wide berth."

Mrs. Jameston squeezed her hand. "I just don't know what to do for him anymore. He's resentful of anything I try. Hopefully he won't be with us for long. I'll encourage him to leave as soon as his leg is on the mend. In fact, I'll pay for him to go elsewhere if need be. I simply cannot have him upsetting my household once again. Even if he is my son."

Cassie patted her arm. "I hate to see you this way, Mrs. Jameston. It's not good for your constitution."

Mrs. Jameston met her gaze. Her brows knit together and wrinkles lined her forehead. "I feel terrible. Sebastian is my own flesh and blood, but there is no joy in having him here. He has proven himself to be untrustworthy on so many occasions, I have, in fact, actually come to fear him."

"Well, you needn't worry now. I'm here. I'll see that you are safe."

Mrs. Jameston shook her head. "You don't understand. Sometimes I fear that boy is in league with the devil himself."

From the moment they met, Mark found he very much liked August Westmoreland. The man was rather stocky in build, with curly red hair that belied his fifty-some years of life, despite the occasional marks of gray. He welcomed Mark from the start with an enthusiasm that immediately put the younger man at ease.

"You must call me August. Everyone does."

"They do indeed," the man's widowed sister said. "I'm Nancy Wenger."

"Mrs. Wenger." Mark gave a brief bow. "I'm pleased to meet you both."

"You came highly recommended," August declared, eyeing Mark as if sizing him up for some future reference.

"As did you," Mark countered, meeting August's gaze. The two men nodded, seeming to understand the underlying truth of why Mark had come.

Since then, Mark had found the room and boardinghouse to be comfortable and consistent with his needs. Not only did August and Nancy keep a tidy house, they put on a generous meal. August also offered a place for Portland to board with his own horses at a very minimal fee.

"So are you heading out today?" Westmoreland asked as Mark came down the rather steep stairs, hat in hand.

"I am. I thought to ride around the town a bit and familiarize myself with the streets. I appreciate the map you drew for me."

"No problem at all. Should you want to go riding with me sometime, I'm sure I can get Nancy to watch over the house."

"Maybe another time. Thank you," Mark said, moving to the door. He had in mind to ride past the Jameston house once again and wasn't yet compelled to share his mission with the older man. He popped the hat atop his head and smiled. "I shouldn't be long."

He found Portland and a pair of matched ebony geldings in the small corral in back. There was a lean-to type shed to offer shelter from the rain, but otherwise the arrangements were meager. Still, Mark thought the animal would prefer it here in the open to the shared quarters of the livery.

"Well, boy, are you ready for a little journey?" He quickly saddled the animal, all the while talking. "We have a little business to take care of." Portland gave a soft whinny as if in acknowledgment of the work ahead of them. Mark led him from the corral and mounted, giving the horse a quick pat against the neck.

The skies were clear and blue as Mark made his way up Spruce Street. The air smelled of spring with the undeniable scent of flowers and budding trees. *Philadelphia is indeed a beautiful city,* he thought. Not only that, but the history of the town fascinated him—just as Boston's did.

He tried to imagine the city as Benjamin Franklin might have known it. He wondered if the old gentleman loved the city as much as he loved the idea of freedom for the country.

Did he take long rides in the afternoon and soak up the sights and sounds around him? Did he have any idea of what his work would bring about in the not-so-distant future?

Heading north, Mark watched the neighborhood change. The docks and bustle of Front Street gave way to neighborhoods of redbrick row houses and cobblestone streets. At one time, this had been where the wealthy had enjoyed stately homes, but as the years passed, the rich took themselves north and west. That was where Mark would find the Jameston house.

He'd ridden by the Jameston property on two other occasions but tried to keep from looking obvious. He knew he would find a subtle opulence that only the very wealthy could afford. Often it seemed people of less capital overindulged to impress, whereas the truly rich had no need.

Mark thought again of Richard and wondered if he'd taken this same route to catch a glimpse of the Jameston house. It was hard to think of Richard gone. They had been close friends for so long. Richard had helped Mark to go on living after the death of his beloved Ruth. When Mark had wanted to turn to drink, Richard had helped him, instead, turn to God. Now God seemed strangely absent. Richard was gone, and in so many ways he'd taken God with him.

Lost in his thoughts, Mark very nearly missed the Jameston address. He focused on the four-story mansion and wondered which of the ornate windows belonged to Sebastian.

The lawn was well manicured with lovely flower beds and tall, majestic trees. The landscaping seemed to beckon him to come and share in its peaceful tranquillity. But Mark knew he'd find no peace there.

He kept his gaze fixed on the house, watching for any sign of movement or occupants. There was nothing, however. He supposed he couldn't be so lucky as to have Sebastian Jameston just happen to wander outside.

He urged Portland forward, but all the while watched the property. It wasn't until the horse whinnied and snorted that Mark put his attention back on the road. Only it was too late. His mistake played out in front of him as a young woman rounded the corner abruptly and screamed as Portland reared in uncharacteristic fear.

CHAPTER 5

The last conscious thought Cassie had was of being stomped to death by the reddish beast. She let the black calm take her and felt as though she were floating. Was this what death was like? Funny how there was no pain.

"Miss?"

The voice sounded faint at first. It held a warmth and concern that greatly appealed to Cassie's senses. She felt the fog lift as he continued to call to her. Did the voice belong to God?

"Miss. Open your eyes."

She tried to, but they felt ever so heavy. Surely God could just open them for her if He wanted them to be open.

Little by little, the feeling was coming back to her. She felt something wrapped around her back. Had God given her angel wings?

"Are you all right, miss? Please wake up."

Cassie opened her eyes and stared up into the handsomest face she'd ever known. God was certainly dashing. She chided herself. Of course God would be dashing. He was, after all, God.

But what had happened? For a moment, she couldn't remember anything, but the more she concentrated, the clearer it became that this was not heaven, and the handsome man was not God. The reality of it all was quite disappointing, for she wouldn't have minded spending eternity in the presence of one so lovely to look upon. The man's dark blue eyes held her captive, while his frown assured her that her injuries must have been grave.

"Am I . . . how badly am I hurt?" she asked, trying to detect any pain in her body. The absence of it was almost unnerving. More disturbing still was the warmth of the stranger's arms around her as he knelt beside her.

He smiled, and Cassie felt mesmerized. "I don't believe you have any injuries, miss. I'm afraid you fainted dead away when Portland began to fret."

Cassie tried to remember what had happened. The horse! She could see those horrible hooves coming down on top of her and gripped the man's arm without meaning to. He pulled her closer.

"I wasn't thinking . . . I mean . . . I was, but not about where I was going." She realized how intimately he held her and felt her heart skip a beat. "I was upset. It was silly. Oh bother." Pushing away, she refocused on the moment. "Am I truly without injury?" She scrambled to her feet and smoothed out her skirt.

The man chuckled and got to his feet as well. "I don't know for certain. Perhaps you should tell me."

Cassie shrugged. "I suppose the only thing truly injured is my pride."

This caused the man to laugh all the more. "Well, I speak from experience when I say that such things mend quite quickly if left alone."

Cassie smiled. "I suppose you saved my life from that brute."

The man sobered. "Portland is not a brute. You startled him. That was all."

"He started it," Cassie countered. "He startled me with his stomping and snorting. It was like some kind of demon possessed him."

"Now, stop. He's just over there, and he might hear you. You'll hurt his feelings." The man's teasing voice was not at all what Cassie had counted on.

She watched as he walked to where the horse awaited him. He took up the reins and drew him toward Cassie. She immediately backed up until she was pinned against a large maple tree.

"No. Get him away." The terror in her voice was clear even to her own ears.

"I don't understand," the man said. He seemed sympathetic enough and stopped in midstep. "My horse is quite friendly. He won't hurt you."

"My father was killed in a riding accident. The horse threw him and then trampled him to death. I watched the entire thing," Cassie said, drawing her arm up as if to shield herself.

"I'm so sorry. No wonder you have such an irrational fear."

This bolstered Cassie a bit. "It's not irrational. I have a very good rationale for my feelings."

"Yes, I suppose so. But they aren't reasonable. Our entire society is dependent upon horses for transportation and work. You cannot merely go about being terrified of them the rest of your life."

Cassie relaxed a bit and shrugged. "It's suited me well enough for ten years."

"But it would suit you better to overcome such fear. Now come here and make up with Portland."

Cassie felt her eyes widen as she caught the large brown eyes of the horse. "Sir, I do not know you, and I have no desire to know your mount."

He laughed. "I am Marcus Langford, but my friends call me Mark. And you are . . . ?"

"Cassie. Cassandra Stover."

"And where do you live, Miss Stover?"

"There," she said, pointing to the Jameston mansion. She saw him frown and wondered why her response seemed so unappealing. "What's wrong? It's a wonderful house. I am Mrs. Jameston's companion. She's the older woman who owns this property."

"I see. And how long have you been her companion?"

Cassie thought the question strange, but at least it kept him from forcing her to meet his horse. Goodness, but why did some men think they had to fix everything? "I've only just started. I've been there for about two weeks."

"And do you find it to your liking?" He reached up and stroked his horse casually.

"I do. Well, I did until her son came back to stay. He was injured, though, and there was no putting him from the house. He's caused all sorts of upset, however. No one likes him." She clenched her jaw shut and shook her head. "I'm sorry. I should be more careful about speaking my mind."

Mark laughed. "I like a woman who speaks her mind. It makes her more honest and her company more enjoyable."

"I doubt that is true of me. I do try to refrain," she said with a sigh, "but sometimes . . . like now . . . it just pours out of me."

Cassie eyed the horse again. She was surprised at how calm the animal had remained at Mark's side. He appeared perfectly safe, but she couldn't allow herself to believe that.

"I see you are reconsidering Portland. He's a fine gelding. And actually, he's very mild-mannered. When you came running out around that shrubbery, he was taken by surprise. That's all. He meant you no harm."

"You talk as if you understand what he's thinking," Cassie said, returning her gaze to the man. He was dressed well in a dark blue frock coat and trousers with a bit of a green striped waistcoat peeking out from against a nicely starched white shirt. His face was clean-shaven, and his wavy brown hair was cut close and combed back under his hat.

He allowed her scrutiny for a moment. "I hope I pass inspection."

Cassie was slightly embarrassed but made the best of it. "I believe for a rescuer, you cut a fine figure."

He smiled and tipped his hat in her direction. "And for a damsel in distress, you could not play the role any better."

Giving him a curtsy, Cassie laughed. "I guess we now know that we're both hopelessly silly."

"If we remain in the street much longer, the entire neighborhood will know that much. Now come here, Miss Stover, and meet Portland. You truly have nothing to fear."

Mark led the mount to the Jameston drive and waited for Cassie to react. She watched him for a moment, shuddered, and then pushed away from the tree.

I might as well get it over with, she thought. *He isn't going to forget this nonsense.* She walked very slowly toward the man and his horse.

"What was that?"

She looked up and smiled. "Nothing. Nothing at all."

"Sounded like something," he teased. "I thought perhaps you were issuing a prayer."

"I should," she agreed, stopping within a foot of the man. "I hardly believe this is necessary."

"Of course it is. Now give me your hand."

Cassie frowned and pulled her gloved hands together. "Why?"

Mark laughed. "So that you can pet Portland."

She looked at the horse. He seemed to tower over her. "I think not. He might decide he's hungry instead."

With lightning-fast reflexes, Mark reached out and locked a hold on her wrist. "Stop being so ridiculous. Here, see for yourself. He's not going to eat you."

Cassie closed her eyes, and Mark pulled her hand to the horse's neck. She felt the firm-muscled animal beneath her hand and trembled.

"He really won't hurt you," Mark whispered against her ear.

Shivering all the more, Cassie's eyes flew open. She was speechless as Mark maneuvered her hand to stroke the animal's mane. She wasn't exactly sure whose nearness was most disturbing—Mark's or the horse's.

"See now? He's perfectly calm. He likes you."

"I'm sorry that I cannot return the feelings," Cassie barely managed to say.

"You need to overcome your fear so that things like this won't happen in the future."

Cassie knew he was probably right, but at the moment she couldn't think clearly. A part of her longed to flee the presence of this intimidating beast, while an equally encouraging part wanted to remain and enjoy the company of this dashing young man.

Mark finally released his hold on her, and Cassie reluctantly stepped away. Portland turned to nuzzle her, causing Cassie to jump.

"I thought you said he wouldn't eat me!" she said, closing her eyes tight.

Mark watched the young woman with amazement. She was truly terrified of Portland. He'd never seen such a fear of horses prior to this.

"He won't eat you. He's trying to see if you have a treat for him. Here." Mark reached into his pocket for a lump of sugar. "I shouldn't spoil him so, but give him this."

Cassie looked at him hard. "And how do you propose I do that?"

"Hold out your hand." She did so and Mark placed the sugar on her gloved palm. "Now feed it to him."

"You can't be serious. Look at the size of his mouth—his teeth. He could bite off my hand in one move."

"But he won't," Mark said with a grin. "Just open your hand flat and lift it to him. I promise he will not amputate any part of you."

Cassie did as she was told and nearly shrieked when Portland gobbled up the offering. He pushed against her for more, but Mark took charge.

"That's enough, you greedy old man." He turned to Cassie. "There. That wasn't so bad, was it?"

"Compared to battling lions in Africa, I suppose it was quite simple," she answered.

Mark couldn't help but laugh. "And what would you know of battling lions in Africa?"

"Only that it would terrify me and leave me without hope of survival. Come to think of it—that's exactly how I feel about your horse."

Mark took her by the arm. "Come. Why don't you let me escort you to the door? Just in case a lion . . . or another horse . . . jumps out."

She giggled and lowered her head as if embarrassed once again. "I suppose it would be the safe thing to do. But I'd rather you leave . . . him." She motioned with her head toward Portland.

Mark nodded and dropped his hold on her. He quickly tied Portland to the iron gate and walked casually at Cassie's side. "So, you said that you had no liking of Mrs. Jameston's son."

"No one but the cook does, as far as I can tell. Apparently, the man is quite exasperating."

"In what way?"

Cassie shrugged. "In most, I suppose. Even his friends have a tendency to shoot him—or so it would seem."

"What do you mean?" Mark looked at her and was surprised to find her watching him.

"Well, apparently there was some sort of play between him and his ruffian friend. A gun went off and the bullet went through Mr. Jameston's thigh. It appears to be a very invasive wound, but he's on the mend, according to his companion, Mr. McLaughlin."

"But what does the doctor say?"

"Oh, he won't allow for one. Said his friend was perfectly capable of treating the injury. He said it was just an accident amongst friends, but frankly, I think someone's temptation got out of hand."

Mark nodded. "There are folks who incite that kind of thing."

"He was the reason I wasn't paying attention to where I was going. He had yelled at his mother and upset her just before I came out here for a walk. Mrs. Jameston is a wonderful woman whose gentle nature compels me to feel overly protective of her, I suppose. I'm afraid I was thinking ill thoughts as I stormed from the house. It serves me right to find myself in peril." They had reached the front steps, and Cassie turned and gave him a smile. "Thank you again for saving me, fair knight."

He bowed. "I like rescuing damsels in distress. In fact, if you have no qualms about it, I would like to stop by tomorrow morning and inquire after your health. You might yet find yourself injured, and I would want to take responsibility for any cost you might endure."

She laughed. "Feel free to stop by, but I assure you I am fine."

He watched her walk up the steps and pause at the door. Something about her made him feel rather breathless. Her delicate features glowed when she smiled, and her dark brown eyes seemed to twinkle with delight or amusement.

He stood there for a moment, even after she'd closed the door. Mark couldn't help but wonder about the woman. She certainly had no lost love for Sebastian Jameston, and that might well work in Mark's favor. At this point he had plans to see her in the morning. That would at least get him inside the house.

Walking over to where Portland stood, Mark couldn't help but glance back at the house. A figure looked down at him from the second-story window at the far end. Was this Jameston? Mark felt his pulse quicken. He pretended not to notice the man as he mounted his horse.

Directing the animal down the street, Mark began to speculate. Sebastian Jameston was injured. Shot in the leg. The timing was right, and Mark couldn't help but suspect that he'd been wounded in the fight with Richard. The police had stated that Richard managed to fire his own weapon before dying.

"This just adds to the clues," he said aloud. Sebastian had no doubt been the one to kill Richard. "But how do I prove it?"

CHAPTER 6

The next morning Mark knocked on the Jameston door and waited with a sense of excitement for the meeting to unfold. He had considered this moment throughout the night. Not only did he enjoy Cassie's company, but he was hopeful to catch a glimpse of Mr. Jameston. This would give him an added advantage. He would have the ability to survey Jameston's domain, perhaps even get a chance to meet the man himself. Surely under such circumstances Jameston would never suspect that Mark's presence had anything to do with investigating Richard's death and the fraudulent insurance claims.

A stately older man opened the door. "Good morning, sir."

"Good morning." He handed the man his card. "I am Marcus Langford. Miss Stover is expecting me."

"Very good, sir. Please come this way."

Mark followed the man into the foyer, where the butler took his hat and gloves. "The ladies are awaiting you in here," the man said, leading the way to an open door.

"Thank you." Mark waited until the man announced him.

"Mr. Marcus Langford has arrived."

Cassie got to her feet, but the older woman remained seated. "Mrs. Jameston, this is the man who saved my life yesterday. Mr. Langford, this is my employer and dear friend, Mrs. Jameston."

Mark bowed in greeting and Mrs. Jameston smiled and nodded. "We are quite grateful to you, young man. Cassie has become invaluable to me, and I would truly have hated for anything to cause her harm."

Smiling, Mark caught Cassie's gaze. "I was glad to render service."

"Please be seated," Mrs. Jameston instructed. Cassie returned to the red fan-backed chair beside the older woman and smoothed out her dark green skirt.

"Thank you for allowing me to visit. I had worried that Miss Stover might have found injuries after further investigation."

"I'm happy to say there are none, with exception to a little soreness in my . . . on my . . ." Cassie blushed and muttered, "A little soreness."

Mark suppressed a laugh and caught Mrs. Jameston's amused expression. Clearly the older woman wasn't without a sense of humor.

"Tell us about yourself, Mr. Langford. I know little outside of the fact that you rescued Cassie and ride a massive red beast that all but spits fire."

Mark did laugh out loud at this. "I would never want to contradict a lady's recollection, but I assure you my mount is completely passive. As for me, I hail from Boston."

"Another city of liberty," Mrs. Jameston commented. "I have been there several times. I found it quite enjoyable. What brings you here?"

"Business. I'm here for a time on business."

"I see. Well, what is your line of business? What does your father do?"

Mark was glad for the second question. He hadn't really considered how he might reference his own line of work. Of course, he did dabble in investments. It was more of a hobby than anything. Then, too, he owned a part of his father's hotel business.

"My family owns the Imperial Hotel in Boston."

"I see. And are you planning to move your business to Philadelphia as well?"

A knock on the door saved Mark from having to reply. They all looked up and Mrs. Jameston cocked her head. "What is it, Mrs. Dixon?"

"Your son would like to see you. He's . . . asked . . . for you to come immediately."

Mark saw the older woman clench her jaw as her brows drew together. She rose and so he quickly got to his feet. Seeing him do so, she turned to Cassie. "Why don't you two go into the garden? I've arranged for us to have a light refreshment there. Hopefully I will not be gone long."

Cassie got up and nodded. Mrs. Dixon turned to lead the way as Mrs. Jameston crossed the room. Cassie turned to Mark. "If you follow me, I'll show you to the garden."

He quickly drew alongside her and offered his arm. "I'd much rather escort you."

Cassie smiled and took hold of him. "You are very kind, fair knight. I accept."

He laughed and walked with her through the house. "So you truly are without injury?"

"Yes, I am fine. I did, however, have nightmares last night. I cannot say my experience was a pleasant one, but I have survived physically unharmed."

"How old were you when your father died, if I might ask?"

Cassie seemed not to mind the question at all. "I was fifteen. It was ten years ago this June. My sister, Elida, was but a few weeks old." Cassie led the way into the garden and smiled as the sun's warmth touched her face. "It is so very pleasant here. I hope you'll enjoy it."

"How could I not?" He smiled at her and noted that Cassie's face flushed.

"This is Mrs. Jameston's favorite place, and it's rapidly becoming mine as well. The air seems so sweet here."

She led him to an iron settee and chairs. Beside this, a cloth-covered table stood with glasses of something that looked quite refreshing.

"Would you care for lemonade? Mrs. Jameston had it made special for your visit."

"Thank you." He took a glass from Cassie and followed her to the chairs. She sat and he followed suit by taking the chair directly across from her.

"Mrs. Jameston comes here every day the weather permits," Cassie offered. "She says it won't be long before the honeysuckle and hyacinths will be in full bloom. Already there are beautiful tulips. I don't pretend to know much about it all, but Mrs. Jameston promises to teach me."

"And what do you know much about?" Mark asked in a teasing tone.

Cassie thought for a moment. "Honestly, not a great deal." She frowned. "I had to stop going to school when my father died. My mother found herself rather destitute. She sold off the extra property we had, as well as my father's mercantile, but there were expenses to pay. Eventually we had the house and a small bit of money, but no hope of more income in the future. My mother turned to the one thing she knew she could do—laundry and mending." Cassie offered him a bittersweet smile.

"And this saw you through?"

Cassie nodded and took a sip of the lemonade. "We worked together. Elida was just a baby. My mother and I took turns working with the laundry and caring for her. Little by little, we had enough business to support our needs."

"Your mother sounds very brave. Many women would give up—or turn to male relatives to provide."

"There were no other male relatives. I think my mother might have given up, except for Elida. With a baby so dependent upon her for everything, Mother had no choice but to go on."

"Would she not also have wanted to continue for your sake?" he asked, watching her closely.

"Oh, to be certain. I do not mean to suggest she cared for me any less than my sister. However, because of my age and temperament, I believe she thought I could handle anything. Truth be told, I was still suffering greatly from what I'd seen, but I knew she needed me."

"It must have been terrible to witness your father's accident."

"Yes. It haunts me even now."

Mark couldn't help but wonder at this remarkable young woman who harbored such horrible memories. Obviously she had a strength deep within that allowed her to press forward, but she also had a remarkable sense of humor.

"How did it happen?" he finally asked.

Cassie lowered her gaze to the glass in her hand. "I had gone with him to visit friends. There was a new horse he was thinking of buying from them. He wanted to try it out first. I sat and watched as he mounted the horrible animal and began to ride. At first nothing went amiss, but something happened to startle the beast. He reared and my father was thrown. Apparently, seeing my father on the ground caused the horse even greater distress. He assaulted my father, vigorously pounding down upon him before the groom could come and quiet the animal."

Her voice had grown so quiet, Mark had to lean forward to hear her. Her golden brown hair fell in tendrils against her face and framed her sad features. "I am sorry," Mark said in a hushed manner. "I cannot imagine anything more horrendous for a child than to witness her father's death."

"I fainted, and when I came to, I was certain it had all been a bad dream." Cassie looked up and Mark could see the moisture around her eyes. "But of course, it wasn't. I've been terrified of horses ever since. They had to sedate me even to transport me back home in the carriage."

Essie emerged from the house with a tray of pastries and cakes. "Mrs. Jameston said I was to serve you." She placed the tray on the table and took up a small plate. "What would you like?"

"Nothing for me," Cassie said, "but thank you."

"Thank you. I'll have one of the fruit tarts. They're a weakness of mine," Mark declared.

Essie skillfully maneuvered the tart onto the plate and handed it to Mark with a fork and linen napkin. As quickly as she'd come, Essie disappeared back into the house.

Mark sampled the tart. "This is very good. I will have to stop by more often. The refreshments are good and the company, delightful."

"I'm sure you are welcome here. Now, where were we?"

"You were telling me how you have nothing to do with horses. I suppose you walk everywhere?" Mark asked.

Cassie nodded. "It isn't as if we lived far away from anything important. I will take an occasional carriage ride, but only if the driver and horse are very experienced."

"Well, I hope to change that for you. As I said yesterday, you cannot go around fearing horses all of your life."

"I hardly see why I cannot. After all, I've done quite well these ten years. And I have ridden in the carriage to church with Mrs. Jameston, so I am not without the ability to travel when I must. In fact, she doesn't even know about my fears."

"But riding is such a pleasant diversion. I think you would find it quite entertaining."

Cassie smiled. "Mr. Langford, there has not been much occasion in my latter years for pleasant diversions, entertaining or otherwise."

"Sorry to have been gone for so long," Mrs. Jameston announced as she joined them. She glided elegantly across the lawn, the epitome of refined womanhood.

"Is everything all right?" Mark asked as he once again got to his feet.

Mrs. Jameston took her place on the settee and nodded. "My son is not known for his patience. But all is well. I see Cassie has amply occupied you. She is a marvelous addition to my life. Like the daughter I never had—or perhaps granddaughter." She smiled fondly at Cassie.

"I am, however, to leave in a short time," Cassie interjected. "Mrs. Jameston has graciously given me Saturdays to spend with my mother and sister. I'm only here because you said you would come this morning. I didn't think to suggest otherwise."

"May I escort you to your home?" Mark questioned.

She shook her head. "I simply plan to walk and enjoy the day."

"I offered her the carriage, but she declined," Mrs. Jameston remarked. "I'm sure I've never known a young lady who liked to walk more than Cassie, unless it's me."

Mark nodded. "Miss Stover mentioned that your son is quite ill. I hope he is recovering."

"As best as can be expected," she said with a frown. "My son—forgive me for my boldness—is a scallywag. He is the product of overindulgent parents who learned much too late in life the dangers of giving in to the demands of an out-of-control child. I'm afraid my son fears neither God nor man."

"I have known men such as this. Is this his residence? I thought Miss Stover mentioned something about his being newly arrived."

"He travels a great deal and, unfortunately, has a residence with his mistress. Unless, of course, he's on the bad side of her, and then he makes his way home."

Mark made a mental note to figure out where Jameston's mistress resided. He started to comment, but Mrs. Jameston quickly continued.

"I do not mean to be shocking or vulgar, Mr. Langford. It is common knowledge that my son acts in an abominable manner. I see no need to pretend it is otherwise."

"Sometimes," Mark said, "it is best to deal with a matter in a straightforward fashion."

"I completely agree. Which brings me to another topic, Mr. Langford. Since you are new to our city, have you yet found a place to worship? If not, I would like to invite you to join us tomorrow at Christ Church."

He hadn't been prepared for that. He looked at his glass of lemonade and realized that getting close to Cassie and Mrs. Jameston would further his efforts more than any other plan he had at the moment.

"I haven't yet explored my options; however, I would be happy to join you. That is the church where Mr. Benjamin Franklin attended, is it not?"

Mrs. Jameston smiled approvingly. "Indeed. George Washington and many others attended there as well. A great deal of praying went on in that church for the independence of our country."

"I have read as much. It would be my honor to join you there."

Cassie smiled and got to her feet. "I hate to be rude, but I really must be on my way."

"But Essie is just now bringing a little more substantial fare," Mrs. Jameston said as the young woman approached with a tray.

"Perhaps Mr. Langford would remain and keep you company," Cassie said. "I promised my mother that I would luncheon with her and my sister. I hope you understand."

Mark had already gotten to his feet. "I completely understand. Thank you so much for the time you've already given me. I would be happy to walk you home."

"Didn't you bring the beast?" Cassie asked with a hint of a grin.

"I did ride Portland, but if Mrs. Jameston were not to mind, I could leave him here and come back for him after I saw you safely delivered."

Cassie shook her head. "No. I couldn't ask you to do that. It's nearly two miles away. I assure you, I'll be just fine." She went to Mrs. Jameston and gave her shoulder a light squeeze. "I shall be back soon."

Mark didn't want to appear too forward. He waited until Cassie had made her way back inside the house before looking to Mrs. Jameston. "I suppose I should go."

"Nonsense. Enjoy some refreshments with me. Silas is a wondrous cook and always manages to make something quite pleasing."

Mark looked at the table where the serving girl had already laid out the sumptuous fare. His mouth watered at the thought. "I suppose I could stay for a short time."

"I'm certain I won't be as pleasing to you as Cassie might have been, but I would like to know you better."

"Really? Why is that?" Mark asked, retaking his seat.

Mrs. Jameston smiled. "Because you are obviously interested in my Cassie."

Cassie sat at her mother's table and listened to Elida go on and on about the mounds of laundry she'd had to help wash and iron.

"It's been like a war," Elida said in a dramatic manner. "Just when I think we've defeated the enemy, more comes to wipe us out."

Cassie laughed. "You've been in the company of the Radisson boys, haven't you? Your analogy of war is better fitted to the male gender than your own."

Mother brought a pork roast to the table and smiled. "I thought we'd have this wonderful treat. I bought it with the money you left last week."

"Oh, it smells delicious," Cassie said, spying the apples and currants in the sauce. "And what of your wonderful potatoes?"

"I have them as well," Mother said. "Bread too. We're enjoying quite the feast."

Elida nodded. "We've planned it all week. I'm so glad you're here. I did so tire of chicken and dumplings."

"But Mother makes such a wonderful recipe," Cassie said. "I could eat them all week long."

Her sister scrunched up her nose. "Do not even speak of such things." She tossed her braided hair over her shoulder. "I would surely waste away."

Cassie laughed. "You hardly look to have suffered." Elida seemed to have grown several inches in the past month—and certainly had become even more of a dramatic actress than she'd been prior to Cassie's departure.

"So tell me everything I have missed."

"Mrs. Blanchard is having another baby," Elida announced. "Her servant told Mother when she came to pick up the linens."

"What number will this make?" Cassie asked, trying to remember.

"Fourteen," Mother replied. "And her youngest is not yet six months."

Cassie shook her head. "That must be a real challenge."

"She should open a laundry," Elida commented as Mother filled her plate with food.

Laughing, Cassie helped herself to the roast. "That would be too much competition. Washing bedding and linens for the Blanchard family is a large part of Mother's business."

"I know, but with the money you give us, we don't have to work as hard."

"Elida!" Mother protested. "We aren't going to sit back and do nothing while your sister labors to care for us. Now let us pray a blessing for the food and speak nothing more of money and work. I want us to enjoy our time with Cassie."

Cassie bowed her head, but when she closed her eyes, it was Mark Langford she thought about rather than grace. She could still remember his smile and those wonderful eyes. How charming he was, and gracious.

"Cassie?" Elida called.

Startled, Cassie opened her eyes and looked up sheepishly. "Sorry."

"I thought you were going to pray all day," Elida replied, handing her the potatoes.

"Well, I don't suppose it would hurt any of us to do such a thing," Cassie answered. "After all, the Bible does admonish us to pray without ceasing."

She caught her mother's smile and decided to move the conversation to something else. "So tell me about school, Miss Elida. Are you still managing to be the best reader in your class?"

CHAPTER 7

Cassie stared in silent amazement at her reflection in the mirror. She wore one of her new gowns of layered pink silk and marveled at the delicately embroidered flowers that ran along the neckline.

"I'm sure I've never owned anything quite so pretty," she told Ada. Turning to catch a look at the back of the gown, she shook her head. "It just seems to float when I move."

Ada laughed. "I'm certain you will turn the heads of all the young men at church." She brought Cassie's bonnet and gloves. "It's nearly time to leave."

"Please go ahead and see to Mrs. Jameston; she's already downstairs. I'll be right there."

With a nod, Ada exited the room, while Cassie noted the hat and gloves. They were just as well made and beautiful as the gown. Why, the white gloves even had the same style of embroidery running up the center.

Moving into the hall, Cassie thought of Mark and wondered if he would find her attractive. She thought him very handsome, but she realized she still knew very little about him. Had he escorted her home the day before, they would certainly have had more time to talk privately, but Cassie wasn't certain that would have been entirely to her advantage. She didn't want to get her hopes up that Mark might consider her worthy of courtship. He was, after all, of a different town and social circle. He was here for the purpose of work, and once that was complete, he would no doubt head back to Boston.

She tied on the bonnet and was just pulling on her gloves when she heard a thud come from the end of the corridor. This was quickly followed by a string of curses and loud moans. Pausing at the stairs a moment, Cassie knew the noise had come from Mr. Jameston's room, but she wasn't at all sure what to do about it. Surely his friend would come to his aid.

But the moans only continued, and now they were interspersed with calls for help. Cassie pulled on her second glove and drew a deep breath. Apparently she was the only one in the vicinity who could hear Sebastian, for no one else was appearing to help him.

"I'll just see what the problem is and then find help for him," she said aloud as she moved down the long corridor.

She knocked lightly on the bedroom door and then opened it just a bit. "Mr. Jameston, are you all right?"

"No. I've fallen. Help me."

Cassie pushed back the door and found Sebastian fighting to get up off the floor. His nearly shoulder-length brown hair hid his face from view as he struggled. She went to him immediately and offered her arm. He latched on to her as though he were a drowning man.

"Your fever is back," she said, feeling the warmth of his body through his nightshirt.

He pushed the hair from his face and flashed a gaze with his piercing blue eyes before he gripped her tightly. His hands were possessive in the way he touched her, and Cassie couldn't help but cringe.

"Where is your friend?"

"Robbie went to the kitchen to create one of his concoctions. But I don't mind. Look what it's merited me." His hand stroked her waist. "You are a trim but strong little thing."

He pressed his face toward hers, but the bonnet prevented contact. Cassie tried to maneuver Sebastian toward the bed, but he refused to move.

"Just let me regain my feet for a moment," he suggested in a husky whisper. "You needn't flee like a scared rabbit."

"I'm not afraid; I'm late. Your mother is waiting for me to join her for the ride to church. It is Sunday, after all."

"She'll wait. She's a very patient woman." Sebastian trailed his fingers against Cassie's neck. "You, on the other hand, don't seem very patient at all."

"I'm not," Cassie declared. She pulled away, hoping he would stand on his own, but instead Sebastian began to slip to the floor again. Putting her arm around him once more, Cassie bore his touch as best she could. "You must help me get you back to bed."

"I would certainly go there if you were to join me," he said with a suggestive laugh.

"Your comments are completely inappropriate, Mr. Jameston."

"I know," he said with a grin. "I'm a bit of a rogue."

"To say the least." Cassie forced him to move by pressing her hip and shoulder against him.

Sebastian allowed her help but did nothing to assist. He slumped against her as though he had no strength whatsoever. His legs seemed to be made of rubber.

"You could be my companion," he said, smiling. "I'm really pleasant company when you get to know me."

"But I do not wish to know you."

"You feel so good in my arms," he murmured. "I could remain like this for some time."

"And if you did so, you would probably lose that leg," she chided. "You are very sick, Mr. Jameston. You're lucky your limb has not had to be removed altogether."

"Please call me Sebastian. Better yet, call me Sebbie. That's what my intimate friends call me."

"Intimate friends like your mistress?" Cassie immediately regretted her comment but tried not to let Sebastian see it in her expression or tone.

He laughed and straightened ever so slightly. "I see my mother has already spoiled your good opinion of me."

"I had no good opinion to spoil, Mr. Jameston."

They were finally to the bed, and Cassie turned without warning to position Sebastian so he would fall back against the mattress. What she hadn't counted on was having him pull her down with him.

Without thinking, she slapped him hard against the face and scurried back onto her feet just as Robbie entered the room.

"What's going on?"

"She couldn't resist me," Sebastian said with a laugh. "I told her I was much too weak to fend her off, but she didn't care."

Robbie laughed. "You do have a way with women."

"He has no such thing. He fell, and you were not here to help him. Now you are, and I will no longer bear his abuse nor allow any ridicule from you." She marched to the door, then turned. "The next time you fall, I'll leave you to your curses and moans."

The men laughed as she hurried from the room. Cassie slammed the door closed behind her and muttered under her breath, "Mrs. Jameston was right. He is a scallywag."

Cassie tried to compose herself as she walked slowly down the stairs. Sebastian's actions had unnerved her. No man had ever taken such liberties with her. She felt her face grow hot remembering the way he'd touched her. She found herself longing for another bath to wash off any reminders.

"Goodness, child, I thought I'd have to send Ada in search of you."

"I'm sorry," Cassie said, her gaze fixed on the floor.

"Are you all right?"

Mrs. Jameston's concern was comforting. Cassie didn't want to upset her, so she went to where Brumley held her shawl. "I'm fine." She pulled the light wrap around her shoulders. "I'm sorry to have delayed us. I hope we won't be late."

The older woman eyed her questioningly but said nothing. It was only after they were settled in the carriage that Mrs. Jameston spoke again.

"You might as well tell me what's wrong. I can read in your expression that something has greatly upset you."

Cassie knew it was senseless to try and keep it from her. "Sebastian fell, and I went to assist him when I realized no one else was coming to his aid."

"Oh dear, what did he do?"

"Well, he was on the floor so I helped him back up. He mauled me all the way as I helped him back to bed." She looked away, feeling her cheeks grow quite warm. "Then I pushed him back onto the bed, hoping to free myself from his clutches, but he dragged me down with him."

"I am so very sorry," Mrs. Jameston said quietly.

"You warned me, but I thought with his injury he would be less of a threat. It was my mistake. I should have called for someone. But little harm was done. It merely shook me. I've never been touched by a man in such a forward manner."

"I will speak to him. In fact, I will pay for him to move into a hotel. I won't have you threatened with his behavior."

Cassie held up her gloved hand. "Please do nothing on my account. My pride is smarting once again, but nothing else has been damaged. I couldn't bear to be the reason you sent your only child away."

Mrs. Jameston sighed and leaned back against the leather upholstery. "I thought things would be so different. I thought Sebastian would be a comfort in my old age. I had two other sons who died, and I always worried that Sebastian would follow suit. Instead, he lived, but he became a complete abomination in light of everything I believe and hoped he would learn."

"Tell me about your other children. Tell me about your husband," Cassie said, hoping it would cause Mrs. Jameston to focus on something other than the incident.

"I was given in an arranged marriage to a man nearly twenty years my senior," the woman began. "I thought it a tragedy, but in time I came to truly love Worther Jameston. Bristol was born two years after we wed, and I'd never known greater joy. We moved to the Federal City—Washington—where my husband worked as an aide to the president."

"How exciting. You must have enjoyed that a great deal."

Mrs. Jameston nodded. "For a time. Plymouth was born in 1808. They were two of the sweetest boys. So loving. When Bristol was seven he fell from a tree and broke his arm. The break was quite severe and he developed a blood infection. He died in my arms a few weeks later." She turned to stare at the passing houses. "I was devastated, as was my poor husband."

Cassie patted her hand lovingly. "I cannot imagine how awful it would be to lose a son."

The older woman drew a deep breath. "When the British invaded the capital, I had to flee with Plymouth on my own. My husband was elsewhere, and although we had a plan for escape, I was terrified. It was a night unlike any other. People were hysterical and the terror was contagious.

"I took Plymouth and went to where Mr. Jameston had arranged for us to cross the Potomac under the guard of Federal soldiers. Halfway out, however, Plymouth fell from the ferry and nearly drowned. A soldier jumped in after him and saved his life. The irony of the entire matter was that Plymouth developed a deep love of swimming and boating after that." She smiled sadly. "He was always in or around the water. He loved it so, but it took his life the summer after he turned twenty-one."

"What happened?" Cassie asked softly.

"He was lost at sea. Drowned during a fierce storm. Sebastian wasn't yet two years old, otherwise I might have walked into the ocean and drowned myself. I was beyond grief. I felt that nothing could ever comfort me again. Mr. Jameston tried, but he was grief-stricken as well. He focused on his work, and I tried to put my attention on Sebastian. Unfortunately, I either ignored or overindulged him, depending on the state of my mind. When I was so deep in sorrow, I couldn't even bear to be with him. I feared loving him, only to lose him. Mr. Jameston was much the same. In time, as our grief subsided, we wanted to make up for our mistakes and indifference. We were somehow convinced that if we showered Sebastian with enough gifts and indulged his desires, he would equate it all with our love for him."

Cassie could understand the older woman's reasoning. People were strange in the ways they chose to deal with grief. She easily remembered the way she and her mother had possessively doted on Elida after their father had died.

"You've certainly had to endure more than your share of tragedy and injustice," Cassie finally said.

"But despite all of that," Mrs. Jameston replied, "I learned to trust God. There seemed no other alternative. At first I wanted nothing to do with Him, but in time, I felt such emptiness that I could not bear my sorrow."

"I know how that is. I was so angry with God when my father died. I thought He had abandoned us. My poor mother sat there with her new baby and didn't speak for days. I thought she might go completely to pieces, but she had to stay strong for Elida."

Mrs. Jameston nodded. "In time, I came to see that I needed to be strong for Sebastian, but by then, I suppose it was too late." She sighed. "He hasn't always been the person you see now. He was a good child. Loving and kind—at least for a time."

The carriage pulled to a stop at Christ Church. Cassie spied Mark Langford waiting for them. He came over quickly and opened the carriage door before the driver could move.

"Good morning, ladies."

"Good morning, Mr. Langford," Mrs. Jameston replied. "Forgive our tardiness." She allowed Mark to help her down, then turned. "Does not our Miss Stover look absolutely charming this morning?"

Mark smiled as he met Cassie's gaze. She felt her cheeks flush once again as he spoke. "She does indeed. That gown is lovely, but surely no more beautiful than the occupant."

Cassie allowed him to assist her from the carriage. "You are both quite kind. However, I believe the gown has far more to do with the beauty of my appearance than you give it credit. I'm certain I have never known anything so lovely. The seamstress outdid herself."

"Pshaw," Mrs. Jameston said with a chuckle. "She makes my clothes, as well, and I do not look half so good." She immediately turned to Mark. "Mr. Langford, I am pleased to see that you have joined us. I do hope you will accompany us home for luncheon after services."

Mark nodded and held out his arm for her to take. "I would be honored. Thank you very much."

Cassie seemed greatly preoccupied as the sermon concluded, and Mark couldn't help but wonder what she was thinking. As he escorted the ladies from church, he contemplated how he might approach the matter.

"Mr. Langford, I'd like you to meet my mother, Mrs. Dora Stover." Cassie pulled her mother forward. A young girl was quick to follow. Cassie smiled and hugged her close. "And this is my little sister, Elida."

Elida gave a deep curtsy. "I am charmed to the depths of my being."

Cassie laughed. "My sister tends to be a bit eccentric with her language at times."

Mark smiled at the little girl. She was very much like Cassie in appearance—same broad smile and big eyes. "I am charmed to meet you as well, Miss Elida." He gave her a little bow, then turned to her mother. "And you, Mrs. Stover." His bow was a little more formal as Cassie's mother curtsied. "It is a pleasure to meet you."

"Dora, would you and Elida care to join us for luncheon? Mr. Langford has already agreed to come," Mrs. Jameston interjected.

"Oh, may we please, Mother?" Elida pleaded. "I'll simply languish away if we have to eat pork roast again."

Cassie elbowed her sister. "I thought it was chicken and dumplings you had tired of."

Elida smiled up in an innocent manner. "You can languish away from more than one thing."

Mrs. Stover rolled her eyes heavenward. "I am certain no one is in jeopardy of languishing. I also cannot think of anything more pleasurable than sharing a Sunday dinner with friends."

"Nor can I," Mark said with a grin. "I counted myself blessed to have the company of two lovely ladies, but now I'm doubly blessed to have four such companions."

"Why don't you ride with us, Dora? I know you walked to church, but it's a considerable distance to my house. We'd love to have you and Elida with us."

Elida clutched her gloved hands together under her chin. "Oh, that would be divine!"

"I think so too," Cassie's mother replied, shaking her head at Elida's melodramatics. "We shall be happy to join you, Mrs. Jameston."

As they journeyed to the Jameston residence, Mark on his mount and the ladies in the carriage, Mark hoped he might have time to speak privately with Cassie and approach the subject of Sebastian and his dealings. He wanted to discover whatever details Cassie might share, but at the same time, he didn't want to push her into a place that would ruin any chance he might have of furthering the relationship. After all, as long as he could continue to see Cassie, he would have the ability to be close to Sebastian.

He felt a twinge of guilt as they reached the house and the women were helped from the carriage. Cassie deserved to know the truth. He didn't want to simply use her for whatever information she could give. Still, what if he told her the truth and she revealed it to Mrs. Jameston? Or worse, told Sebastian what he was up to?

Portland snorted out a puff of air as if he could read Mark's thoughts. Dismounting, Mark gave the gelding a gentle pat on the neck. "I know, boy. I know." He tied off the horse, then followed the women into the house. Mr. Brumley awaited him and quickly took charge of his hat and gloves.

"Cassie, why don't you take everyone out into the garden? I'll see to our dinner and join you very soon."

"I'd be happy to," Cassie said. "Mother, you will love Mrs. Jameston's garden."

"I love her house," Elida said in complete awe. "Look at that beautiful staircase!" She stood gape-mouthed as she gently stroked the polished wood.

"Close your mouth, Elida," Mrs. Stover said, laughing. "Mrs. Jameston will believe you were raised to have no manners."

Mark followed behind the women, amused at the animated way Elida danced down the hall. Her imagination seemed to run wild in the face of such luxury.

"Imagine living here, Mama. It would be like you were royalty. Oh, Cassie, is it just wonderful? I would swoon every day if I lived here."

Cassie laughed and gave her sister a hug. "Then it's good that you do not live here. But you are right. It is quite wonderful. I've never known such beauty and elegance. Mrs. Jameston bought me new gowns, like this one, and all new shoes and hats. I cannot even begin to tell you how amazingly generous she is."

Cassie opened the French doors leading out onto the beautiful cobblestone walkway. "Mrs. Jameston told me this was her favorite place, and I believe it has become mine as well," Cassie told them. "The trees offer such restful shade in the afternoon.

Mrs. Jameston said that when everything is in full bloom, it's like a little sanctuary back here."

"Little? But it's so big," Elida said as she ran out into the grass and began to spin, her arms flapping up and down like a bird. She stopped and laughed as if amused by some private joke. "And look at the flowers! They're so beautiful."

Mrs. Stover followed her daughter and chuckled. "Yes, this is a lovely garden. Why don't we go and explore?"

As the twosome walked away, Mark said to Cassie, "While they are occupied, I wanted to ask if you are well. You looked upset this morning."

Cassie frowned. "I was upset, but truly, I am fine. I had a bit of . . . an imposition forced upon me."

It was Mark's turn to frown. "What kind of imposition, if I might be so bold as to ask?"

"Well, I hate to say this, but I had some unsavory interaction with my employer's son. I went to help Mr. Jameston after he fell in his room. There was no one else around, and when I went to him, he was . . . well . . . overly friendly." She flushed. "I can't believe I just told you this."

"Someone should speak to him," Mark said gruffly. "That's hardly something to be allowed."

"Oh, I know. I spoke to his mother, and she offered to send him to a hotel, but I couldn't let her do that. She already struggles with her feelings for him. He's her son, and he's sick."

"He's well enough to molest helpless young women."

"I'm hardly helpless. When he pulled me into bed, I slapped him quite vigorously."

"He pulled you into bed?" Mark felt his anger stirred.

Cassie bit her lip and shook her head. "That sounded so awful—which it was, but nothing happened." She smiled. "Let's just forget about it. It was upsetting, but I shall know better than to assist him next time."

Mark nodded. "I hope you will stay away from him."

"I will. And what of you and your business in Philadelphia? Will you be with us much longer?"

"Why don't we sit? I would very much like to explain something." Mark offered his arm and they walked to where the iron settee and chairs were positioned.

Cassie took a seat on the settee, but Mark found it served his purpose to stand. "I don't know quite where to begin, but it has to do with the loss of my best friend."

"I'm so sorry. When did this happen?" Cassie questioned.

He heard the sincere concern and sympathy in her voice and smiled. "A few weeks back. We had been friends for many years, and losing him has been most difficult to bear."

"I know how that can be." She held his gaze and smiled. "I'm sure he must have been quite a wonderful person, if he was your best friend."

Mark smiled. "Richard was a good man. We were working together and he came here to Philadelphia to investigate a problem." Mark chose his words carefully. He was still uncertain how much he could share. "Richard . . . was killed. Murdered."

"How awful." Cassie put her hand to her throat. "I cannot even fathom such a horrific thing. Who did it?"

"That's part of the reason I'm here, but you cannot speak of it to anyone."

"But why? If you are here to find his murderer, why not shout it out to the world?"

Mark paced a bit, then took a chair beside the settee. "There's something . . . well . . . I'm not sure how to say this, but I believe the time has come for me to—"

"Dinner is ready," Mrs. Jameston announced from the French doors. "Why don't we adjourn to the dining room?"

Cassie looked at him for a moment before rising. "Perhaps we should continue this conversation another time."

"I thought you might like to have some of your favorite chocolate cake," Silas said as he slipped into Sebastian's room. "I made it with you in mind."

"You're the only one who ever considers me," Sebastian said, pushing his dinner tray to one side.

Silas brought the plate to Sebastian and smiled. "It seems you've managed to get yourself in quite a mess this time, Sebbie."

"I suppose so," he said, picking up his fork to sample the cake. "Mother was certainly less than happy to see me. Tell me about this Miss Stover. I'd certainly like to know more about her."

The older man shook his head. "I couldn't really say. She seems to be amiable enough. Your mother finds comfort in her company."

"Unlike she does in mine."

This gained him a sympathetic smile from the cook. "I wouldn't seek to contradict you, sir, but your mother has been notably worried about your health."

"Only because she wants to see me leave as soon as possible." Sebastian forked in another mouthful of cake and gave a little groan of pleasure.

"I'm glad the cake meets with your approval. I should return to the kitchen now. They are serving luncheon below, and I could be needed."

"Silas, I want you to do me a favor."

The man paused and looked at him in question. Sebastian smiled. There was very little Silas wouldn't do for him. He was completely loyal. "Find out what you can about Miss Stover. I'd like to know where she lives when she's not here, and who her family is. I want to know it all."

The man nodded. "I'll do what I can, young master."

Sebastian smiled and turned his attention back to the food. "And send me up another piece of cake. I find my appetite has only just been whetted by this offering."

It had been whetted, too, by the appearance of the beautiful Miss Stover, but Sebastian wouldn't yet take action on that. There was too much at stake. First he had to mend from his wound, and then he had to assure his men that their plans were not jeopardized.

"Of course, first I need to convince myself of that matter," Sebastian said aloud. His eyes narrowed as he thought of the problems that had been thrust upon him, including the leg wound. People would pay for causing him difficulties. He would see to it.

CHAPTER 8

A few days later Cassie strolled beside Mrs. Jameston as they went for their afternoon walk. She had come to greatly enjoy her position as companion to the older woman, and she felt a sense of excitement as they discussed some of the upcoming events to which Mrs. Jameston had been invited.

"I'm not always obligated to attend parties," Mrs. Jameston declared, "but the Wilsons are good friends, as are the Beavertons and Isaacs. I should very much like to attend their gatherings and have replied as such to their invitations. You will, of course, accompany me."

Cassie couldn't begin to imagine what such parties would entail. "I hope I will not embarrass you."

"Hardly, child. Besides, people of society do plenty to embarrass themselves. The Wilsons, for example, have a son who is very nearly as much trouble as my Sebastian. We often commiserate. Oh look, the lilacs are beginning to bud! It won't be long now before they are flowering in full."

Cassie let her gaze travel to the bushes, heavy with the promise of springtime flowers.

"I love to have huge collections of them in every room. It makes the house smell so sweet," Mrs. Jameston admitted. "But I digress. The Wilsons will have a party in May to celebrate Henrietta's birthday. She hasn't been all that healthy of late, but she does love to celebrate her birthday. We will attend the dinner, and then if it seems the party is going well, we might stay for the dance."

"What do you mean, if the party is going well?" Cassie asked.

"As I mentioned, they have a son who is quite unruly. His name is Franklin, and he has ruined more than one of his mother's parties. He never comes for the dinner but generally shows up at the dance to cause enough of a commotion that most of us make plans to leave prior to his arrival."

"How sad that he should ruin what means so much to his mother."

Mrs. Jameston nodded. "He has always been jealous of his mother. She holds his father's affections in full, and Franklin has often felt left out of their circle. It isn't true, of course, for his five sisters seem to feel no such abandonment, but Franklin is frustrated by his mother's influence over his father. She often advises him in matters of business, and Franklin feels he should be the only one attending to that. But enough of such miseries."

She began to walk again and pointed toward a large house with her silver-tipped cane. "That is the Isaacs' house. They have been in Philadelphia since before the war. Of course, the house was less grand back then. Mr. Isaacs made a fortune in railroad investments and built this beautiful stone estate for his new bride."

Cassie had seen the grand mansion on several occasions during her private strolls. She couldn't imagine what it would be like to have a husband who loved you so much that he would spend that kind of fortune to please you. Mark's image came to mind and she felt her stomach give a flip.

Memories from Sunday remained strong in Cassie's mind. Mark had been about to tell her something important when Mrs. Jameston had called them to dinner. He had never found the opportunity to speak on the matter again, and for that Cassie was sorry. He appeared to be quite vexed about it, and why not? His best friend had been murdered, likely cut down in the prime of his life. Cassie could not begin to imagine how awful it would be to have to seek out the man who'd killed your friend.

"I do not believe you have heard a word I've said," Mrs. Jameston said. She stopped and looked at Cassie with a grin. "Whatever—or whomever—is on your mind?"

Cassie shook her head. "I am sorry. I don't mean to be so preoccupied. I suppose it's because I'm nearly a year older." She laughed.

"You are about to have a birthday?"

"Yes. This Saturday, the twenty-fifth. I'll be twenty-five. The same number as the day. Mother teased me that this was a lucky birthday. She said that when you had a birthday that matched the date you were born, you would be extra blessed with God's good gifts."

"What a pleasant thought. Oh, but we must have a party for you."

"No, that's quite all right. I wish to celebrate with my mother and sister." She put her hand to her mouth. Speaking through her gloved fingers she apologized. "I didn't mean to sound ungracious. Of course I'd love celebrating with you as well. I just know that my mother plans to make my favorite meal."

"She can make it at my house, or we can have Silas make it and give her a rest."

"You are so generous. How kind."

"We shall also invite that nice Mr. Langford. I think he has an eye for you, Cassie. He seems such a decent sort."

"I find his company . . . easy to bear," Cassie said.

Mrs. Jameston gave a knowing laugh. "Easy to bear . . . yes, yes. And he's handsome too."

Cassie laughed. "Yes. That had not escaped my notice."

This only made Mrs. Jameston laugh all the more. "We shall have a grand time of it. I will send word immediately to your mother, as well as an invitation to Mr. Langford. Should we invite anyone else?"

"No," Cassie said, smiling. "There really isn't anyone else with whom I would rather spend my day."

Mark checked his pocket watch as he made his way into the boardinghouse. He'd had no luck locating the address of Sebastian Jameston's mistress and was feeling a great sense of urgency to accomplish something more than he'd already done.

"Evening," August Westmoreland greeted as Mark entered the front parlor.

"Good evening." Mark nodded to the proprietor.

The stocky man gave his chin a scratch, then struggled to his feet with the help of a sturdy oak cane. "You were certainly gone for a long time. I hope the time merited you well."

"It did not, unfortunately." Mark took a seat as Mr. Westmoreland continued to watch him.

"You seem concerned." Westmoreland tilted his head. "Is there naught that I can do to offer you aid?"

Mark considered this for a moment. Perhaps it was time to put him to work. "I understand you used to work as a police officer," he started.

"I did," the man said. He went to the window and closed it before hobbling back to his chair. "It's going to rain. I can feel it all the way down my spine. My leg only acts up when it rains," he continued, as if Mark had demanded some sort of explanation for the cane.

"I thought the air felt rather heavy," Mark replied. "I'm sure you are right about the weather."

"Most everyone is out for the evening. My sister has made a wonderful dinner of lamb stew, but if you'd like to delay here a bit longer, you can explain what kind of help you need that you would bring up my former situation."

Mark nodded. "I was told you were a good man to see about private matters that needed further investigation. I was told you were able to keep information in confidence—as well as do a good job for a fair price."

The man grinned and ran his hand through his hair. "Aye, that I am."

"Well, I am in need of such a man."

"Then let us discuss your situation over supper. I'll send Nancy to visit her friend, as she ate earlier with the others. We'll have the house to ourselves, at least for a time."

"That sounds perfect," Mark replied.

"When does the next shipment come in?" Sebastian questioned. Robbie had just finished re-dressing his leg. The wound looked much better, and Sebastian knew his fever was nearly gone.

"The twenty-seventh. The ship was delayed after it left France. They had trouble and had to make port temporarily in Plymouth. They weren't long detained, but long enough that it set our schedule back."

Thunder rumbled as a light rain began to splatter against the windowpanes. Sebastian motioned to Robbie to close the window. "Have the police stopped nosing around regarding that insurance investigator's death?" Sebastian narrowed his eyes. "I won't have that mess rearing its ugly head again."

Robbie returned from the window and shrugged. "There have been no further questions. I've found no one else to be snooping around the docks. The boys would have told me if there was a real threat. So far, no one has come to bother them."

"Good. That's what I like to hear. Still, I'm certain they will not just set it aside. Unless I miss my guess, they'll send someone else as soon as they decide how to go about it. Now, tell me about this next shipment."

Robbie fanned through some papers before pulling one sheet from the pile. "The original freight had nothing more than rubber boots, tea, and other incidentals. However, it has been insured as being a far more valuable cargo." He grinned. "As it now reads, it contains expensive china, crystal, and rare pieces of art, including those that are supposedly being sold from one collector to another."

"Good. Still, given the trouble we've had in the past, I'm inclined to believe it might be time for a change. We should definitely consider ending our work here and moving on to another location."

Robbie crossed the room and sat down on the edge of Sebastian's bed. "Do you know how long it will take to secure and train another group of dock workers? It will also be quite expensive, and I hardly think we're prepared for that."

"That's true. Unless I can get money from my mother," Sebastian stated, easing back against the pillows. "I'm certain to be able to get some support from her, but whether it will be enough is another question. However, I already know the location. Baltimore."

"Baltimore? But why?"

"Because we have mutual friends there who have served us well in the past. I believe they would prove useful in securing a force to assist us," Sebastian declared.

"I hadn't thought about it before, but I suppose you are right." Robbie seemed to think about the matter for several minutes. "Baltimore would be a reasonable location."

"And some of the men we work with here would most likely be happy to follow us," Sebastian said, grinning. "After all, it's not so very far away."

"But what if the insurance company just sends someone else after us?"

"I've thought about that as well. I believe it is time for change—there are other insurance companies; perhaps it would behoove us to do a little investigating of our own and locate a more . . . accommodating company. Say, one that has an employee who would like to benefit from our organization."

"A true inside man?" Robbie questioned. "That could also be very dangerous."

"It could be," Sebastian agreed, "but if we offer the right price, I believe we can purchase all the safety we need. I believe it's where we've failed in the past. That insurance investigator—that Adkins fellow—could have been very useful to us . . . if we could have found his price. If we could have won him over to our side, he could have reported back to his people that there was nothing out of line. Now, however, things are different."

Robbie ran a hand through his hair. "You're laid up with a wound that nearly cost you a leg, and there are no doubt other investigators who will be sent to seek out the truth of what happened."

"I believe we covered things up well enough. It looked like a simple robbery and nothing more. Even the police were happy to call it so. Don't make more of this than is necessary."

"I wish I could feel as confident as you are," Robbie admitted. He got up and walked to where he'd left his coat. Shoving papers into a pocket, he pulled on the coat and shrugged. "I suppose I must make my way to the docks and check in with the fellows there. Do you want me to mention the idea of Baltimore to them?"

Sebastian considered this for a moment. "I think it would be a bit premature. I'm still a few weeks away from being able to fully function as I once did. The less we say for now, the better. The shipment will come to us in four days' time. If all goes well, tell them there will be something special in it for each man."

Robbie nodded. "I'll do exactly that."

Sebastian waited until Robbie had been gone for a full half hour before getting up to test his leg. Robbie would have him lie about and do nothing all day, and Sebastian knew that would only lead to additional weakness. He hobbled around the bed, careful to hold on to the framework for support.

The throbbing started up with his sixth step, but Sebastian wasn't about to let it stop him. He had to regain the use of his leg. He had to get himself back in business as soon as possible. Otherwise he would lose too much. Money would be funneled elsewhere to more competent schemers, and he couldn't let that happen.

He made it to the far window without too much trouble. Pushing aside the drapery, he looked down upon the front lawn to find the beautiful Miss Stover walking with his mother. They seemed to be taking note of the flower beds.

The memory of her body against his caused Sebastian to smile. She was a tasty dish, one he intended to sample.

Of course, she had proven difficult so far, but that was to be expected. He grinned.

"I needn't worry about you, dear little Cassie. You'll do my bidding soon enough."

His mother had warned him about bothering her staff, but Sebastian cared little for her concern. He knew how to handle his mother. She was frail and weak and not long for this world. That thought alone gave him reason to smile. An idea that had once been cast aside began to brew again. If his mother were to die, he would inherit everything. He'd been careful to bide his time.

Sebastian's gaze again focused on Miss Stover. He loved the way her hips swayed as she walked. He noted her figure was slender, and she was taller than most of the women he knew. Sebastian liked that fact very much as he, too, was tall.

It was dangerous, he thought, to have his mind so divided, but he couldn't help himself. That Stover woman had captured his imagination in the worst way. He would have to see about putting himself in her company.

Silas had learned where her mother and sister lived, along with the fact that Cassie's father had died many years ago. The family had lived quite meagerly after that, and Sebastian wondered if expensive gifts might entice Cassie to think more fondly of him. It was obvious she was raised to be a lady, but even ladies were generally known to submit to seduction—if the price was right.

He laughed and retested his leg as he hobbled back to bed. "I will have to find that price and pay it. Or perhaps just steal what I want, as I often do."

CHAPTER 9

Cassie couldn't help but touch the folds of her silk gown once again. The yellow shade was one that Mrs. Jameston insisted she have, and Cassie had to admit she loved it. The neckline was rounded in a modest manner and trimmed in ivory lace that had also been sewn along the corded ribbing that formed a V along the bodice to the waist.

"I've never seen such a pretty gown," Elida said. "It's just like you're a princess."

"Mrs. Jameston gave me the dress as a gift," Cassie told her little sister in a whisper. "Perhaps we can have one in a similar shade made for you, and you can be a princess too."

"I would like that." Elida giggled. "I've always wanted to be a princess."

Cassie laughed. "Me too."

"What are you girls giggling about over there?" Mrs. Jameston asked with a smile.

"We were talking about princesses," Cassie admitted.

"Did I ever tell you that I once attended a party where Princess Victoria, now Queen Victoria, was also present?" Mrs. Jameston questioned. "Her mother kept her very secluded, but on this rare occasion she was allowed to attend. I cannot even remember what the party was all about, but I do remember her. She was so elegant and stately. A finer monarch England has never had."

"You met a real princess?" Elida said in awe. "Did she wear a crown?"

"Of course," Mrs. Jameston said with a smile.

Just then, Mr. Brumley appeared at the door. "Mr. Langford," he announced.

Cassie looked up to see Mark in his dark brown suit. He looked so handsome, and Cassie couldn't help but feel her heart skip a beat. He made her feel special, and no other man had done that since her father was alive.

"Mr. Langford, we're very honored you could attend the party," Mrs. Jameston declared. She stepped forward, and Mark gave her a bow.

"The honor is all mine. I feel quite blessed to have been included. It's hard to be a stranger so far from home." He smiled and met Cassie's gaze.

For a moment, she felt embarrassed that he'd caught her staring but realized that it was only natural. Everyone was looking at him. She calmed her nerves and returned his smile.

"Happy birthday, Miss Stover."

"Thank you. I must say this is such a treat. Mrs. Jameston has been most generous. I'm very glad you could attend." She didn't dare say more, or she might ramble on and on about how she couldn't think of anything but seeing him again.

"Cassie got a new princess dress," Elida stated as if Mark couldn't see for himself. "Isn't she grand?"

"She is quite pretty." He held Cassie's gaze.

Elida sidled up to him as if they'd been the best of friends for years. "I always think Cassie is pretty," she said rather conspiratorially, "but today, she is *incomparable*."

Cassie felt her face grow hot even as she wanted to laugh at her sister's choice of words.

"I would have to agree," Mark said, giving Cassie a wink.

She could only pray that they would change the subject or that perhaps the floor would open up and swallow her whole. It seemed so awkward to be embarrassed so completely by the attention of a handsome man. Of course, it had never happened to her before. She remembered the glances and affections of young men when she'd been but a girl, but those men seemed to rapidly vanish from her circle after her father died and their social status dropped considerably.

"I believe I'll go check on the meal," Cassie's mother announced. "Your cook seemed upset at having me in his kitchen, and I would hate to add further insult to him by ignoring the meal."

"I have something to see to as well," Mrs. Jameston added. "I'm certain Cassie will keep you amply entertained." She looked at Mark with a grin. She seemed to enjoy the discomfort that all this attention was causing Cassie.

"I am certain she will." Mark's tone betrayed amusement.

Once the women had left the room, Elida surprised Cassie by taking hold of Mark's hand and dragging him toward one of the settees. "Cassie said you are going to teach her not to be afraid of horses. Can you teach me about horses too? I've always wanted to ride, but Cassie and Mama are too afraid of them. I'm not afraid, but I need someone to show me how. I'll positively expire if I do not learn how to ride." Her brown ringlets danced down her back as she whirled and plopped down on the seat.

Mark sat beside her and replied seriously, "We cannot have that, Miss Elida. If your mother agrees, I will do what I can to see the task done."

"Can you come every day?" she asked with great enthusiasm.

"Elida, Mr. Langford also has work to do. He is here, after all, on business." Cassie took a seat in the chair nearest her sister.

"I can easily divide my time," Mark said. "Oh, I nearly forgot." He reached into his pocket and pulled out a brown paper–wrapped parcel. "This is for you. Happy birthday."

Cassie took the package and shook her head. "But you shouldn't have."

"And why not? It is your birthday, and it seems perfectly appropriate to give a gift."

"Open it, Cassie. Let's see what he got you," Elida demanded.

"It isn't much, but it has special meaning to me," Mark told her.

Cassie unwrapped the paper and turned over a burgundy book. Embossed in gold letters were the words *Poetry for the Ages*. "It's lovely." She opened the volume and perused several pages before she looked up to meet Mark's eyes. "Thank you so much. I know I'll enjoy this."

"My wife gifted me with a copy years ago. I always enjoyed the poems there."

Cassie felt her heart sink. "You have a wife?" she blurted. How stupid she felt. She thought he had come here out of interest for her. But instead he was married. Her mind began to race.

Mark frowned. "She died years ago. I thought I had mentioned her before. I'm sorry."

Cassie calmed and refocused her attention on the book. "I'm the one who is sorry. Might I ask how she died?"

"Cholera," Mark replied. "She was just twenty-five."

"That's how old Cassie is today," Elida said, jumping up. "And I'm going to be ten on May the second." Cassie looked up to reprimand her sister, but she had no chance. The fact was, she was glad Elida had changed the subject.

"You are? How very exciting," Mark said, seeming to shake the sadness from his voice as he smiled at the child. "That's a perfect age to learn about horses. By the time I was ten, I could ride nearly as well as my older brothers."

"Dinner is nearly ready," Cassie's mother announced. Mrs. Jameston was on her heels as they returned to the sitting room.

"Look what Mr. Langford gave Cassie," Elida said, pointing to the book of poetry.

"How very kind. What a thoughtful gift," Cassie's mother commented.

"Since we are giving gifts, I'd like to share my gift with Cassie," Mrs. Jameston announced.

"But you've already given me this gown and so much more," Cassie protested.

"Nevertheless, there is more. Come to the garden."

Mrs. Jameston led the way and didn't wait for anyone else to respond. "Mr. Langford, you bring Cassie."

Elida danced down the hall after her mother and Mrs. Jameston, while Mark assisted Cassie to her feet and took the book from her hands. "We can leave this here for now. There's no telling what Mrs. Jameston has in mind."

Cassie liked the way Mark took hold of her arm and tucked it against his side. But Cassie found herself longing to know more about his wife. Without thinking, she said, "Will you tell me more about your wife sometime?"

He stopped and looked at her oddly. For a moment, Cassie thought that once again she'd made the mistake of speaking without thinking. To her surprise, however, Mark smiled.

"I'd love to. Ruth was a wonderful woman."

Cassie nodded. "I'm sure she was. You must miss her very much."

"I do at times, but it's been seven years, and I find that my heart has mended. I am surprised, I must admit, that you make such a request. Most women do not like to hear stories of other women—even wives dead and gone. It seems strange that you would want to know more."

It was hard to explain why she wanted to hear more. Cassie supposed it was because she longed to know Mark better. Still, she could hardly say that without having to explain herself.

"I . . . well . . . I enjoy people," Cassie began. At least that much was true. "I find stories about people to be fascinating. That's why I love to read." She shrugged. "I suppose I'm a bit of a bore."

Mark laughed and pulled her along to the garden. "Not at all. You care about people and what is important to them. That makes you special. Not a bore at all."

Once they were in the garden, Mrs. Jameston motioned to Mark. "Cover Cassie's eyes. I don't want her to see her gift before the time is right."

Cassie looked at Mark, who raised a brow and gave her an impish grin. He dropped his hold and moved to stand behind her. He stood so close that the skirt of Cassie's gown billowed forward a bit.

"This could be great fun," he murmured against her ear. "I feel like it's my birthday."

Cassie trembled when he put his warm hand over her eyes. She wanted nothing more than to lean back against him, and for a moment she pretended to do just that. How wonderful it would be if she were married to Mark and had the right to let him hold her so intimately.

"All right, Wills. You may bring the gift out," Mrs. Jameston called.

A gasp from her mother drew Cassie's attention. "Oh dear," her mother said, causing Cassie to stiffen.

"There might be a problem," Mark said as he put a hand on Cassie's arm. He whispered against her ear, "Don't be afraid."

"Whyever would there be a problem?" Mrs. Jameston questioned.

"Because Cassie doesn't—"

"Hush, Elida!" their mother commanded.

This was Cassie's undoing. She was already trembling from Mark's whispered breath on her skin. The nearness of him was overwhelming her. She pulled his hand down and found a dapple-gray horse standing not three feet away.

She couldn't halt the scream that escaped her mouth, causing the horse to start. The groomsman fought to keep the beast under control while Cassie turned quickly to bury her face against Mark's shoulder.

"Whatever is the matter?" asked Mrs. Jameston.

"Cassie is afraid of horses," Mrs. Stover told their hostess.

Cassie hated the way her heart pounded in fear, but she found Mark's hold soothing. He patted her back while whispering words of comfort.

"You're all right. The horse will not harm you. Look, she's calmed now."

"Cassie witnessed her father's death," her mother began to explain to the confused Mrs. Jameston. "He was thrown from a horse and trampled to death. She's been afraid of horses ever since."

"Oh, my dear. I am sorry," Mrs. Jameston declared. "Wills, take the mare back to the stable. Cassie, I wish I had known. I feel so bad. I could not have chosen a worse gift."

"On the contrary, Mrs. Jameston," Mark stated. "Miss Stover had already agreed to let me help her get over her fear. This will be perfect. I can come here and work with her, and eventually take her out riding. It is the perfect gift."

"And if Mama agrees, he's going to teach me to ride too," Elida announced.

Cassie drew a deep breath and squared her shoulders as the groomsman led the animal away. She could see the worried expression on Mrs. Jameston's face and knew she would have to put her fear aside.

"Mr. Langford is right. I do plan to overcome my fear. Your gift is not only thoughtful and overly generous, but perfectly appropriate." She went to Mrs. Jameston and kissed her on the cheek. "Thank you so very much."

"It hardly seems like something you should thank me for."

"Miss Stover is right," Mark offered. "It is very appropriate, and she's quite a handsome mare. She'll suit very well, I'm sure."

Mrs. Jameston still didn't look convinced, but said nothing more. She moved quickly toward the house. "Why don't we go back inside and have our dinner. Later, you may want to see the horse again. Perhaps with the animal in its pen, you will feel less fear."

"Perhaps," Cassie said, forcing a smile. She glanced at Mark, who gave her a wink. "Perhaps the horse will also sprout wings and fly away."

Mark gave a hearty chuckle, causing everyone to turn and stare. Cassie merely shrugged her shoulders. "He's a very happy fellow, is he not?"

Mark couldn't remember the last time he'd enjoyed a day as much as he had this day. Watching Cassie with her sister, he was touched by her patience and genuine affection for the child.

"Your daughters seem quite fond of each other," he told Mrs. Stover as they relaxed in the garden.

"Oh goodness, but they are. Cassie has been a second mother to Elida. They love each other dearly. Don't tell Cassie, but Elida cried almost every night for over a week when Cassie moved here to live with Mrs. Jameston."

"I wouldn't dream of mentioning it," Mark promised. Mrs. Jameston had taken leave of them to attend to her son's demands, and Mark was quite glad for the time to speak privately with Cassie's mother.

"When I lost their father, the girls were all I had to keep me going. Sorrow nearly swallowed me whole."

Mark nodded. "When my wife died, I felt the same way. My friend Richard helped pull me through, but it was the most difficult thing I've ever had to do."

"You must have been quite young." Mrs. Stover offered him a sympathetic smile. "Of course, to my eyes, you seem young even now."

"I feel as if I've aged a decade of years past my thirty-two. I only recently lost my friend Richard as well. It has been most difficult to endure, but I find Cassie has been a pleasant diversion." He smiled as she played tag with her sister.

"Cassie is a dear girl," her mother agreed. "I hope you will be kind to her. She's never allowed herself to be courted." Mrs. Stover looked hard at Mark. "She's never allowed herself much fun at all. Not since her father's death."

"I can well imagine. She seems to take responsibility very seriously."

"Yes—even responsibility that doesn't belong to her."

"If it comforts you, I have only the best intentions. I would never purposely hurt her." But even as he spoke, Mark felt a twinge of guilt. While he found Cassie fascinating, even special, he was also here because of Sebastian. He reminded himself that Mr. Jameston had to remain the focus of his attention.

Mrs. Stover smiled. "I didn't believe you would. But she is rather naïve about matters of the heart. I only ask you to treat her kindly and with great respect."

"I give you my word," Mark declared.

Cassie came to join them just then. Elida seemed to have endless energy, but Cassie made it clear that she was spent. "I have to catch my breath. You've worn me out."

Mrs. Stover laughed. "We must make our way home, Cassie. Mrs. Jameston has offered her carriage for us, and I told her we would be ready to leave by four."

"Oh, do we have to go?" Elida moaned. "I love it here. It's so cheery. Not dark and gloomy like our house."

"Elida!" Cassie waggled her finger. "That is unkind. Our little house is quite nice."

"We don't have a garden like this," Elida muttered. "And the roof leaks."

"We'll soon set the roof right, and perhaps if you were willing to do the work, you could have a very pleasant garden too,"

Cassie chided. "Gardens are very time consuming. Wills spends a good deal of time out here trimming and planting. His wife, Miriam, helps as well. Later in the summer, Mrs. Jameston even hires a couple of other young men to come and help. It takes a great deal of effort to develop something like this."

"Come, Elida. We need to get home." Her mother stood and smiled down at Cassie. "I left your birthday gift in your room. Mrs. Jameston took me there earlier."

"You shouldn't have brought me a present. You made us lunch, after all."

"And a wonderful lunch it was," Mark added, getting to his feet as well.

Mrs. Stover smiled and pulled on her bonnet. "I'm glad you enjoyed it."

Cassie kissed her mother good-bye. "I will see you at church tomorrow."

"Can't I stay?" Elida begged.

"Perhaps sometime you may," Cassie replied, "but for now I think you should accompany Mother, or she might grow too lonely."

Elida reluctantly sighed and nodded. "Good-bye, Cassie. It hasn't been any fun at all without you at home. I've missed you so much."

"I've missed you, too, but everything will work out. You'll see." Cassie gave her sister a hug and then kissed the top of her head. "Come on, I'll see you to the carriage."

"Nonsense," her mother said, waving her off. "I know the way, and you have a guest to entertain. Please give Mrs. Jameston my regards."

"I'm sure she will be sorry to have missed your departure. Her son has taken up a great deal of her time of late."

Mrs. Stover nodded. "It is no bother to me. Just let her know what a wonderful time we had."

"I will."

Mark waited until they were gone before speaking. "Maybe we could visit your mare for a few moments. She really did seem gentle."

Cassie looked at him and rolled her eyes heavenward. "So do rabid dogs—until they decide to attack."

Mark laughed. "And how many rabid dogs have you encountered of late?"

"Well . . . I suppose to be honest . . . none."

"And I have never dealt with one either, so I believe that to be a rather poor analogy."

"Perhaps, but you understood my position nevertheless."

He took hold of her arm. "Indeed I did. But, for the sake of pleasing Mrs. Jameston, why don't we pretend that you adore her gift and have never wanted anything as much as you do that dapple gray."

"I'm good at pretending," Cassie told him. "I just don't know if I'm that good."

"Well, you'll never know if you don't at least give it a try."

By the time Cassie fell into bed that evening it was quite late. Her mother's gift of a new handmade shawl lay neatly across the end of the bed, while Mark's book of poetry was tucked beneath her pillow. She supposed it was silly, but she'd thought to put it there much like a piece of wedding cake—to encourage dreams of the one she might one day marry.

Her fingers touched the binding as she closed her eyes. "I know I'm being silly," she whispered into the night, but she left the book there nevertheless.

CHAPTER 10

"Well, well. This looks to be a cozy family luncheon," Sebastian said, eyeing Cassie and his mother. He hobbled into the dining room, with Robbie following behind. "A quiet Sunday dinner it would seem. Am I to be excluded?"

"I didn't expect you to join us, but I can have Essie set two more places," Mrs. Jameston replied with a frown. "Are you certain you are well enough to be out of bed?"

"I am greatly improved," Sebastian said as he took his place at the table. "And I needed a change of scenery." He gave Cassie a seductive wink. "I find this scenery is greatly improved over that in my bedroom."

Essie entered the room carrying a tureen of soup. She nearly dropped the fine china piece at the sight of Sebastian. Cassie quickly took the soup from her and placed it on the table.

"Essie, we need two additional place settings," Mrs. Jameston instructed.

Cassie watched as Essie lowered her gaze. "Yes, ma'am." She hurried from the room.

"Such a little mouse," Sebastian commented. "She always has been rather skittish."

Robbie took his seat beside Sebastian and laughed. "You seem to have that effect on a lot of women."

Sebastian laughed. "Miss Stover, do you feel that way? Do I make you skittish as well?"

"I have no feelings toward you, skittish or otherwise." Cassie picked up her linen napkin and placed it on her lap. "Mrs. Jameston, would you like me to offer grace?"

Just then Essie returned and hurriedly put down two place settings of china and silver. She pulled linen napkins from her apron pocket and offered them to each of the men.

"Essie, you naughty thing, you haven't yet come to visit me," Sebastian said, taking hold of her hand as she extended the napkin.

Cassie couldn't help but notice the frightened way Essie looked back and forth from Sebastian to his mother.

"Sebastian, unhand her. You know better than to act in such a way," his mother admonished. "Essie has no purpose or reason to visit you. Now leave her alone."

"We were once very close," he told Robbie as he finally dropped Essie's hand. "Very close."

"Not by choice," Mrs. Jameston interjected. "Now, Cassie, please offer our prayer of thanks."

Cassie muttered a quick prayer, but her mind was hardly on the words. She couldn't help but remember the way Mr. Jameston had handled her when she'd gone to help him. She could still remember the feel of his hands on her body, and it repulsed her greatly.

She concluded the prayer and looked up to see Sebastian watching her closely. His scrutiny made her feel uncomfortable, but Cassie did her best to disguise it as she removed the lid from the soup tureen.

"Silas has made us an oyster soup," Cassie announced.

"I asked him to," Mrs. Jameston said. "We're soon to be into the summer months. April is the last good month for oysters until September."

Essie bustled back and forth to the table several times to bring additional dishes of food. She was careful to steer clear of Sebastian, which made an awkward placing of all of the food on one side of the table.

Mrs. Jameston didn't admonish her for this, however. She merely dismissed the girl and proceeded to serve herself.

"I am glad to see you on the road to recovery, Sebastian," Mrs. Jameston began. She passed a plate of bread to her son and added, "Perhaps it would be a good time to consider moving elsewhere. Say, to a hotel."

Sebastian frowned. "Why would you suggest that? This is my home, isn't it?"

Mrs. Jameston focused on a platter of roasted lamb. "To be quite honest, it isn't. You made that choice some time ago. You only return here when you are in need. Otherwise, I scarcely even know if you're alive or dead."

"What a horrible thing to say to your only living child." Sebastian appeared greatly offended, but Cassie could see the underlying hatred in his eyes. "Would your mother ever treat you so poorly, Robbie?"

Robbie looked first at Sebastian and then at the bowl of candied sweet potatoes being offered him by Cassie. He took the food and smiled. "She might, if I were remiss in visiting or attending to her needs."

"But Mother has no needs. She has hired a complete stranger to share her company and has more than enough money to buy anything else she needs," Sebastian countered. "She has no need of my company. At least that's what her comment would suggest."

"I had great need for your company, at one time. You chose to turn away from me," his mother replied.

"You were the one to turn away first, Mother. After my brother died, you scarcely acknowledged having another son in the house. My nanny took more interest."

"But it wasn't always that way," Mrs. Jameston said in her own defense. "I've never been able to understand why you can't find it in your heart to forgive me my mistakes. I've lived these long years with the consequences, grieving the loss of our relationship."

"Just as I grieved the loss when a small boy."

Cassie felt sorry for the man. For a moment he almost seemed vulnerable, and then she saw him harden again as he watched his mother's reaction. Was it all just a game?

"Can you not forgive your father and me?"

Sebastian's eyes glinted as they narrowed. "And that would make it all better? Would that ease your conscience, Mother?"

"Why must you always act with such hostility?" she asked. "I acknowledge that you were wronged, and whether you believe me or not, I am deeply sorry. I regret my actions of long ago."

"You should regret your actions now. You treat me like a stranger. You don't even want me here."

"I don't wish to endure the trouble you cause whenever you are in residence," Mrs. Jameston said. Her own bright blue eyes narrowed. "You are not respectful of others, and I will not have my household turned topsy-turvy for the sake of your entertainment. Not only that, but you refuse to adhere to my rules. Mrs. Dixon found several bottles of alcohol in your room. You know my feelings on such things."

"I'm a grown man who happens to be in a great deal of pain. The liquor was for that purpose. Would you begrudge me relief from my misery?"

"I offered to get you a doctor, but you wouldn't hear of it. Why should I feel bad about such a matter when you refuse to take the help offered? If you are in pain, it is of your own doing, not mine."

"Such a kind comment from a loving mother, to be sure."

Noting that Sebastian's anger was mounting, Cassie thought perhaps it would behoove her to intercede and change the subject. "I want to thank you again for a lovely birthday party, Mrs. Jameston. I know my mother and sister were delighted."

Mrs. Jameston looked away from Sebastian and met Cassie's eyes. "It was my pleasure. I am sure Mr. Langford enjoyed himself as well."

Cassie looked down at her plate. "I certainly hope so."

"I would have enjoyed a party," Sebastian said rather accusingly. "Why was I not invited?"

His mother helped herself to a portion of sautéed greens before addressing the question. "You stood to benefit more by resting."

The answer didn't set well with Sebastian, but to Cassie's surprise he turned his attention to the food. They ate in silence for what seemed an eternity. Robbie never even bothered to raise his focus from the plate, while Cassie hardly tasted her food. Mr. Jameston's anger seemed to hang thick in the air and made her uncomfortable even though she was sitting across from him—out of his reach.

Cassie felt confused by all that had just taken place. For a moment she had actually felt some sympathy for Sebastian, but there was something about his reaction that seemed less than sincere. Even now watching him, she could see the anger in his expression, but not the pain she might have expected. To Cassie's way of thinking, he didn't appear nearly as wounded by his neglect as he let on. Essie came into the room, casting a hesitant glance in Sebastian's direction. She checked the platters and asked Mrs. Jameston if they would need more bread.

"No, Essie. Why don't you take yourself upstairs for a rest? We can see to this."

The young woman looked noticeably relieved and nearly ran from the room without another word. Sebastian sat back and wiped his mouth almost ceremonially.

"You treat the servants better than you treat your own son. Something seems very wrong with that."

"Sebastian, if you wish to discuss this matter further, I will see you in private. There is no need to ruin everyone else's dinner." She raised a brow as if in question as to what he preferred. When Sebastian didn't reply, Mrs. Jameston dabbed her lips with her napkin. "Perhaps it would be to our mutual benefit to leave off with this subject altogether."

"I do not wish to leave off with it," Sebastian said, throwing down his napkin. "You treat me abominably. Robbie knows it, and now Miss Stover knows it as well."

"I do not wish to further your embarrassment by continuing this conversation." Mrs. Jameston picked up her teacup and appeared to dismiss her son.

Sebastian hit the table with his fist. "I am hardly embarrassed by your lack of motherly love and concern. That is your embarrassment, madam."

Cassie watched as the older woman continued to sip her tea. Robbie put his hand on Sebastian's arm and whispered something.

"I don't mean to calm down. I've been rejected in my own home." He got to his feet.

Cassie watched him as he struck an indignant pose. It was almost as if he were an actor playing a part. Something about the entire situation rang false.

"You put yourself from this house," his mother said, setting her cup down. "You refuse to accept my apology or my love. You refuse to forgive a past that I clearly admit having handled poorly. You molested my servants and brought shame upon yourself."

"Your serving girls threw themselves at me, then cried foul when I took them up on their wanton behavior. Essie parades around here like a wounded soul, but believe me, she was willing enough when I took her to—"

"Enough! I will not have such talk at my table!"

Sebastian laughed. "Of course not. We wouldn't want your dear companion to see the distasteful side of life in the Jameston palace." He stormed from the room, and Robbie followed silently.

Mrs. Jameston drew a deep breath and looked to Cassie. "I apologize. That should never have taken place. I will go to him and see if I cannot bring about a truce at least." She rose from the table and smiled. "Please feel free to continue your meal."

Cassie immediately got to her feet. "Let me assist you."

"No, please do not leave on my account."

Cassie took hold of her arm and walked with her into the foyer. "You're trembling. Are you all right?"

"I'm fine, my dear. Please enjoy your meal in peace."

Cassie hesitated but let Mrs. Jameston go her own way. A part of her longed to go with the older woman and give Sebastian further comeuppance for his behavior, but an equally strong part wished to have nothing more to do with the man.

"How can he be so cruel?" she muttered as she crossed the foyer to find solace in the front sitting room. *It's obvious he was only saying those things to upset his mother. I could see in his eyes that he was playing us all for fools.* Of course there was no way to prove that, and Mrs. Jameston was clearly overwhelmed by the guilt she felt for the past.

Brumley opened the front door as she passed, and Cassie was surprised to find Mark Langford standing on the other side. She knew her expression must surely have suggested her emotional state, for Mark's face immediately tensed.

"Are you all right?" he asked, stepping into the house.

"No. Not in the least," she admitted.

"Would you care to walk with me?"

Cassie drew a deep breath and nodded. "I'd like that very much."

Brumley turned. "I will tell Mrs. Jameston that you've gone out. Should she need anything, I will attend to the matter."

"Thank you, Mr. Brumley." Cassie didn't even bother to retrieve her bonnet and gloves. "I'll be back shortly."

She walked in silence beside Mark until they had gone nearly half a block. She barely noticed the scenery around her as she struggled to figure out how to tell Mark all that had happened.

"What's wrong?" he asked softly.

"Mrs. Jameston's son."

Mark stopped her and turned her to face him. "Has he acted inappropriately again?"

"He's a dreadful man," Cassie blurted out. "He treats Mrs. Jameston with great disrespect. He is a cad of the worst kind, and I fear he means her harm. I wish there were some way to put him out of the house and away from her."

Mark seemed to struggle for a moment with the news. "There is something I should tell you, Cassie. Something that you cannot speak of to anyone."

"Not even Mrs. Jameston?"

He shook his head. "Especially not Mrs. Jameston."

"I don't want to live with secrets. Mrs. Jameston has been good to me, and I am completely devoted to her."

"I promise you, this is not the kind of thing she would desire to know—at least not at this juncture."

Cassie considered him for a moment. His eyes seemed to plead with her for understanding. "I don't pretend to know what this is about, but very well. I will not speak of it with Mrs. Jameston unless the time comes when I feel it is in her best interest."

Mark offered a nod. "Fair enough. The truth of the matter is, I need your help. I know that God put us together for just such a reason."

"I would like to be helpful to you." Disappointment edged her tone. She would much rather have heard him declare his affection for her instead of his need of her assistance. "To what does this pertain?"

"Sebastian Jameston."

She shook her head and frowned. "I have no interest in anything that deals with that man."

"But that's exactly why I need your help," Mark declared, his tone sounding desperate. "I am here in Philadelphia to see Jameston put behind bars—hopefully for the rest of his life."

CHAPTER 11

The first of May dawned warm and sunny. A slight breeze brought a strange blend of aromas—fish, water, and freshly baked bread—to the boardinghouse. Along the waterfront and up Market Street, Mark watched the bustle of daily activities as people went about their business.

Mark, too, was about his duties. Earlier he'd received a telegram from Nelson and had ridden to the telegraph office to send his reply. Nelson feared for him, as Jameston had struck again. It wasn't news to Mark, for Westmoreland had already delivered that information the night before. The fact that a man had been killed trying to protect the insured cargo was the worst of it. Now Nelson Stafford had written to say that he was concerned Mark might be next if he continued to investigate on his own. Nelson even suggested that perhaps Mark should just return to Boston.

"Well, that's not going to happen. Not until I accomplish what I came here for."

He retrieved Portland from where he'd been tied, all the while contemplating his message to Nelson.

HAVE MATTERS UNDER CONTROL STOP WILL REMAIN HERE STOP

It was short and simple, but Nelson would understand. They had to be very careful about the information conveyed in their messages. There was no telling who might turn out to be a friend of Jameston and share the information.

Mark's plan for the morning was to see Cassie and get her answer as to whether or not she would help him. He'd given her very little information regarding Sebastian. He wanted to make certain she would agree to work with him on the investigation before sharing too much. A part of him feared drawing her into the plan, but another part was delighted for the opportunity it would present to see Cassie in his company more often.

Portland craned his neck toward his master as Mark drew the reins and started to mount. Mark pushed the gelding back. "No treats just yet, old boy. You have to earn your keep first."

The horse gave a bit of a prance but settled quickly as Mark climbed into the saddle. There was a great deal to consider. Mark wasn't yet sure how he could utilize Cassie's situation to his best advantage. Neither one of them wanted Cassie in Jameston's company any more than she had to be. Still, if Sebastian Jameston was responsible for the men stealing the cargo and killing people, Mark needed to act quickly to see him brought to justice.

"But she might not like my idea," he mused. He'd been working on the plan ever since his second visit to the Jameston house. Cassie might be offended by his suggestion, and that would put them back at the starting point.

One way or another, he had to convince her to play the game his way. He knew what men like Sebastian Jameston were like—what they could do without warning. Cassie had already gotten a taste of the man's character; given that much, Mark hoped it would give him an edge in convincing the beautiful Miss Stover to see things his way.

"So it went well?" Sebastian asked Robbie.

"I believe it went perfectly. The cargo has been secured elsewhere in the city and the police are happy to look the other way, thanks to the contribution we made. The man we killed was a nobody. No family or friends to speak of; just a loner down on his luck."

Sebastian nodded and flexed his leg. "Good. Move the cargo as soon as it's safe." He really had no concern for or interest in the man they'd killed. He only wanted to send a message to anyone who might yet be investigating the missing cargo.

Robbie plopped down in a chair opposite Sebastian. The well-worn pieces were placed in front of the fireplace, and Sebastian stared into the empty hearth as though there were flames to watch.

"I've given a great deal of thought to the matter and am convinced it's time to move on, as well as expand. There's no reason we cannot set up additional companies along the coast to insure our cargoes through various organizations. Insurance is becoming more and more popular."

"It does seem to be a rather advantageous business," Robbie replied. "Especially from our side of the board."

Sebastian chuckled. "What can I say? I am a man of opportunity. They have provided a means for me to better my station, and I won't ignore it. I think we can easily put our friends to work up and down the coast. It will require a bit of investment money, but I believe I can soon have that in my pocket."

"Your mother?" Robbie questioned, raising a brow skeptically.

"Yes. She isn't well, you know." Sebastian smiled and shrugged. "If she dies soon, I will inherit everything. It will give us the foundational investment to allow for a worldwide enterprise. There are a great many cargoes that are vital to this country. Cotton alone is a huge industry. We can begin to invest in that, as well as other commodities."

"I can see what you have in mind, and I suppose if you are able to get a great deal of money together, we could proceed without risk."

Sebastian nodded. "I want you to get word to the men. All of them. The team here, of course, as well as our connections in New York City, Norfolk, and Charleston. See what you can discover about making additional allies in other cities. We'll also need to contact our friends in England and France, but I will see to that myself."

"All right. What do you want me to say?"

"Tell them we're expanding. Tell them instead of merely having someone to contact in those towns, we're seeking to put together a group of men who can work with us on a permanent basis. We can arrange to meet with them here in Philadelphia; perhaps by the end of the month. See what their feelings are on the matter and get back to me as soon as possible."

"I'll do what I can, but my present financial situation is no better than yours."

"I've already thought of that," Sebastian said with a smile. "Under my bed there is a pillowcase filled with some of the family silver and other trinkets. I believe you can sell those for a tidy sum. That should give you the travel funds you need."

Robbie got to his feet. "I'll be off, then. I'll get as much accomplished as quickly as I can."

"Good. I'm certain by the time we have everyone in place, I'll have the additional money we'll need to see this through. Now I must go see Silas on an important matter."

"Since when has the kitchen become your interest?" Robbie laughed.

Sebastian fixed him with a serious look. "Since it occurred to me that many of my problems could be solved through culinary efforts."

"I don't understand, Sebbie. What is your meaning?"

Jameston smiled. "It isn't important. Go to your business and leave me to mine."

Cassie walked beside Mark to the stable, a sense of anxiety building as they approached. The smell of hay and straw mingled with the animal scent that clearly reminded her of all that she'd been avoiding these past ten years.

"Elida's birthday is tomorrow," Cassie offered to keep her mind occupied.

"Yes, I remember. I've purchased her a gift."

"That was very kind," Cassie said, looking up at him. "You didn't need to, however."

"I have it with me. I left it in my saddlebag. Could you perhaps deliver it for me?"

Cassie nodded. "Certainly. Mrs. Jameston is having her driver take me to the house tomorrow night."

"That's even better. Might I accompany you?"

Cassie stopped and studied him for a moment. "I suppose you could. I know Mother would not mind another guest for our little celebration."

"Wonderful. What time shall I come?"

"Five. I'm leaving here at five."

He smiled, and it warmed her through and through. "Are you ready to see your new horse?"

"Not really," Cassie replied as she stared into the stable. "Nevertheless, I suppose I must. I did give my word."

Mark led her into the building. "I think you will be surprised at how easy this will be. I've already spent time talking to Wills about your gift. He said the mare is very congenial and quite docile. You should get along famously."

"I hope someone suggested the same thing to the animal." Cassie could see the gray peeking out from her stall just down the way.

"I believe Wills had a long talk with her when he brought her here today, Miss Stover," Mark said.

"Would you do me a favor?" He stopped and looked down at her, and Cassie felt a catch in her throat. Goodness, but his eyes were so blue.

"Anything."

She heard such tenderness in his voice that for a moment she nearly forgot what she'd wanted to request. "Please . . . ah . . . call me Cassie. I know all the proprieties demand otherwise, but I hate the formality. I wasn't raised with it, and well . . . it seems . . . I mean, I like to think we've become friends."

Mark laughed and patted her arm. "Of course we're friends. I would love to call you by your first name. And you must call me Mark."

"I'd like that . . . Mark." She was thankful he couldn't see how her knees were knocking together. Just being near him caused her to forget most everything else.

"Now Posie is waiting for your formal introduction."

"Posie?"

"That's the mare's name. Didn't Mrs. Jameston tell you that?"

Cassie eyed the animal's large head. Reality began to sink back in. The mare's eyes seemed intent on watching her. "No. No one told me her name."

Mark reached up with his left hand to pet the mare's face, all while pulling Cassie closer with his right hand. "See, she's absolutely gentle."

"That's because she recognizes a person of strength. You are a man and quite a brave one. She obviously knows that, just as she will know I am afraid."

"I am certain she will sense your fear, and that is why you must cast it aside. You have to take charge and let the animal know that you are the boss. She will yield to you once she understands that point."

Cassie shook her head. "I hardly see how that could be true. She's ten times my size and hasn't any need to adhere to social rules."

Laughing, Mark rubbed the mare's muzzle, then drew Cassie's hand up to do likewise. Cassie stiffened beside him but let him guide her hand. The animal's nose was like velvet to touch.

"See, she likes you," Mark declared.

They stood there for some time, just stroking the animal. Mark told Cassie a great deal about horse care and shared stories of his childhood when he had first learned to handle such animals.

"Each animal has his or her own personality. You have to remember that. Learn what upsets them and what comforts them."

"There was a time," Cassie said, remembering for the first time in years, "when I thought horses were wonderful. I liked them very much."

"Your tragedy was painful, but unusual. While such beasts do need a firm hand and a wide berth, they are generally manageable. You should have a healthy respect for them, but not a crippling fear."

Cassie knew he was right, but it didn't ease her concern. That would only come in time, she thought. Once she could put aside the memories of her father's ordeal, perhaps then she wouldn't be afraid.

"I just keep seeing my father on the ground being trampled." She pulled away and buried her face in her hands. She smelled of horse, and that only served to make the memory stronger. "I couldn't help him. I couldn't do anything but watch him die."

"Cassie . . ." Mark came up behind her and put his hands on her shoulders. "Sometimes things like this happen. I don't expect you to put aside your fears overnight."

She trembled at his touch. She knew he would feel her shaking but hoped he would believe it had more to do with Posie than anything else. "I will try," she whispered.

He turned her and pulled her hands away from her face. "Let's go for a walk," Mark suggested. "We've done enough here today, and I would very much like to discuss something with you."

"I presumed you might. I told Mrs. Jameston that we might take a stroll after we visited the stable."

Mark smiled. "And what did she say?"

Cassie felt a flush come to her cheeks. "That she was glad to see two young people getting to know each other better."

"Then let us make her deliriously content." He looped his arm through Cassie's. "I'm certain you'll stop trembling if I get you away from Posie."

More likely, I'll stop trembling if I get away from you, she thought, but remained silent.

They ambled from the stable and through the garden. At the back, an alleyway allowed them a means of exit from the yard. Mark walked at her side as though they had done this a million times before. Cassie couldn't help the race of emotions that coursed through her mind. She was losing her heart to this stranger—this man who intended to see her employer's son sent to prison, if not hanged.

"So have you considered my proposal?"

"Your what?" Cassie asked, startling at the comment.

"The idea of your helping me to capture Mr. Jameston."

Cassie steadied her nerves and nodded. "I have, but I need more information. I do not pretend to understand how I can be of use to you."

Mark led her to a small park and pointed to a bench. "Why don't we sit, and I will explain."

Cassie couldn't help but feel a sense of relief as he let go of her and remained standing as she took her place on the seat. His nearness was most difficult to deal with in her present state of mind.

"Sebastian Jameston has been in trouble with the law in various ways for most of his life. His mother and father had enough money to keep him from prison for his petty offenses, but now he has expanded his crimes to include murder."

"Murder? Whom exactly did he kill?"

"My friend Richard Adkins." Mark's features darkened.

Cassie started. "The one you told me about?"

"Yes. Richard and I worked for the same insurance company. Over the course of several years, there were a great many claims put in from various companies here in Philadelphia."

"Claims?"

"Yes. You see, we insure ship cargoes, as well as the ships themselves. When a cargo is stolen or lost at sea, there are often insurance policies against such losses. When there is a loss, the company who insured the cargo puts in a claim. The claim is to reimburse them for the monetary equivalent of their property loss."

"And Mr. Jameston was responsible for these claims?"

"Ultimately, yes. As far as we can figure out, he heads up a group of criminals who steal cargoes and then demand reimbursement from the insurance company. Sebastian Jameston is the leader. Richard learned that much. I believe it was because he was getting close to catching Jameston that he was killed."

"I am sorry. I cannot say that such a thing would surprise me about Mr. Jameston. But I am heartbroken for his mother. She is a good woman. I am certain she has no idea of his committing such crimes."

"Perhaps not, but he was shot. She cannot help but wonder how that came to be. I believe Richard was the one who shot him. The police said Richard had fired his pistol."

"I knew it hadn't happened while engaged in some type of entertainment, as he professed. Although if I were long in his company, I might very well want to shoot Mr. Jameston myself."

Mark laughed. "I do like the way you speak your mind."

Cassie shook her head. "It's not a quality to admire. I speak far more than I should. And I certainly should not make light of something so serious as shooting a man."

Sitting beside her, Mark took hold of her hand. "I need your help in this, Cassie. I am confident that if I can just get close enough to Jameston, I am sure to be able to get the proof I need."

Cassie couldn't help but stare at his hand holding hers. "And how do I help you do that?"

"Well, that's easy. We pretend to be courting. If I am courting you, then I will obviously be in your company as much as possible. Mrs. Jameston doesn't seem to mind having me at the house, so you could encourage this. Get her to invite me to dinners and gatherings. Anything that would help me to have opportunities to explore the house and Jameston's activities."

Cassie felt a lump form in her throat. *Pretend to be courting. Just pretend.* She drew a deep breath and sighed. "I'm quite good at pretense. I suppose it could work. I do not like deceiving Mrs. Jameston, however."

"There is a difference in this kind of deceit. You said yourself that you fear for her life. I do as well. Jameston is a desperate man, and there is no telling what his next move might be."

"Very well. Then I will do as you say. But I must tell you, I don't know much about being courted. I've never had a suitor."

"I find that hard to believe." He looked at her as if to ascertain if the comment was nothing more than a joke.

She pulled her hand away from his and clasped her fingers together. "It's true. I've been far too busy. My mother desperately needed my help after Father died. So I quit school and went to work in our laundry service. And I helped care for Elida. . . . Besides, I was afraid to let anyone in my life. I couldn't bear the thought of losing them."

"I know how that feels. When Ruth died, I found I didn't want to continue my life without her love." Mark's voice deepened. "Richard was the one responsible for helping me to get through my pain. He wouldn't let me give up on life."

"He sounds like a very good man to care so much."

"He was. He helped me to turn to God instead of drink or sorrow. His death caused me to . . . well . . . I suppose I shouldn't say this, but when Richard died, it felt like he took God with him."

Cassie considered his words for a moment. "I had similar feelings when Father died. I couldn't understand why God would take someone I loved so much, someone who loved Him so much. Father's death was violent and senseless. I felt as though God no longer cared about us, and I grew quite angry. Mother helped me to overcome my anger, but it wasn't easy."

Mark met her gaze, and Cassie felt as if she couldn't draw a breath. He was so very handsome and very near. It was almost as if he'd cast some kind of spell over her, but Cassie didn't believe in such things. Still, his dark eyes seemed to beckon her trust—her acceptance. She tried to look away but couldn't. "Why don't you come early tomorrow? You can speak a bit with Mrs. Jameston and familiarize yourself better with the house."

"I'd like that. Then we can go see your sister and mother. It will seem natural if we are courting."

Cassie frowned. "I know it's for a good cause, but I will feel strange lying to my mother about our situation. Pretense is only fun when no one gets hurt."

Mark gave her hand a gentle squeeze. "Many people court and nothing comes of it. Let us court and perhaps a greater good will evolve." He winked.

"It will still be nothing more than pretending," Cassie said, daring him to correct her. When he said nothing, she got to her feet. "We should go back. Mrs. Jameston will worry about me."

Later that night, Mark sat at the table with Westmoreland. He was intrigued by the information the man had picked up among his friends.

"I believe I know the identity of at least one of the men involved in the latest cargo heist," Westmoreland said. "With a little luck, we can corner him and separate him from his friends."

"And you believe we can get information out of him?"

"If he's the same weasel of a fellow he was years ago, I believe he will tell us everything we want to know rather than be incarcerated."

"Good. We'll have to set something up. For the time being, I have some new connections of my own. Connections that I believe will deliver the ringleader into my hands quite neatly."

Westmoreland lit his pipe and nodded. "If you cut the head off the snake, he's no longer a danger."

"Well, all we can do is hope and pray that the snake doesn't learn of our efforts and disappear." Mark got to his feet. "For now, I'm going to bed. Tomorrow should be a busy day."

In the quiet of his room, Mark thought of his encounter with Cassie. She hadn't minded the idea of pretending to court him. The only real problem was that Mark wasn't at all sure that he wanted it to be pretense. He was starting to have feelings for the woman—feelings that were vaguely familiar—feelings he'd vowed to never have again.

CHAPTER 12

"I'm delighted that you could attend the party with us," Mrs. Jameston told Mark. Cassie watched his reaction with a bit of apprehension as the older woman continued. "I believe you and Cassie make a perfect couple. I knew from the moment I met you that you held more than a passing interest in our Cassie."

Mark seemed completely at ease. He gave Cassie a smile as he leaned closer to Mrs. Jameston. "I'm very glad to have been asked to join you lovely ladies. I have to say that I've thoroughly enjoyed myself."

Cassie looked out across the sea of people. Henrietta Wilson smiled and nodded as various people stopped by to wish her a happy birthday. The woman was quite pale and thin, but seemed happy enough. Mrs. Jameston had told Cassie that the troublesome son would not be making an appearance at the party, which had led to a more relaxed atmosphere. It seemed Franklin Wilson was abroad, thanks to a last-minute suggestion made by his father. Cassie couldn't help but wonder if Mrs. Jameston might follow suit and offer to send Sebastian abroad as well. For the last few days, he'd caused nothing but misery to anyone who dared to stand up to his bullying ways. Cassie knew the situation was taking its toll on her employer. Mrs. Jameston had complained several times of stomach pain and weakness. She thought it nothing more than nerves, however, and refused to see a physician.

"Why don't you two join the others and dance?" Mrs. Jameston suggested. "I'm going to speak with Henrietta." She didn't wait for an answer but moved across the room to her friend.

Cassie looked at Mark with a sense of panic. "I can't dance with you."

He laughed. "But why not? I dance fairly well. I promise not to step on your toes."

"But I cannot offer you the same pledge." Cassie moved away from the dancing and music and made her way outside onto the lawn, where dozens of people strolled and talked.

Mark was at her side immediately. He took hold of her elbow. "What's wrong?"

Cassie twisted her gloved hands together. "I cannot dance. I've never learned."

"Is that all? I could easily teach you. No one will ever know."

She laughed nervously. "I doubt you could keep that secret for long. I'm not at all graceful. In fact, I'm rather clumsy at times. You would be completely aghast."

He shook his head. "I could never be aghast at anything you did. Come along, let me show you how easy it is." He drew her to the side lawn, where there were no people.

"Here?" she asked in disbelief.

"Why not? I can show you some simple moves. Before you know it, we'll be in perfect step together." He tightened his hold on her arm and turned her to face him. "There's really nothing to be afraid of."

"That's what you said about horses." She met his eyes and felt as though he were pleading with her to trust him.

"You haven't suffered from your time with Posie. In fact," he drew her right hand in his as he positioned her left on his upper arm, "you've truly done well. I think the horse is quite fond of you."

"I suppose you'll want me to dance with her next."

Mark chuckled. "Let's see how you do with me first. Keep your arms fixed. Resistance is important so that you can feel the direction I'm taking you."

She felt his hand pressing on her back. "It seems you're always taking me directions that I'd rather not go," Cassie said as Mark pushed her backward. She stumbled slightly, but he held her fast.

"The waltz is a wonderful dance. It allows the couple to remain close, face-to-face, so that they can talk all the while."

"I'll do well to breathe and not step on your feet, much less talk," Cassie declared, trying to look over her shoulder as Mark continued to move her backward.

"Don't worry about what's behind you. That's my job. Your job is to relax in my arms and enjoy yourself."

Cassie laughed nervously. "Sounds dangerous."

Mark winked. "It could be." His voice was husky and bordering on seductive.

She trembled from his nearness. *This is just a game,* she reminded herself. *We're just doing this in order to get information on Sebastian Jameston.*

"See there, you're doing very well. Now as I turn you, lessen the tension in your arms. That's the way," he said as he maneuvered her. "You're a natural. Soon you'll be an accomplished horsewoman and dance partner."

"And then what will you teach me, Mr. Langford?" Cassie questioned, feeling rather breathless.

He laughed and brought their dance to a stop. "I suppose we shall just have to wait and see, Miss Stover. But whatever it is, I am certain it will be pleasurable."

Cassie felt as if she were floating with the clouds. The evening with Mark and Mrs. Jameston had proven to be so much fun. She had learned to dance, and Mark had been so very gracious about her missteps. He seemed to enjoy himself, but Cassie knew it was all a game.

"But for tonight," she told herself as she brushed out her long hair, "I can pretend that it was all real. That the way he looked at me was more than just a game." She looked in the mirror and saw the flush on her cheeks. Her eyes were bright with the joy she felt. No matter what happened in the future, she would always have this one very magical night.

"Cassie?"

She turned from where she sat and found Mrs. Jameston standing in the adjoining doorway. Offering the woman a smile, Cassie put her brush down and got to her feet.

"Is there something I can do for you?"

Mrs. Jameston smiled. "No. I just wanted to thank you for accompanying me tonight. You seemed to have a very good time, and that was as much a blessing to me as anything else."

"I did have a good time," Cassie agreed. "I must say it turned out to be more fun than I had ever imagined."

"I would say your young man also had a good time. He seems quite smitten."

Her comment caused Cassie to sober. Mark had lavished her with attention, but that was all in keeping with their agreement.

"Did you check on your son? Is he all right?" Cassie asked, quickly changing the subject.

"I did, but he's not here. Silas told me that Robbie took him out for the evening but an hour ago. He isn't expected back very soon. I'm not at all certain that was such a good idea, but it's out of my hands." She grimaced and held her hand to her stomach. "I believe I'll retire early. I'm still suffering from whatever malady has my stomach on edge."

"Would you like me to come and read to you?"

"No. I think not. You might just as well enjoy some time to yourself. I pray you have the sweetest of dreams." Mrs. Jameston turned to go and then called over her shoulder, "No doubt Mr. Langford will be having very pleasant dreams of you."

Cassie was glad that Mrs. Jameston couldn't see her expression, for surely it was not very complimentary. She'd scrunched up her nose, as if smelling something rotten.

Thinking of what Mrs. Jameston had said about her son, Cassie wondered if she might have time to do a little bit of snooping. Mark had asked her to try and get into Jameston's room when he was absent and see if he'd left behind any papers or information that might help the case. Cassie didn't like the idea of having anything to do with Jameston or his room, but if the man was out for the evening, it might work to at least attempt a bit of investigation.

She tightened the ties on her robe, then lit a candle. Drawing a deep breath, Cassie headed for the hallway. There wasn't a single sound in the house as she made her way toward Sebastian's room.

Pausing at the staircase, Cassie glanced down to the first floor. Seeing no one there, she hurried past and made her way to Jameston's bedroom. The last time she'd been in his room . . . She shuddered as she remembered his hands on her.

Cassie knocked lightly on the door, deciding that if anyone called back, she'd merely make a run for the servants' stairs. But no one called to her and so she gingerly turned the knob on the door.

The silence seemed overwhelming as she peered into the darkness of the room. She held the candle high and watched as it cast eerie shadows on the walls. Stepping inside, Cassie nearly jumped out of her skin at her own reflection in the window. The drapes hadn't been pulled and the glass seemed to create a perfect mirrored image of her frightened face.

She pulled the drapes quickly, fearing that someone might already have seen the light from the street below.

"I'm not very good at this," she whispered. As soon as the windows were covered, Cassie turned her attention to the nightstand beside the bed. A pair of scissors, some bandages, and a bottle of ointment stood as reminders of Jameston's wounded leg. Otherwise, there was nothing worthy of her attention.

The small round table near the end of the bed drew her attention. There were several pieces of paper on it, and Cassie hurried to view them. One looked to be an invoice for a new suit. A rather expensive new suit, Cassie noted. Another piece of paper appeared to be hastily written notes, but they made no sense.

"Baltimore—six weeks. See Davis about the pier." There were several other scribbled comments, which Cassie quickly committed to memory.

She had just turned to investigate a large trunk that stood beside the door when she heard the unmistakable sound of men talking. Blowing out the candle, she hurried into the hallway and tried to figure out which way she should go.

"It doesn't seem to me," Robbie was saying, "that the men would need all that much time to learn the job."

"If they are smart men—eager men—then no," Sebastian agreed.

Cassie realized they were coming up the main staircase. She could see the golden glow of their lamp as they drew near. She hurried to the servants' stairs and hid in the passageway. The conversation between Jameston and McLaughlin might well be important to Mark, and she didn't want to risk leaving too soon.

"I've seen too many men who were quick to volunteer for good pay but were unable to satisfy my desired level of performance. I need men who are unafraid of the law and what might happen if they're caught. I also need men who can keep their mouths shut."

"I think you'll find these men are trustworthy," Robbie replied.

Cassie clung to the stair rail and tried to slow her panting breath. She prayed the men wouldn't hear her on the stairs; otherwise she would have to face them and make up some sort of story as to why she'd come this way.

"Do you smell smoke?" Sebastian asked.

The candle felt like a dead weight in Cassie's hand. How could she have been so stupid as to have blown it out in Jameston's room?

"The lamp is smoking, that's all," Robbie assured.

Cassie didn't even feel she could draw a breath until she heard the bedroom door close behind the men. Their conversation, now muffled, continued as if nothing were amiss.

She tiptoed past the room and hurried as fast as she could down the hall until she was safely inside the walls of her own room. Breathing heavily, Cassie leaned back against the bedroom door.

"I am about as good at this as I am in dealing with horses," she said, shaking her head. "And about as brave."

CHAPTER 13

A crash of thunder caused Cassie to sit straight up in bed. She held a light coverlet to her neck and waited for yet another flash of lightning. It wasn't but a few seconds before it appeared again, and the thunder followed suit.

B-O-O-M!

The windows rattled ominously, leaving Cassie completely shaken. She eased back against the pillow and tried to slow her rapidly beating heart, but it was no use. The storm outside, however, was minor compared to the one raging deep within. During every waking moment of her life these days her mind and heart were centered on one thing—one man. For more than three weeks, she had been pretending to be completely enamored with Mark Langford. There was only one problem: She knew without a doubt that she was no longer merely role-playing.

"What am I to do?" she asked the emptiness of her room.

Throwing back her cover and tossing the pillow aside, Cassie got out of bed without even bothering to put on her slippers. She walked to the window and stared out for several minutes as rivulets of water streamed down the glass.

"O God, what am I to do? Is this punishment for pretending to be in love?" She wiped a tear from her cheek. "I care so much about him. I've never known these feelings before, and now they're supposed to be nothing more than a game. A game to catch a criminal."

She hugged her arms to her body. The lightweight lawn gown was more luxurious than anything Cassie had ever worn for sleeping. It was just one more reminder of Mrs. Jameston's generosity.

"She's been so good to me, Lord. Am I doing the wrong thing by trying to see her son put in jail?"

Even though she'd asked the question, Cassie knew the answer. She was doing the right thing. Sebastian Jameston had become increasingly ugly with his mother. He'd made it quite clear that he wasn't in a hurry to leave her home. He shamed her daily as he heaped one comment upon another, trying to make her feel guilty about the way she had failed him. It was taking its toll on Mrs. Jameston's health, and frankly, Cassie had begun to worry.

"He can't be put behind bars soon enough," she muttered.

Cassie left the window and sat back down on the edge of her bed. Mrs. Jameston's health seemed to be failing a little more every day. She'd grown quite weak, not even desiring her afternoon carriage ride or stroll in the garden. No one seemed to know what to do. Even Ada was concerned.

"Lord, please show me what I can do to help Mrs. Jameston. I hate to see her—"

The sound of another crash came to Cassie's ears, but it wasn't from the thundering storm. Jumping to her feet, she ran for the door that adjoined her room to Mrs. Jameston's. Opening it only a crack, Cassie called out, "Mrs. Jameston? Are you all right?"

There was no response.

Cassie opened the door fully and entered the room. "Mrs. Jameston?" She looked at the bed, but the older woman was not there.

As Cassie drew closer, it was clear why the bed was empty. Mrs. Jameston was on the floor. Unconscious.

With a presence of mind that Cassie hadn't thought possible, she rang for the servants, then hurried back to Mrs. Jameston's side. She couldn't see well enough to tell whether the woman was injured and quickly went to light Mrs. Jameston's bedside lamp.

Cassie brought the lamp to where Mrs. Jameston had fallen. Relief coursed through Cassie when she didn't find any blood or obvious wound. Mrs. Jameston's fragile form was so completely still, however, that Cassie knew things were not right.

Kneeling, Cassie felt the woman's forehead and called to her once again. "Please wake up, Mrs. Jameston. It's Cassie. I'm here to help you."

She didn't so much as stir and Cassie shuddered. What if she were dead? Cassie quickly bent her head to the woman's chest and listened for a heartbeat. A very faint *thud-thud* could be heard, but it did little to ease Cassie's worries. The beat was slow and very weak.

A knock sounded on the outer door. "Come in!" She knew the urgency in her voice would send someone to her aid.

"Miss Stover?" It was Brumley. He appeared disheveled and confused.

"Mrs. Jameston has fallen, and she's unconscious. I don't know what's wrong with her, but please help me get her back into bed."

The man came quickly to her side. He was clothed in a dark blue robe, but his nightshirt was clearly evident beneath. Cassie realized she hadn't even bothered to don a robe and immediately became self-conscious. She hurried to put the lamp on the nightstand and then went back to help Brumley as he scooped up his employer and placed her on the bed.

"We need a doctor," she told the man. "Can you send someone immediately?"

"I will see to it, miss." He exited the room more rapidly than Cassie had ever seen him move.

In his absence, Cassie went quickly back to her room and retrieved her dressing gown and slippers. She had just returned to Mrs. Jameston's bed and was securing the ties to her robe when Mrs. Dixon showed up. With her mobcap askew, she came to Cassie's side.

"What has happened?"

"I don't know," Cassie said, shaking her head. "I heard a crash and came to investigate. I found Mrs. Jameston on the floor." Mrs. Dixon gasped. "Brumley helped me get her back into bed and then went to send someone for the doctor."

"I'll get more light in here," Mrs. Dixon offered. "Poor dear. I knew she wasn't well. She didn't eat a thing for supper. Said her stomach pained her too much."

"I know," Cassie said, unable to keep the worry from her voice.

"Miss, I've sent Wills for the doctor. It shouldn't be long now," Brumley said as he returned. "What can I do to help?"

"I don't know," Cassie admitted. She sat down beside Mrs. Jameston and took hold of her hand. "I feel completely useless. I am living here so that I can help her, and I have no idea how to make this right."

"You found her, miss," Brumley said in a sympathetic manner. "You have done exactly what needed to be done."

Cassie met his gaze and saw the support in his expression. "Thank you, Brumley." She drew Mrs. Jameston's hand to her breast. "I just wish we could do more."

It was another twenty minutes before the doctor showed up with an anxious Wills following close behind. The doctor entered the room with authority, and just seeing his familiar face gave Cassie a feeling of hope. This man was Mrs. Jameston's regular physician. He knew her better than anyone—at least in regard to her physical health. Surely he would know what was wrong.

"Dr. Riley, I found her unconscious on the floor," she told him as she got up off the bed.

"She hasn't been feeling well for several weeks," Mrs. Dixon offered as she placed two lamps on the nearby dresser. "We tried to get her to come see you, but she thought it nothing more than a summer complaint."

"What were her symptoms prior to the fall?" he asked as he took out some of his instruments from a well-worn bag.

"She complained of pain in her head earlier in the day, and her stomach has bothered her for some time," Cassie told him.

Mrs. Dixon nodded, wringing her hands. "Yes, and she's also been tired. She takes more naps now."

Dr. Riley immediately began to examine her, and as he did, Mrs. Jameston moaned softly and began to regain consciousness. She looked rather startled at the gathering, then turned her attention to the doctor.

"Goodness . . . what . . . whatever has happened?"

"You might well tell me that, Mrs. Jameston," the doctor replied. He listened to her heart and breathing, then straightened to examine her eyes. "Do you remember falling?"

She considered the question for a moment as the storm once again rattled the windows. "I remember the thunder. I got up to make certain my window was closed, as I feared the rain would ruin my draperies. I just felt so weak. I don't know anything else."

"Your heartbeat is very weak. I believe you may have damaged your heart."

Mrs. Jameston shook her head very slowly. "I am an old woman. Such things shouldn't surprise either one of us. I think this is much ado about nothing."

Cassie came around to the other side of the bed and sat on the edge. Reaching out, she took hold of the woman's hand. "Mrs. Jameston, you gave me quite a start. I hope you will listen to the doctor and do as he says. You hired me to be your companion and help take care of you, but I cannot do that if you will not cooperate."

She met Cassie's eyes and nodded. "Very well. I suppose you are right."

"I'd like everyone to leave now so I can better examine my patient," Dr. Riley said in a tone that suggested he would brook no argument on the matter.

Brumley and Mrs. Dixon immediately left the room, but Cassie was slower to follow. "I'll be just outside the door if you should need anything."

Mrs. Jameston nodded, then closed her eyes as if submitting heroically to her fate. *She's almost like a lamb being led to slaughter,* Cassie thought. She leaned against the doorjamb and tried to pray. It was only a matter of minutes, however, before she heard someone join her. She thought perhaps Mrs. Dixon had returned, but when she opened her eyes she found Sebastian Jameston staring at her like a wolf about to devour its prey.

Cassie crossed her arms to her chest as if to ward off his intense gaze. "What do you want?"

"I'd like to know what all this commotion is about. And maybe why you are standing here in your nightclothes. Were you hoping I might come along to . . . entertain you?" He chuckled.

"Hardly. Your mother fainted a little while ago and fell on the floor. The doctor is with her now."

"The doctor? Why is he here?" Sebastian seemed rather upset by this and kept glancing back and forth between the door and Cassie. "Old people faint all the time."

"He's here because we sent for him. Your mother hasn't been well for weeks. Not that you would notice."

"You're awfully impudent for a servant," Sebastian countered. He stepped closer to Cassie, backing her against the wall. "But I happen to like cheeky wenches."

"I really have no interest at all in what you like," Cassie said, lifting her chin in a defiant manner. "Your indifference toward your mother lessens my already poor opinion of you."

"Miss Stover," Dr. Riley called from behind the closed door. "Would you join us?"

"I have to go," Cassie said, pushing him away.

Sebastian reached out and took hold of her arm. He lowered his voice so that Cassie had to strain to hear him. "I'm not at all indifferent toward my mother, Miss Stover. I hope she dies and does so soon. I have a great many things to give my attention to once she's out of my way."

Cassie narrowed her eyes and scowled. "You are a hideous man, Mr. Jameston. Your poor mother deserves a much better son."

He let her go and shrugged. "Then she should have been a much better mother. Nevertheless, when she is gone, I shall be your new master, and I shall take great pleasure in that position."

Cassie could still hear his threatening tone the next morning when Mark showed up with flowers to brighten her day. She was greatly impressed by the bouquet of hothouse roses but reminded herself that Mark was only using these as a prop for his grand scheme.

"Thank you. They're lovely."

He looked at her oddly. "What's wrong?"

"Did I say something was wrong?" she asked, burying her face in the roses. They smelled sweet.

"Your mouth might have refrained from it, but your expression did not." He smiled and gently took hold of her. "Come sit with me and explain what's happened."

Cassie let him lead her into the sitting room. She sat in one of two chairs positioned by the window that looked out over the street. Mark took the other chair, flipping up his dark blue coattails before seating himself.

"Now tell me, why you are frowning on such a perfect day?"

Cassie glanced toward the doorway and then back to Mark. "I'm not sure that we should speak here." She got to her feet. "It has to do with the topic we've often discussed."

Mark took her cue. "Perhaps we should walk in the garden, then, if you are to whisper sweet words in my ear." He grinned and stood.

Cassie crossed the room without looking behind her to see if Mark had followed. She ran into Essie in the foyer and handed her the bouquet of pink roses. "Would you mind putting these in water for me?"

The young woman bobbed a curtsy. "No, miss. I'll see to it right away."

Mark took hold of Cassie again and led her down the hallway to the French doors. "I'm starting to sense that something is very wrong. I hope your feelings for me haven't changed."

She looked up at him, mesmerized by his nearness and the scent of his cologne. "No. They haven't changed," she whispered.

Was it a lie? Could she honestly say that without there being some falsehood in the matter?

Outside, the brilliance of the sun sent them to the shade of a large white oak at the far end of the gardens. Rather than sit, Cassie broke away from Mark and began to pace. "Mrs. Jameston is ill. She collapsed last night in her room. I found her unconscious."

"I'm sorry to hear that."

Cassie shook her head. "She's been feeling poorly, as you knew, but this was something different. The doctor has put her to bed and wants her to receive very few visitors. He wants to keep her calm."

"Sounds sensible."

Mark watched her closely and Cassie couldn't help but feel a sense of protection under his scrutiny. She stopped directly in front of him. "Mark, there's something else. I was sent to wait in the hallway while the doctor examined her. It was the middle of the night and only a few of the servants had been awakened. They were gone at that point, and in their absence, Mr. Jameston made an appearance."

It was Mark's turn to frown. "What did he want?"

"Me," she blurted. Rolling her eyes, she began to pace again. "His nearness forced me back against the wall, but that wasn't nearly as upsetting as what he said."

"Which was what?" Mark asked in a very low voice.

Cassie stopped and stepped closer lest anyone hear her. "I chided him for his indifference toward his mother's condition. He told me he wasn't indifferent at all; he hoped she would die and soon. And he added . . ." She stopped and met Mark's gaze.

He took hold of her and pulled her close as a suitor might dare to do when certain that he wouldn't be discovered. "And he added what?"

Cassie trembled. "That once his mother was dead, he would be my master, and that he would take great . . . great pleasure in that position."

For a moment Cassie saw rage in Mark's expression, but it passed rather quickly as he pulled her against his chest possessively. The action so shocked her that Cassie couldn't speak. "He'll never be your master, nor will he take any pleasure with you. I'll see to it. Do not fret or be afraid."

"That's easy to believe when I'm here with you," she said with a sigh. "So long as you are nearby, I know I needn't worry."

Mark dropped his hold and stepped back just a bit. "Cassie, I don't want to have to tell you something, especially in light of what's happened."

She stiffened. "Just tell me. I want no other games between us."

"I have to go to Boston. My employer has asked me to look at some evidence and information they've recently laid claim to. I have to go, but I wish I didn't."

She nodded, feeling a chill come over her. "We all have our duties." She knew the words sounded rather stilted, even indifferent. Cassie quickly turned away. "Please don't worry about me. My attention must be on Mrs. Jameston. I wouldn't have time for our walks or work with Posie anyway."

"Cassie, if I didn't have to go, I wouldn't." Mark took hold of her again and turned her to face him. "Believe me. I do not wish to leave you here."

Letting her guard down once again, Cassie nodded and met his gaze. "I know."

In Boston two days later, Mark looked over the deposition taken by a customs man who had given the latest stolen cargo a quick inspection before it left New York for Philadelphia.

"They were uncertain why the ship went to New York first. But while it was there, one of the customs inspectors came aboard and gave a cursory look at the cargo before being chased off by another inspector," Nelson told Mark.

"And this was what he found?" Mark asked, looking up. "Rubber boots and umbrellas?"

"Among other common things. Certainly not the vast number of art pieces and artifacts that the other customs inspector suggested."

"Obviously the other man is working with Jameston."

"That's what I surmised," Nelson said. "However, when I interviewed the man, he simply suggested that the other inspector had no time to get to the areas of the hold where the most valuable cargo was secured."

"And what of the information I shared with you—the notes Miss Stover read?"

"We're still uncertain. My guess is that Jameston also has some sort of scheme going on in Baltimore. Probably with a different insurance company."

"Gentlemen, I've asked Miranda to bring tea," Mark's mother said as she interrupted their discussion. Both men got to their feet.

Mark had chosen to stay with his parents rather than go back to the lonely house he'd shared so long ago with Ruth. He smiled his gratitude and nodded, but Nelson announced otherwise.

"I'm afraid I cannot stay. I would like you to come to the office tomorrow," he told Mark. "I have some other things to share with you. Read the rest of the information and then we can discuss it."

"Very well. I will see you tomorrow."

Nelson smiled at Mark's mother. "Thank you for your generous hospitality, Mrs. Langford."

"You are most welcome. Any friend of Mark's is always welcome in our home."

"I'll see myself out, Mark. Enjoy your tea," Nelson said as the serving girl arrived with a tray.

"Set it over there, Miranda," Mark's mother instructed.

With Nelson gone, Mark gathered up the papers and tucked them inside a book he'd been reading. "What delights have you ordered for us today, Mother?"

"I had your favorites made," his mother admitted. "I thought it might serve as a bribe." She took a seat and motioned Miranda to leave. Once the girl was gone and Mark had taken a seat across from her, his mother continued.

"I know something is troubling you deeply. It's more than Richard's death and this horrible job you have taken on to find his killer. I want to know what has happened in Philadelphia to occupy your thoughts so completely."

"I never could hide much from you."

"A mother does not do a proper job of rearing a child if she cannot read him like a book." She smiled. "What is troubling you so?"

"I find myself in a difficult situation. There is a young woman in Philadelphia—"

"How wonderful!" his mother exclaimed. "Have you fallen madly in love with her?"

He shook his head. "Not exactly." He wasn't entirely sure that was the truth, but he was trying hard to keep his thoughts from jumbling. "I asked for her help. You see, she lives at the residence where the man I'm investigating lives."

His mother's expression fell. "Oh dear. Is she . . . well . . . one of those women?"

Laughing, Mark leaned forward. "Goodness, no. She's as prim and proper as any refined young lady. She is the companion to this man's mother. She was living there prior to the man returning to the house. He was injured—probably when he killed Richard—and he went there to recuperate."

His mother relaxed and nodded. "I see. And exactly what kind of help did you ask of her?"

"I asked her to pretend we were courting. If I had a vested interest in going to the house, I would be able to better observe the suspect."

"And she agreed?"

"Yes." Mark reached out and took a fruit tart without benefit of a plate or napkin. "Her name is Cassandra, but she's called Cassie. She's a beautiful woman, kind and loving. She has even convinced me to attend church on Sundays with her and her employer."

"And is that a pretense as well?"

"I don't know exactly," Mark admitted with an embarrassed smile. "I've found myself listening a little more each time. I don't wish to keep my heart hardened against God." He paused and met his mother's compassionate gaze. "I'm just still so confused by it all. Richard's death. Cassie's appearance in my life. This man's threat to her well-being, as well as that of his mother." He took a large bite of the tart and nearly swallowed it whole.

His mother nodded and poured the tea. "I suppose it would be useful to take each matter in separate doses. Consider them apart, rather than forcing them all in one container. God has a way of working out the details in bits and pieces, and before we know it, He has dealt with the overall scheme of things."

She extended a cup and saucer to Mark. He took the tea and put the half-eaten tart alongside the cup. "But I don't know where to start to sort it all out."

"Start with the thing that is uppermost on your mind. I suppose that would be Richard's death."

Mark shook his head. "To be honest, I find Cassie there."

"Indeed," his mother said in a nonchalant manner. "And what does she do there?"

"Consumes me," Mark admitted. "I find myself drawn to her like I've been with no other woman since Ruth."

"Perhaps you should make your game of pretend a more substantial arrangement," his mother said, smiling in a coy manner. She sipped her tea as if quite satisfied with her son's announcement.

"But what if she has no interest in such things? I mean, I know she finds my company pleasant enough, but she wants to see this man behind bars as much as I do. What if that's all there is to this?"

"I believe everything will sort itself out in time, dear boy. However, if you truly want to make this woman permanent in your life, why not try turning on the charm that you are so capable of, and woo her?"

Mark put the cup and saucer on the table. "She's not from a socially elite family. Her father was a merchant who died some ten years ago. Her mother has since made a living taking in laundry. Cassie is working as a companion. None of that matters to me, but I wouldn't wish to make things uncomfortable for you and Father."

"Pshaw. Your father once mucked out stables to make a living. You know we've never cared about such things. The upper class here still turns its nose up at the Langford name. They frequent our hotel often enough but seek to keep us firmly in our place otherwise. I cannot possibly imagine that your father would feel any differently than I do. We only want to see you happy. You've been alone much too long, and if this Cassandra woman makes you happy, then that is good enough for me."

"It might mean my moving permanently to Philadelphia," he said, knowing that wouldn't sit well.

To his surprise, his mother shrugged. "I would miss you, of course, but I would not seek to stop you from true happiness. After all, Philadelphia is not so very far away. We could always come for visits, as could you."

Mark reached out and touched her arm. "Thank you. I knew your counsel would put my mind at ease. I've been trying to reconcile how I would deal with the situation if courting Cassie for real caused some kind of separation with you and Father."

"Then wonder on that no longer." She smiled broadly. "See there—we've already eliminated one of your problems. Go back to Philadelphia and win the heart of your young lady."

CHAPTER 14

"You're doing very well," Mark told Cassie. He had finally convinced her to sit atop Posie and allow Mark to lead them around the yard. Her fear of the animal had diminished somewhat, and he now knew it would only be a matter of time until she could overcome it completely.

"I don't feel all that confident up here," Cassie replied. "Sitting sidesaddle is not exactly easy. You really should try it sometime."

He chuckled at her awkward seating. "I'm certain I would not care for it."

Cassie gripped the reins with both hands. "I'm convinced it would be easier to ride backward."

"Well, if that's what you'd like to try . . ."

She shook her head and the ribbons of her riding bonnet flared out in the breeze. "Perhaps another time."

Mark smiled. He'd been back in Philadelphia for over a week and had thoroughly enjoyed spending most of that time in Cassie's company. She, too, seemed content. At least with him. She wasn't at all happy that Sebastian had decided to remain in residence.

"You started to tell me about Mr. Jameston earlier. What were you going to say?"

Cassie frowned. "He's quite recovered, but he refuses to leave. Mrs. Jameston is much better now, as well, but not at all happy about her son's refusal to go. He tells her it's his concern for her recovery, but we both know he's up to something far more self-motivated. He's had unsavory characters to the house at all hours of the day and night."

"Have you overheard any conversations?"

"No, but he certainly has hushed discussions aplenty with that Robbie McLaughlin. They are often doing something in Mr. Jameston's room until the wee hours of the morning. I know this only because of the light shining from under his door at the end of the hallway. Oh, and some of the noise as they go up and down the stairs."

Mark brought Posie back toward the stable, where Wills awaited them. "Miss Stover, you're doing very well," Wills encouraged. "You look like a proper horsewoman."

"I feel like . . . well . . . I shan't say. I do know I would not be long for this saddle without suffering some terrible affliction," she announced as Mark lifted her from the horse's back.

"I remember only too clearly how I used to beg my father to let me ride astride."

"You'll get used to it again," Mark told her. "Before you know it, you'll be jumping fences. Here, feed her this," he directed and handed Cassie a piece of apple. "She'll love you forever."

"Is that all it takes to make someone love you?" Cassie blushed and looked away.

She fed the fruit to Posie, not at all the same fearful young woman she'd been when Mark had first introduced them. She was obviously embarrassed by her outburst, but he found that charming about her.

"See there," he said softly. "She adores you."

"I'll see to her," Wills announced, taking the reins from Mark. He led the horse away, leaving Cassie and Mark to stroll the gardens.

June's warm weather had brought everything to full bloom. A variety of roses filled the air with such sweet scents, as did irises and other flowers unfamiliar to Mark. The Jameston garden was a peaceful sanctuary of blossoms and greenery, and having Cassie at his side only made it more so.

"Did your wife like to ride?"

Cassie's question surprised him. "Yes, but it wasn't as convenient for us to ride in Boston as it might have been elsewhere. There were the parks, of course, but Ruth preferred the open space of the countryside, and it was often difficult to get away."

"So you lived in the city?"

"Yes," he said, nodding. He walked beside Cassie and paused when she bent to study a yellow rosebud. "We had a small house, not far from my parents. I own it still, but I'm rarely there. In fact, while I was in Boston this last time, I actually considered selling it."

"But where would you live?" she asked, straightening to meet his expression.

"I'm not sure. I find that I like Philadelphia very much." He studied her for a reaction and was pleased when she smiled.

"I'm certain Philadelphia would enjoy having you remain here as well."

He chuckled. "Is that so?"

Cassie's cheeks reddened as if she'd revealed too much. "So how did you meet your wife?"

"We were childhood friends. Our parents were very close, and I cannot remember a time when she wasn't a part of my life."

"How special to have that kind of history between you. It must have made her feel very safe."

"Safe?" He looked at her quizzically. "That seems a strange way to put it. What of love?"

Cassie nodded enthusiastically. "Oh, of course. Love would definitely be a part of it. I didn't mean to suggest your wife didn't love you."

"I didn't think you were, but the issue of safety is also not one I would have thought to equate with our relationship."

"Safety is very important to a woman," Cassie countered. "A woman needs to know that she is safe and protected—that she'll be provided for and cared for. My mother . . ." She sighed and seemed to wrestle with how to best speak her thoughts. "My mother always felt so content—so safe—while my father was alive. But when he died, everything changed. A woman's entire world changes when her husband dies."

"I'm sorry, Cassie. That must have been very hard."

"It was. It was a loss of something familiar and good," she said, growing thoughtful. "You and your wife knew each other's past. You weren't concerned about surprises that might rise up to separate and divide you. There were no secrets or unpleasant ordeals to hide from each other."

"I suppose you are right on that matter. Although I've not ever truly considered it. Of course, she made me feel safe in other ways. I knew my heart was safe with her." He smiled, feeling rather bittersweet. "Of course, she did betray me."

"Oh, surely not. What did she do to betray you?" Cassie questioned, touching his arm lightly.

"She died."

The realization dawned on Cassie, and she nodded as one who completely understood. "Yes, that sometimes happens. Like with my father."

"I felt a similar betrayal when Richard died. He had been such a stalwart friend, especially after Ruth died. Losing him was like losing her all over again. Not to mention the separation it made me feel with God. I suppose I had come to trust God through Richard, instead of learning it for myself."

"I don't understand. How could you trust God through another person?"

He saw the genuine concern and interest in her expression. "I can't completely explain that even to myself. My mother suggests it's something to do with having to make my faith stand on its own. I had known God through my parents to begin with. Then Ruth had a deep faith, and so I naturally came alongside.

When she died, I was bitter, but Richard's faith helped me to see that God hadn't deserted me in Ruth's death."

Cassie nodded. "I see what you mean. It was the same for me with Father's death. I thought I understood about God and His place in my life as a heavenly Father. I suppose when my earthly father died, however, it caused me to fear that perhaps I would lose God as well. I know for some time I felt alone and frightened. I didn't know what the future might hold for us. Elida had just been born, and mother was still weak from giving birth. I was only fifteen and knew that everything would change. It was as if I took on the weight of the world."

"Yes," Mark agreed. "It's just like that."

Her expression changed quickly from one of compassion to fear—almost anger. "What's wrong?" he asked.

"It's Mrs. Jameston's son. He's watching us." Cassie pressed a little closer. "He's at the French doors and is just standing there, as if waiting for us to do something. Oh, I do wish he would go away."

"Not until I can be the one to see him taken away," Mark said, surprising himself and Cassie by reaching out to sweep her into his arms. "Why don't we give him something to talk about?"

His face was only inches from hers, and Cassie had to lift her chin to see into his eyes. He heard her breathing catch and was certain that she was enjoying his touch as much as he enjoyed holding her.

"What do you mean?"

"This," Mark whispered and lowered his mouth to hers.

He hadn't expected the feeling that jolted through him like a white-hot flash of lightning. Nor had he expected Cassie's arms to go so eagerly around his neck. She was trembling from head to toe, but she leaned into the kiss with great abandonment.

In that moment, he thought of nothing but Cassie and how much he'd come to care about her. There was no haunting image of Ruth as he pulled away and gazed into Cassie's eyes, nor was there any sense of regret as he had once imagined there might be.

There was only Cassie.

Mark's kiss had left Cassie breathless and paralyzed with an emotion she could not even begin to understand. She had never been kissed by a man, but it was certainly all that she had hoped it might be. Her own reaction, however, shamed her greatly. She'd latched on to him like . . . well, she didn't like to think of how wanton the act must surely have seemed.

"I . . . I'm . . . sorry." She stepped back, noting that Sebastian was no longer watching from the French doors.

"Sorry?" Mark asked softly. "For what?"

"I . . . well, that is to say . . . I don't . . . I mean I've never . . ." She shook her head. "Oh bother." For once, she was unable to just speak her mind, which was probably to her advantage this time.

He laughed and looped his arm through hers and pulled her out of view from the house. When they stopped under the large white oak, Cassie sat down rather hard on the bench. She tried to gather her thoughts.

"Are you all right?" The concern in Mark's tone made her feel guilty for some reason.

"I'm fine. I know it's silly, but you see—" she drew a large breath—"I've never been kissed before. I always dreamed of the moment—of that first time."

She forced herself to look up at Mark. She felt certain he would laugh and make light of the moment and their pretense, and she fought to steel her heart against breaking when he did so. Instead, he quickly sat beside her and shook his head.

"I didn't know. I'm so very sorry. I never meant to take such a liberty. I just thought with Jameston watching it would be the easiest way to convince him of our feelings."

Cassie knew that Mark had no understanding of her feelings whatsoever. "I told you it was silly. I'm fine, really. It just took me by surprise."

"It isn't fine. I do apologize. It was thoughtless." He appeared agitated, even somewhat nervous.

Seeing him that way, Cassie wanted to crawl into a hole. *Why couldn't I remain silent? What a fool he must think me. An immature old maid who goes all weak in the knees at the first touch of a man.*

"It wasn't thoughtless," she said, getting to her feet. "We had a deal, and it was the right thing to do given that Mr. Jameston was keeping us under such close scrutiny. But I really should go now. I'm sure Mrs. Jameston will have awakened from her nap."

Mark jumped to his feet and took hold of her. "Cassie . . . I . . . there's something I should say."

She smiled and shook her head. "I'm fine. Honestly. I was just startled, and perhaps . . . well . . . a bit ashamed for the way I acted. I hope you'll forgive me."

"There's nothing to forgive," he protested.

It's just a part of our game, Cassie told herself. She wanted nothing more than to stay there—to find her way into his arms once again, but she wanted it for real and not just because Sebastian Jameston might see them. "I must go."

Hurrying toward the house, Cassie wanted to die a thousand deaths. Why couldn't she have just kept quiet? Why did she have to act like an inexperienced schoolgirl?

"Because I *am* inexperienced," she muttered. She fled through the French doors and hurried down the hall toward the stairs, only to find a human obstacle in her way.

"You give yourself quite freely to Mr. Langford. Should I suppose he has just proposed and you have accepted? Or are you just that kind of woman?" Sebastian sneered.

Cassie tried to get around him, but he moved to block her. "Would you please let me pass?" She looked up at him in anger. "I have no desire to explain myself to you. Not now or ever."

"Ah, but when I am the lord of the manor, you will have to answer to me."

"When you are lord of the manor, I will be gone. I am only here for your mother's sake."

"But couldn't I entice you to stay even a short time with me? I assure you I can show you a far better time than poor Mr. Langford." His eyes bore into her, leaving Cassie chilled to the bone despite the sweltering June heat.

"As I said, Mr. Jameston, I am only here to be a companion to your mother."

"Then I shall have to find a way to persuade you to consider other pursuits. I happen to find you quite intriguing, and I have yet to be bested by a milksop like Langford when it comes to the pursuit of women."

Now Cassie was angry. She put her hands to her hips and shook her head. "You have no right to speak with such disdain toward my suitor. Mr. Langford is a wonderful man who holds my heart completely. My love for him runs deeper than anything you could understand."

The words were no sooner out of her mouth than Cassie realized just how true they were. The declaration, however, seemed to stop any further aggression by Jameston. He narrowed his eyes at her, then leaned back against the stair rail to let her pass.

"Oh, then this is truly a matter of the heart and not just lust. I suppose I mustn't stand in the way of true love," he said in a snide tone.

Cassie hurried past him and ran the full length of the stairs to seek her consolation elsewhere. She felt a sense of relief when she reached her room and could lock the door behind her.

"Why can't I learn to keep my mouth shut?" she called out.

"Cassie? Is that you?" Mrs. Jameston called from the adjoining room.

Cassie could see that the door was open and realized that Mrs. Jameston had probably heard every word she'd said.

"It's me," she replied. Squaring her shoulders, she moved across her bedroom to peek into Mrs. Jameston's room. "Do you need me?"

The woman smiled from her bed. "Yes. I wonder if you might read to me. I'd like to hear something from the Psalms. I know it would comfort me."

Cassie nodded and picked up the Bible from Mrs. Jameston's dresser. "It comforts me as well. I would be happy to read to you."

She took a seat beside Mrs. Jameston's bed. For the last couple of weeks, she had kept vigil in this chintz-covered chair. The floral pattern had been traced and retraced as Cassie had prayed for the older woman's recovery.

"You seem . . . deep in thought," Mrs. Jameston said as Cassie thumbed through the pages of her Bible.

"I am," Cassie said honestly. She looked up and smiled. "You have been much on my mind. I can hardly wait until you are fully recovered and able to take strolls in the garden or accompany me to church. I have missed our talks."

Mrs. Jameston smiled and reached out her delicate hand. "I have missed them, as well, but I feel stronger every day. I am certain it won't be long before we are able to resume our routine. Now, why don't we start with Psalm 118. I find it such a wonderful chapter."

Cassie nodded and carefully tucked her thoughts of Mark away for safekeeping. There would be time enough to sort through her heart and the effect he had on her.

CHAPTER 15

Even several days later, Mark still kicked himself for having kissed Cassie. The scent of her hair and the softness of her lips were still very much on his mind, as well as the realization that he had crossed a line he'd never intended to cross.

He tried to convince himself that the moment had been necessary for their ruse, but in truth he knew better. He could have simply embraced her. He could have lovingly touched her face, all while speaking to her about how that should convince Jameston that they were madly in love. But her lips . . . her eyes . . . they had driven him to that kiss.

He stared out on the street below and relived the moment. Since losing Ruth, he'd found little interest in other women.

It wasn't that he mourned her so much now seven years gone; it was more that he couldn't find her equal. Ruth had been compassionate and gentle, yet she had the ability to stand up to him—to help him see reason when he wanted to jump into a bad situation. Most of the women he'd gotten to know since his wife's death were shallow or overly controlling. There seemed no middle of the road. Until Cassie.

But being with Cassie was supposed to be nothing more than a game of pretense in order to capture Jameston. Cassie had agreed to the ordeal because she loved Mrs. Jameston—not because she wanted Mark to court her. Now things were seriously complicated, and he wasn't at all sure what to do about it.

"I've made a real mess of this," he said, shaking his head.

Despite his mother's advice to win Cassie's affections, Mark thought perhaps his feelings had been nothing more than a fluke—a sort of response to being without feminine company for so long. But when he returned from Boston and first saw her again, Mark knew there was far more to this than he could have ever imagined.

"I wanted to kiss her," he admitted to himself. "I wanted to kiss her from the first moment of my return."

He dropped his hold on the curtain and walked away from the window. For the last few hours he had been trying to figure out his next move, and staring out on the busy street had done nothing to lend him direction.

"And she wanted me to kiss her," he muttered as he sat down at a small desk Westmoreland had arranged for him. "But did she want me to kiss her for the sake of Jameston—or because of something more? She's played the game well, but is she really that great of an actress? Or could she have feelings for me as well?"

In his heart, he felt certain she'd enjoyed the kiss. Still, she'd been shocked by it. She'd never been kissed before, and her reaction could have been nothing more than surprise.

Mark ran his hands through his hair, almost hoping he could actually push the matter from his mind. "I can't focus on Jameston if I'm thinking about her and that . . . ridiculous . . . foolish . . . wonderful kiss." He sighed and gathered his things. He needed air. He would take Portland and give him a good stretch of the legs. It might do them both a world of good.

"You are looking much better," Cassie told Mrs. Jameston as they sat together in the parlor. It was the first day in weeks that Mrs. Jameston had been able to come downstairs.

"I feel much improved, although I find my limbs quite weak," the older woman replied. "In time, I'm sure to regain my strength."

"That would be wonderful, but the doctor did fear that your heart was damaged."

Mrs. Jameston waved her lace handkerchief as if shooing away unwanted flies. "I'm certain the doctor was wrong about damage to my heart. I think it was probably nothing more than the grippe."

"Let us hope so." Cassie wasn't really convinced, but she didn't want to discourage her friend. "Shall we continue reading *The Wide, Wide World*? I know we usually read in the morning, but the afternoon light is quite nice in this room."

"In a moment. I want first to know that you are all right. You've been preoccupied these last couple of days. Has Sebastian been bothering you again? I know he's had many people in and out. Mrs. Dixon keeps me informed."

Cassie had hoped to keep the matter from Mrs. Jameston, especially since she didn't know what Sebastian had been up to. "I've found I can hold my own with your son."

"He's a cad, Cassie, and if I know my son, he's merely planning his strategies. One of the last lengthy conversations we had was just before I fell ill. He was arrogant and self-assured, but also demanding, wanting to know why I couldn't simply release his inheritance to him and sell this huge house. He wants everything he can get his hands on—even my mother's jewelry and the pieces his father bought me. He even suggested I turn everything over to him and let him care for me, but we both know how that would go."

"Why does he think himself entitled? He treats you cruelly and then expects you to put your life in his hands?" Cassie shook her head and put down the thick volume she held. "I don't want to speak ill against your son, Mrs. Jameston, but I cannot help it. He has said things that have been . . . well . . . rather threatening."

"I've no doubt of it," Mrs. Jameston replied. "I suppose . . . I suppose it would be better if you left me."

Cassie leaned forward and patted Mrs. Jameston's hand. "I am not leaving you. I do not fear for myself. I fear for you. He's always talking about when this shall all be his. He speaks of being my master once you are gone. I do not like the way he talks about you. I must say, Mark—I mean Mr. Langford—feels the same way."

Mrs. Jameston smiled. "What of your Mr. Langford? Are things becoming serious between the two of you? I believe it will just be a matter of time before he proposes, and what a story you shall have to tell your children!"

Cassie startled. "What do you mean?"

The older woman chuckled. "That you met when he nearly ran you over with his horse. And then he taught you to love horses again."

"Well, I cannot pretend I love them, but at least I can tolerate them more readily. He wants us to ride in the park next Sunday, but I'm not at all comfortable with the idea."

"Oh, you'll do fine. You should go and enjoy the afternoon."

Cassie frowned. "But I do not like leaving you alone. I'm not trying to frighten you, but I am worried about your son trying to do you harm."

Mrs. Jameston's expression saddened. "I'm too tired and weary of the fight. Sebastian will do what he will do. We cannot hope to stop him from that."

"That's ridiculous!" Cassie immediately glanced toward the parlor door, hoping no one had heard her outburst. She lowered her voice and continued. "I am here to help you—to be a strength for you to rely on. I won't give up this fight without at least trying to keep you from harm. If your son shows himself to be a danger in a way that I can counter, I will." Cassie paused and lowered her voice even more. "Even if it means he goes to jail."

Mrs. Jameston sighed. "I am convinced that is where he belongs. Sadly enough, I know his deeds have not been good.

Worse still, I know that I have shared responsibility in what he's become."

"Everyone is accountable for their own deeds, Mrs. Jameston."

"True, but had I been a better mother, Sebastian might not have turned away from what was right. I neglected him, Cassie. I allowed my grief to separate me from him when he needed me most. As the years have gone by, his behavior has caused me to pull away even more. Had I been more loving, he might not have turned down the road he's chosen.

"I can see in his eyes that he has done a great deal to be ashamed of, yet he's proud. I pray for his soul, Cassie, but I fear he is lost to the powers of this present darkness."

Cassie shivered. She believed it was true, as well, but she'd not really applied a spiritual element to the matter. "We shall have to pray all the more that God will protect you from harm."

"And you, my dear. I've seen the way he looks at you. You are in danger from his advances. I wasn't going to tell you this, but I feel it only fair and right. Sebastian took Essie against her will long ago. That's why she is terrified of him. I caught him in the act, but the damage was already done. I threatened to call the police, but he swore it would never happen again—that he would leave her alone. I should have done something more, but I felt . . . well . . . he was my son, and I hated to think of his suffering in jail. Not that they would have necessarily done such a thing to him given Essie was a servant and has dark skin. But even so, his reputation would have been damaged and . . ." She let the words trail off.

For several minutes, Mrs. Jameston fixed her gaze on a portrait that hung over the fireplace. "There's no sense in talking about it now." She straightened. "It is enough for you to know that he is not to be trusted, Cassie."

"I know that very well. But I also know it is true for you. I do not wish to lose my dear friend."

Mrs. Jameston smiled. "That could never happen. Now let us put aside sad matters and share a pleasant afternoon."

But that was not to be. The words were no sooner out of her mouth than Sebastian Jameston strode into the room.

"Mother, I wish to speak to you."

"Very well." Mrs. Jameston stiffened, and Cassie saw her fix a stern expression on her face.

Cassie turned her attention back to Jameston. He had dressed in a dark suit as if ready for a day on the town, and the irritation in his tone left no doubt that he was in a hurry. He glared at Cassie momentarily, then returned his focus to his mother.

"I wish to speak to you alone. I'd like Miss Stover to leave." It wasn't really a request so much as a demand.

"There is nothing you can say that I would not allow Cassie to hear. I prefer she stay," his mother replied.

This did not bode well. Jameston heaved an exasperated sigh and crossed the room in two long strides to take the chair across from the women. "Perhaps you do not care that she hears our conversation, but I do." He looked at Cassie and narrowed his eyes. "Go."

Cassie lifted her chin and squared her shoulders. "No. Mrs. Jameston is my authority, not you." She hoped he felt the full impact of her statement. He could not—would not—control her, and Cassie felt it imperative to stand her ground.

For a moment, Sebastian watched her. Cassie could only imagine what he was thinking. His gaze swept over her body. Taking his time, he finally met her eyes and smiled. "Very well."

While he said nothing more than those two words, Cassie felt certain there was some sort of implied threat. She could just as easily have heard him say, *You'll pay for this.*

"So what was so urgent that you felt it justified interrupting our afternoon of reading?" Mrs. Jameston asked her son.

Sebastian leaned back and crossed his legs. "I see you are recovered."

Cassie watched the exchange between mother and son. They might as well have been enemies, and that might have described their relationship more accurately than any other word. The tension between them was thick.

"I am better," Mrs. Jameston replied. "Although not recovered. I am still quite weak and only able to be up for a short while."

"Long enough for a ride to town, I'm sure."

"Hardly that," Cassie interjected. "This is her first day to come downstairs."

"Besides," his mother continued, "I have no need to go to town, and no desire for a carriage ride."

"But I have need," Sebastian declared. "I need money."

Cassie could hardly believe that he'd come to bother his mother over money. She started to speak her mind on the matter, but Mrs. Jameston quickly answered.

"I've not even been able to pay my staff these last weeks due to my illness. I cannot give you money for frivolities and not pay them first. When I am able to, I will have Cassie and Wills take me to the bank."

"I need the money now."

His statement was delivered without emotion. He didn't care that his mother had come close to death; he only cared about his personal desires. At least that was how Cassie saw it.

"In a day or two perhaps," his mother told him.

"No. I need the funds today. I've had an investment go bad, and I must have the cash immediately."

"Exactly what do you do for employment, Mr. Jameston?" Cassie dared to ask. "You've been here for some time now, and I have yet to see that you occupy any job at all."

He gave her a cold, hard smile. "I didn't know that you cared enough to watch over my actions. Suffice it to say I am an investor. I invest myself in the properties, situations, and interests of others. When I am successful, it plays out very well for me."

"And when it does not, you take advantage of your mother?"

The smile faded and Sebastian's expression became menacing. "You would do better to stay out of things you have no place in."

"Enough. I won't have you berating Cassie. She is only concerned for me," Mrs. Jameston interjected.

"And have I not shown concern as well, Mother? I have remained here and risked my investments in order to assure myself of your recovery."

"Let us not play games. You've stayed here because it suited your purpose to do so. You have never been known to handle your affairs in any other manner." She turned to Cassie. "I believe I am ready to return to my room. I'm quite exhausted."

Cassie nodded and put the book aside. She rang for Brumley while Sebastian protested his mother's decision.

"I have responsibilities, and I need my money. Why can't you just give me my inheritance now? In fact, why not sell this house and everything in it and live in a smaller place—a place where I could look in on you from time to time? You have no need of a companion and this many servants, and you certainly have no need for a house this size."

"Enough, Sebastian. I have no interest in selling my property. This house was your father's gift to me, and I cherish it." She got to her feet, but Sebastian remained seated. Cassie came quickly to her side to offer support.

Sebastian watched the women with narrowed eyes. Cassie forced herself to hold his focus. She wanted to prove her strength to him and hoped it might act as a means to ward off his further threats and attention.

To both women's surprise, Sebastian got slowly to his feet and came to stand only inches away. He lowered his voice and spoke in a barely audible manner. "You are neither one strong enough to keep me from what I want. Tomorrow, whether you are recovered enough or not, Mother, you will accompany me to the bank—alone. I have no need of your pretty little companion to poison your mind against me."

"And if I refuse?" his mother questioned, meeting her son's evil expression.

"Then you will both suffer for it. You will suffer in a most heinous manner." He turned to Cassie and grinned. "Especially you."

"Enough," his mother said. "I want you out of this house. No one threatens me, my friends, or my servants."

"You may want whatever you choose, but I would weigh my choices carefully. I, too, have friends. If you try to force my hand in this matter, you will find yourself left with very little. It would be a pity, for instance, if this house were to burn down."

Cassie felt an icy shiver run down her spine. Sebastian was serious. He would see them all dead if he had his way. Just then Brumley appeared at the door.

"You rang, ma'am?"

Sebastian stepped back and smiled. "My mother is feeling a bit tired. Would you be so good as to help her upstairs?"

Cassie marveled at the way Sebastian instantly changed his countenance. She kept watching him even as he moved away from them. He was a dangerous adversary, and now he had made a direct threat toward them both. Cassie knew it was the kind of thing she would have to share with Mark.

But there is nothing he can do. He cannot stay here and watch over us, and he doesn't have the information he needs to put Jameston in prison. She sighed. There seemed no simple answer, but Sebastian Jameston was dangerous, and if she wasn't careful, she might well be the focus of his next attack.

CHAPTER 16

Cassie sensed something was wrong from her first waking moment. The memory of Sebastian and his vile threats had left her restless throughout the night, but joy had not come with the morning. In fact, what had come was the memory of Sebastian threatening to force his mother to accompany him to the bank.

Dressing without Ada's help, Cassie hurried next door to see how Mrs. Jameston had fared. She was shocked to find the adjoining bedroom empty, however. Fear coursed through Cassie as she raced downstairs, nearly running Ada over in the process.

"Where is Mrs. Jameston?"

Ada shook her head. "Mr. Jameston woke her early, then demanded she accompany him to the bank. At least he waited long enough to let her eat. She's still quite weak, though."

"This is ridiculous. I cannot believe he's doing this. I know he doesn't care if she lives or dies, but this is outrageous." Cassie hurried outside to find the carriage nearly ready to go.

"I'm afraid Mother will have no need of you this morning," Sebastian said as Cassie tried to make her way to Mrs. Jameston's side.

"This is pure nonsense, Mr. Jameston. Your mother is not well." Cassie came to where he stood and squared her shoulders. "We already know you are ruthless and without concern for anyone other than yourself, but this goes beyond cruelty. The doctor has told your mother that she is to remain quiet and at rest."

"I am well aware of that, Miss Stover, and once she has done her duty by me, she can rest all she likes."

"She owes you nothing," Cassie declared.

"That is where you are wrong," Sebastian countered. "She owes me everything."

Mrs. Jameston had been sitting on a bench by the carriage house, but now she stood and made her way to where Cassie and Sebastian argued.

"Please do not fight on my account, Cassie. As Sebastian pointed out to me, he can leave more quickly once he has money in hand."

"That's still no excuse. You are in no condition to go out."

As if to prove Cassie's point, Mrs. Jameston began to sway. "Oh dear."

Cassie pushed Sebastian aside and went to help support his mother. "Wills!"

The man left his work harnessing the horses and immediately noted the problem. He lifted Mrs. Jameston in his arms just as the woman went pale and nearly lost consciousness.

"Take her back to bed. I'll be right there."

Cassie turned to Sebastian. "If you want that money you so crave, perhaps you would do a better service to go after the doctor than to remain here sulking."

She started to go, but Jameston took hold of her, bruising her wrist with his grip. "I warned you to stay out of my affairs. I can make matters exceedingly unpleasant for you." He lifted a brow. "On the other hand, I could make you mistress of everything here. You could live quite happily with me after my mother is deceased. Imagine it: You could have everything you've ever desired."

"You have nothing I could desire. Besides, I could never love you," Cassie said rather haughtily.

Jameston laughed and released her. "Love? Who said anything about love? I hold no store in such fairy-tale ideals. I merely *want* you. I have no love for you."

Cassie felt as if he'd slapped her across the face. She stood in stunned silence for several moments before managing to gather her wits. "Your mother needs the doctor. I will expect you to go for him immediately. The carriage stands ready."

She didn't wait to hear what he might say. He knew his mother was very ill, and despite his desire to take over her fortune, he knew also that other people had observed his presence. Cassie felt confident that this would cause the man to act to put aside any doubts that the staff might have in regard to his plans for Mrs. Jameston.

But half an hour later, Cassie came downstairs to find him in deep discussion with Mr. McLaughlin. The doctor had failed to arrive, and she wanted very much to know what had caused the delay.

"Excuse me. Did the doctor say when we should expect him?"

Sebastian leaned back, while Robbie rolled up the papers he held. "I have no idea when the doctor should arrive. I didn't have time to do your bidding, Miss Stover."

Cassie felt her stomach churn. "You didn't go for the doctor?"

He smiled. "No. I didn't. Now if you'll excuse us, we have some important business to discuss."

With her hands balled into fists at her side, Cassie stormed from the room. She nearly plowed right through Brumley as she came into the foyer.

"Steady there, miss." Brumley reached out to keep Cassie from falling backward. "Are you all right?"

"No. No, I am not all right. Mr. Jameston was to have gone for the doctor, but he chose instead to do business with his friend."

Brumley frowned. "Would you like me to go?"

"Yes, please. Mrs. Jameston is suffering pain in her stomach. She nearly fainted at the carriage house. I think the doctor should come and see her immediately."

Brumley went to retrieve his hat. "I shall be as quick as possible."

"I know," Cassie said, shaking her head. "It's my own fault for having trusted Mr. Jameston to do the job."

Just then, Miriam appeared. "I heard that the missus has taken ill again. Is there anything I can do?"

Cassie looked at the petite blond and noted the grave concern in her expression. "Pray. I fear it's all we have."

Miriam smiled. "It's all we need."

The house seemed deathly quiet as Cassie paced from room to room, waiting for the doctor and Brumley to return. She had come to love the subtle elegance and charm of the Jameston house. Mrs. Jameston had given the place such tender care. The oak woodwork of the stairs gleamed as if they had been built only yesterday.

Of course, a houseful of servants had seen to most of the needs over the years, but Mrs. Jameston's touch was evident everywhere. Toying with a porcelain figurine of a dancing couple, Cassie couldn't help but think of Mark. Would they ever dance together again?

She replaced the figurine and moved to the window. Mark hadn't come to see her since the day he'd kissed her. Cassie touched her fingers to her lips. She could still feel the warmth of his mouth on hers. Long ago her mother had warned her not to be taken in by men who promised the world with their mouths but failed to produce such with their hands and deeds. She couldn't help but wonder if Mark's kiss might be exactly what her mother meant. That kiss seemed to promise a future of happiness and joy—of true love.

"At least it did to me," she murmured.

The sound of the front door opening sent Cassie running to the foyer. Brumley was just taking the doctor's hat when she approached.

"Dr. Riley," Cassie stated breathlessly.

"Miss Stover. I hear our patient has taken a bad turn."

"Yes. I'm so glad you could come. I'll take you right upstairs to her." She paused only a moment to meet Brumley's sober expression. "Thank you so much, Mr. Brumley."

He nodded solemnly before turning to go. Cassie hurried to the stairs. "Mrs. Jameston had a spell this morning, about an hour and a half past. She was at the carriage house and fainted dead away."

They climbed the stairs together as Cassie continued to explain. "Her son had demanded she go with him to town. We told him she was not up to the trip, but he insisted."

"I've always known Sebastian Jameston to be a selfish man, but this truly surpasses my expectations of him," Dr. Riley said in a gruff manner. "I may need to have a discussion with him after I see Mrs. Jameston."

"I think that would be very helpful. Perhaps he's thought us all rather silly, suggesting Mrs. Jameston remain in bed. If it comes from her doctor, surely he will listen."

They reached Mrs. Jameston's bedroom and found her in bed with Ada at her side. Mrs. Dixon hovered nearby, as if uncertain how to best help.

"I see you have given us all a scare, Mrs. Jameston," Dr. Riley said as he came to her bedside.

"Oh, this is just stuff and nonsense. I suppose I overdid things a bit."

"If you were preparing to go into town, then I can guarantee that you were overdoing things by quite a lot." He began his examination by questioning her. "Do you have pain?"

"Some," she admitted. "My stomach mostly, and my head. It grieves me at times."

The doctor looked into her eyes, then listened to her heart. He continued to ask her a bevy of questions while Cassie paced the rug at the foot of the bed.

"Mrs. Jameston, I cannot say for certain what ails you. You may well have an ulcerated stomach, but I cannot be sure at this point. I want you to eat only the mildest of foods for at least a week." He turned to Cassie. "See that she has nothing stronger than mild broth or simple soup, and diluted oatmeal. If she seems to be hungry for something more, then a bit of milk toast would be acceptable, but only in a small portion."

Cassie nodded. "We'll see to it."

"I hate to be such a bother," Mrs. Jameston declared. She grimaced, and Cassie knew she was in pain.

"Is there anything we can give her for the pain?"

"I have a small bottle here that might help." He popped the cork and poured a small amount. "It's a mixture I've created myself. It's potent, however, and should be given in very small doses. No more than a spoonful every six hours." He gave Mrs. Jameston the liquid then passed the medicine to Cassie. "It should help with her pain, but it will make her sleep more."

Cassie handed the bottle to Ada. "Since you'll be caring for her during the day, you should keep this."

Ada tucked the bottle into her apron pocket. "I'll guard it with my life."

"I'll let Silas know what to prepare," Mrs. Dixon announced as she followed the doctor to the door.

Ada and Cassie crossed the room to join the others in the hall. Even Miriam and Essie had come to hear the news. Dr. Riley looked quite grave as he spoke in a hushed tone.

"I do not know why she remains so sick. She was the picture of health only a few months ago, and while she is advanced in years, there is no reason for this onset of symptoms. I will speak with my colleagues and see if they might offer some thought on the matter. In the meanwhile, give her the medicine and keep her in bed. I will come back tomorrow."

"I'll see the doctor out," Mrs. Dixon offered. "I'm heading to the kitchen anyway."

Cassie waited until the others were gone before pulling Ada to her room. Closing the door, Cassie threw a side glance at the open adjoining door. She went to close it quietly before speaking.

"Ada, I do not know what is happening here, but I fear for Mrs. Jameston's life. Her son made grave threats yesterday, and I think he means her harm."

"Do you believe he's made her ill?" Ada asked in disbelief.

"It wouldn't surprise me, though the doctor has not said such a thing. Still, Sebastian holds such contempt for her. He has continuously implied that he's just waiting for her to die."

Cassie wanted to say more—to let Ada know about Mark's investigation—but she supposed it only fair to speak to Mark about the matter first.

"Ada, I think we need to make sure Mrs. Jameston is never alone. During the day, I want you to lock her bedroom door—and mine—when you sit with her. I will do the same at night.

We should let the other ladies know to do the same. If we all take turns sitting with Mrs. Jameston, her son won't be able to do her harm. At least, I hope he might not be able to."

The maid nodded. "I know we will all do our part. Mrs. Jameston has been so very good to us. No one here would want to lose her."

"No one, save her son."

Later that night, Cassie sat beside Mrs. Jameston and attempted to spoon-feed her some soup. Having known her mother to make a wonderful healing concoction that never failed to rally the sick, Cassie had sent Wills to request that her mother make a batch. He had come back an hour later with the mixture fresh from the fire and the promise that her mother would deliver an additional batch on the morrow.

"I have no appetite for soup or anything else," Mrs. Jameston said apologetically. "I suppose the end of my time has come."

"Nonsense. Do not speak of such things. The doctor said there was really no reason for you to be ill. He was quite baffled, but he believes if you do as you are told, you will make a full recovery."

"But in time, I will die," Mrs. Jameston declared in a barely audible voice. "I am not afraid of that fact, and neither should you fear for me."

Cassie put the soup aside. "I'm not afraid. I simply do not believe it's your time."

Mrs. Jameston smiled and closed her eyes. "Only the good Lord knows that day and hour, I'm sure. Still, there is a weariness to my soul and body that I cannot deny. I fear leaving my staff to fend for themselves. I need to arrange something in my will to see to their needs."

"Then you must remain strong and get well," Cassie said. "Now why don't you try to sleep? The medicine is obviously working, and you should rest. I will leave our adjoining door open. You have only to call for me or to ring this bell," she said, putting the bell in Mrs. Jameston's hand. "I will come to you immediately."

The night air was heavy and hot, but Mrs. Jameston had requested a fire be built in her hearth. Cassie thought the added heat quite oppressive but knew that it benefited the older woman and said nothing.

Getting to her feet, Cassie felt compelled to kiss Mrs. Jameston on the forehead. She bent and did so as a dutiful granddaughter might do. The older woman's eyes opened for a moment, and she smiled.

"Thank you. I've not had such tenderness from anyone since my beloved Worther was alive. I cherish you, Cassie. You are like a daughter to me. I have grown to love you dearly."

"As have I you, Mrs. Jameston," Cassie admitted. "You are family to me, as certainly as my mother and sister."

She left the woman smiling. Cassie felt she had done very little for Mrs. Jameston, yet she knew that this last offering had been more precious than anything else she might have given. The woman was starved for love, and no wonder. Her own son—the only child still living—would give nothing of himself to his mother. He couldn't forgive his mother's mistakes and had made it his ambition to see her paid back in kind. Of this, Cassie was certain. She supposed in Sebastian's mind, it was somehow all very justified. His mother clearly admitted her wrongdoing—the ways she had failed him. But in turn, Sebastian refused forgiveness in lieu of retribution.

Ada came to help Cassie disrobe for the night. Neither one spoke for some time, but when Ada reached for the brush and began to comb out Cassie's long brown hair, the maid finally offered some news.

"I have told the others of your concerns. We all agree that Mr. Jameston is not to be trusted. He has caused so many of us grief, as you well know. We will endeavor to do our best to keep him from Mrs. Jameston—even if we must defy him."

Cassie nodded and got to her feet. "It will most likely come to that. I do not see Sebastian Jameston giving us an easy time of it. I will also speak to Mark and see what help he might offer."

Ada put the brush down and took the bottle of medicine from her pocket. "I'll leave this with you. She might have need of it in the night."

"I'll lock the doors when you leave," Cassie said as she took the bottle. "If you need me, knock three times on my door, then pause and knock three more."

"I will come and relieve you in the morning."

Cassie went to the door with Ada and waited until the maid was down the hall and headed for the servants' stairs before retiring to her room. She locked the door, grateful for the latches that secured the door at the top and bottom. She slid the bars into place, feeling confident that it would be difficult to break down such a door.

She knelt by the bed and murmured her prayers before blowing out the lamp. Her room felt much too warm for covers, so she merely stretched out on top and tried to relax. Sweat trickled down her forehead and neck, making Cassie miserable.

She promised herself a tepid bath in the morning, but it did little to comfort her at the moment.

Little by little, however, exhaustion claimed her, and Cassie felt herself slipping away. She found Mark's image before her as a dreamlike state took over. She reached out for him, but he only laughed and stepped away. Pressing toward him, Cassie soon found herself running.

The dream faded and Cassie awoke suddenly. She couldn't have been asleep for long. She tiptoed to Mrs. Jameston's room and found the woman sleeping peacefully. The fire had died out, so the room was somewhat cooler. Cassie thought about stoking the embers, then decided against it.

She heard the doorknob rattle on Mrs. Jameston's door and froze in place. Ada had not given their agreed-upon knock, so it couldn't be her. Cassie felt her breathing quicken as the door was tried again.

Without seeing him, Cassie felt certain that Sebastian was on the other side of the door. Her fear mounted with every passing moment. Backing away, she edged toward her room when the doorknob went still. She was just starting to breathe normally when she heard the same attempt on her own bedroom door.

Biting her lip to keep from crying out, Cassie prayed that the door would hold. She prayed that God would intercede on her behalf and on the behalf of her employer. God was their only hope, Cassie knew. For only God could battle evil and win.

Sebastian's eyes narrowed. Miss Stover was proving to be more difficult and cunning than he had planned. He headed back to his room, only to be intercepted by Silas.

"Are you quite all right, young master?" the older man asked.

"As well as can be expected. What has you prowling about at this late hour?"

Silas smiled and held out a plate of cookies. "I heard you return and thought you might need a snack. You've put in far too many late nights, Sebbie."

He smiled at the man's kindness and took the plate. "I have indeed, but soon that will be behind me. You were good to think of me."

The man seemed pleased at Sebastian's praise. "If you should need anything more substantial, I could open the kitchen."

"No. I'm perfectly fine. I will make my way to bed shortly." He glanced back down the hall. "How did my mother fare today?"

"I hardly know. Miss Stover decided against serving her anything from my kitchen," Silas said in an obviously offended tone.

"What do you mean?"

"She had her mother create some kind of soup, I believe. She told me that the doctor insisted Mrs. Jameston eat nothing but the simplest of broths and that her mother had a special recipe to help with such matters."

"I'm sorry, Silas. I know that must have deeply grieved you. Especially given that you've cooked for Mother all these years." Sebastian eyed the man sternly. "I suppose next thing you know, Miss Stover will try to take over your kitchen altogether. It seems to be her plan for this household."

Silas nodded. "I have wondered as much myself, Sebbie."

Sebastian reached out and patted the man's shoulder. "You have been like a father to me. Better than my own, to be sure. I will not forget that point when I come into my inheritance."

"No one could see the good in you but my Jeannette and me. You have suffered much."

"Yes, but we all must suffer from time to time," Sebastian said. "Now please get some sleep. Whether Mother will eat from your kitchen or not, I plan to, and to do so first thing. I have an important meeting in the morning."

"I will have your breakfast ready and waiting."

Sebastian slipped into his room without waiting to see whether Silas took himself upstairs to bed or back down to the kitchen. He put down the plate of cookies and shrugged out of his outer coat. Retrieving a map from behind his dresser, Sebastian spread it out on the table and picked up a cookie.

The layout of the dock seemed simple enough. It was an area Sebastian wasn't that familiar with, but he'd been assured it could provide a good source of income. The police force in this particular town would be quite open to bribes—perhaps even more so than he'd found to be the case in Philadelphia.

"There is always someone of a corrupt nature who is willing to see things my way," he said with a smile. "So long as the benefit exceeds the risk."

It was no different for him there at home. There were challenges to be had at every turn. Obstacles that threatened his livelihood and happiness. Still, he was willing to press forward and do whatever was necessary to have things his way. In the long run, it was a benefit he could not ignore—no matter the price.

CHAPTER 17

"Mama!" Cassie declared in surprise. She had been so caught up in her care of Mrs. Jameston that she'd not even taken the opportunity to visit her family. It blessed Cassie more than she could say to see that her mother had taken the time to come to her.

"I was worried about you," her mother said. She gave her bonnet to Brumley, who waited in anticipation. "I've also brought some more soup." She held up the basket.

"Brumley, would you please retrieve Mother's clean jars to take back with her?"

"Certainly, miss." Brumley seemed only too happy to be involved in anything that might aid and assist his infirmed employer.

"How is Mrs. Jameston faring?" Mother asked.

"Better. Your soup has definitely done the trick. She's not only able to keep it down, but her stomach pains have subsided, as well as the headaches. I believe she is on the mend."

"That is good news. I'll be sure and make some additional soup for her and bring it to church tomorrow. That way, you can take it home with you."

Cassie shook her head. "I doubt I'll be there. I feel that I should be here for Mrs. Jameston." Cassie glanced around to see if anyone could overhear their conversation. "Why don't we step into the garden?"

She headed through the French doors. "Mother, how did you know you were in love with Father?" Cassie asked, the words springing unexpectedly from her lips.

Her mother smiled in surprise. "I just knew. Everything about him was exactly what I had hoped for in a husband. He was industrious and yet knew the importance of family. He always made me feel as if I were the most important person in his world. His thoughtfulness touched my heart. He never forgot my birthday or yours. No matter what else was happening, he would see to it that we celebrated the occasion."

"I remember," Cassie said thoughtfully as they sat on the settee. "He was probably the most considerate man I knew."

Her mother turned and raised a quizzical brow. "Why do you ask? Have things gotten serious with your Mr. Langford?"

Cassie shook her head. She wasn't sure what to make of their relationship. It had started out to be more of a business deal than anything. Still, she felt her mother might offer insight, so Cassie began to whisper the entire story to her.

"I wanted to help. I suppose in part because Mr. Jameston caused me such grief and frustration. I've never met a man so cold and unfeeling. Mark assures me that once he is able to get proof that Mr. Jameston killed his friend, he'll have the man arrested. I pray the truth is learned sooner than later, however. I fear for poor Mrs. Jameston."

"I thought things seemed a bit awkward. Still, I think you did the right thing, Cassie. I cannot imagine what a burden Mrs. Jameston has had to bear. What she must suffer."

"I worry that she won't be safe here," Cassie said. "I worry that Mr. Jameston will seek to do her harm."

"Have you told this to Mr. Langford?"

"He's not been around since the day he kissed me in the garden." Cassie got up, wringing her hands. "Mama, I don't know what to do. In the midst of all this intrigue, I've really begun to care for him."

Her mother offered a gentle smile. "He's a good man. I sense a great deal of respect and quality in his character. I do not think he would want to lead you on in matters of the heart. Perhaps if you explained things to him, you might be able to come to some agreement."

"But what if that agreement is that my feelings are wrong and should be changed to fit our original purpose of merely pretending? I don't know how I would be able to handle the situation if that was his comment."

"Cassie, no one can force another person to love them, but if this man has won your heart, he should know that you are no longer playing a game. To do otherwise would show you to be false with him."

"I know you're right. I simply do not know how to tell him. I've had so much to occupy my mind with these past few days, yet his absence has been uppermost in my thoughts."

Her mother got to her feet. "I will pray that God gives you wisdom in the matter, but for now I need to return home. The walk is long."

"Nonsense. I'll have Wills take you in the carriage. It's the least we can do. I know Mrs. Jameston would want you to have that comfort. After all, it's your good soup that has helped her to recover her strength."

Cassie linked arms with her mother and headed toward the stables. "I can also show you the progress I've made with my horse. I'll have you know I've actually sat atop her several times now. And I've ridden her slowly around the yard."

"I'm proud of you for overcoming your fears. Your father would be proud too."

"I hope so," Cassie replied. "It has taken a great deal of courage."

"So will dealing with your heart."

Cassie nodded. "I know. I'm just not sure I can handle both horses and hearts."

Cassie heard a commotion at the front door and realized that Sebastian had once again returned with a group of friends. She glanced up from her book to see half a dozen men following Sebastian into the formal sitting room.

The raucous group seemed highly entertained by something Sebastian was telling them. The men laughed heartily and made comments, but Cassie couldn't quite make out what was being said.

She closed her book and rose from the chair as silently as possible. Tiptoeing to the foyer, Cassie clutched the book to her chest and tried to move close enough to the formal sitting room to overhear the conversation.

"The biggest problem I foresee is the means of getting business done in a timely manner without proper resources," Sebastian said as the men sobered.

"And why has the payment been delayed?" one of the men questioned. "That's never happened before."

"I'm not entirely sure," Jameston replied. "It probably has something to do with the death of their investigator, but they cannot bring that back on our company. For all they know, we're just a small shipping firm that expects to be reimbursed for stolen cargo."

"What about the plans for Baltimore? We're going to have to put forth some investment in order to have any cooperation there," another man declared.

"Baltimore is still on the table. Charleston too."

"I have a friend in New York City," someone else mentioned. "I believe he can be useful to us."

Cassie nearly jumped out of her skin as someone came to close the pocket doors. She pressed back against the wall just in case the person looked out into the foyer. Her knuckles went white as she gripped the book even tighter.

"Now, as for the local river matters, the real issue is the warehouse on Arch Street" was the last thing she heard Sebastian declare. She didn't have any idea what it all might mean but decided it would be best to go write everything down for

Mark. There was no hope of reaching him until he sought her out, but Cassie wanted to be ready nevertheless.

It was several days later before Cassie saw Mark again. She had wondered if he'd been upset with her, but when he arrived and suggested they go for a long walk, he acted as if nothing were wrong.

The warmth of the day had caused Cassie to dress in a layered muslin gown of light blue. The short puffed sleeves and modestly rounded neckline helped to alleviate the heat. Ada had dressed her hair that morning in a wonderful new way that put it all high atop Cassie's head. The style gave her great relief from the damp humidity of Philadelphia, and the wide-brimmed bonnet she tied on over it allowed her some shade from the sun.

"You look very pretty," Mark said as he took hold of her arm.

Cassie forced her nerves to remain even and unaffected by his touch. She didn't want to act like a complete ninny after not seeing him for so many days.

"I've wanted to see you," Cassie admitted, "but didn't know how to get ahold of you."

"We should rectify that," he said with a grin. "Mrs. Jameston has my address, but I will leave it with you as well. You can always send Wills after me with a message." They strolled out along the street looking for all the world as any courting couple might.

Cassie cleared her throat rather nervously. She wanted to address the matter of their kiss, but she felt so self-conscious.

Besides, there was the other information to share. Mark no doubt cared more about Sebastian's dealings than the wanton way she had responded to his kiss.

But I can't keep denying what my heart feels, she told herself. There was an unrest in her soul where Mark was concerned, and she needed to set things right. Yet just as she worked up her nerve, Mark questioned her about Sebastian.

"Have you managed to overhear any of his conversations?"

Cassie sighed and nodded. So much for her decision. "As a matter of fact, things have not been good. He has been desperate for money. I don't know what happened to cause this, but he even forced his mother to leave her sickbed for a trip to the bank. But poor Mrs. Jameston was too weak and collapsed at the carriage house. Meanwhile, there have been many people coming to see Mr. Jameston. I did manage to overhear him say something about a delay of payment and the men needing to get what was due them. He said something, too, about a warehouse on Arch Street, but I don't know the address. It sounded like it might be close to the river, though."

"That's all very good information, my dear," he said, smiling. "I couldn't have done better. You are quite good at this spy game."

The reminder of their situation came like a kick in the stomach to Cassie. She tried hard not to openly react to his comment. At her age, Cassie figured she ought to be able to handle just about anything, especially if it related to her emotions.

"I managed to dig up some information of my own," he told her. "And the delay of payment you heard him mention is in regard to the insurance claim. My company has refused to pay out just yet. In the past, he's received his money fairly quickly once the police verified the theft. This time, however, we are certain the police are cooperating with Sebastian and his cronies, and my company has refused to pay out on their verification alone."

"I have to tell you that Mr. Jameston is getting more and more dangerous," Cassie confided. "He . . . well . . . he threatened both his mother and me."

Mark captured her gaze. "What kind of threat?"

"He came to interrupt us in the sitting room. He wanted his mother to go with him immediately to the bank. He said some investment of his had failed and he needed the money right away. I argued that she was still too weak and that the doctor wasn't allowing her out of the house just yet. This enraged him. He said we would suffer in a most heinous way if we interfered. He even implied that he might burn the house down around us."

"I don't like this at all. I knew Jameston would get desperate, but I hadn't seen it playing out this way. It would appear our little game has taken a deadly turn."

"About our game . . ." Cassie said, feeling the need to declare her thoughts.

"I know what you're going to say," Mark said, pulling her along with him as they made their way back to the Jameston house.

Cassie looked at him as they walked. "You do?" She tripped and would have fallen if Mark hadn't righted her.

"You're going to tell me that the charade has become more than you bargained for." She drew her breath in sharply and knew he hadn't missed her reaction. "See, I knew the situation would become dangerous. I knew it had the potential to lend itself to tragedy anew. You didn't. I should have made it clearer."

Confusion coursed over Cassie's mind. What was he talking about? "I don't . . . I mean to say . . . that isn't—"

He patted her arm as they walked up the expansive drive to the Jameston mansion. "It's all right. I wouldn't blame you if you wanted to put an end to this. I've benefited greatly by having a reason to come here and listen to what you've managed to learn. But I don't want you to feel endangered."

"That isn't going to change—even if I stop trying to overhear what Sebastian Jameston is saying," Cassie replied. "And that isn't what I was going to say at all. I'm glad to help. I just feel it only fair to . . ." Her words trailed off as she spied Sebastian and Robbie as they walked on the westerly side of the lawn. "It's him," she whispered.

Mark pulled her into his arms, but while he bent his head to hers, he didn't kiss her. Cassie had closed her eyes in anticipation of the moment, but she quickly reopened them when nothing happened. Mark smiled. "I'm sure Mr. Jameston can't tell that we're not actually kissing. I felt bad about forcing it on you last time. It was wrong of me. I feel as though I stole something very precious."

"You didn't steal anything. I gave it quite willingly. I'll happily give it again," she said rather boldly, then immediately regretted her words.

Mark, however, grinned. "I've never been one to look a gift horse in the mouth."

"Excuse me? Are you suggesting that—" she started to protest, but he covered her mouth with his own.

Cassie completely forgot about everything with that kiss. She loved the way she felt in Mark's arms. She loved the smell of his cologne and the softness of his lips against hers. She feared her knees would buckle beneath her at any moment.

"Perhaps a quick marriage would suit you both," Jameston declared as he and Robbie made their way to where Mark and Cassie stood. "On the other hand, your wanton behavior might best be served by not marrying at all, Miss Stover."

Cassie pulled away from Mark. She was breathless and couldn't reply. But that didn't stop Mark. She felt him stiffen at her side.

"I beg your pardon?"

Sebastian laughed as Cassie's face reddened. "You two can scarcely keep your hands off of each other. It's embarrassing to watch your public displays. Come along, Robbie. Let us leave them to their cavorting. At least I have the decency to keep my mistress hidden away."

Mark stepped forward and stood in Sebastian's way. "I expect you to apologize to this young woman. She is far from wanton in her behavior and has done nothing to merit your disdain. If there is fault to be placed, it is appropriately put upon my shoulders."

Sebastian's steely eyes never left Mark's face. Cassie watched as just a hint of a smile—cold and calculated—appeared on Jameston's face. "I certainly didn't mean to imply that our Cassie was anything other than chaste in her behavior."

Cassie hated the way he spoke with such familiarity, suggesting she belonged to him. She stepped forward to speak her mind, but Mark was already responding.

"Jameston, you would do well to leave this matter alone. I do not appreciate your sullying Miss Stover's good name by pretending a familiarity with her that you do not have."

"Oh, but don't be so sure. After all, we live under the same roof. Her room is only a short walk from mine." Now Sebastian was grinning from ear to ear. "I would say that I have more than ample reason to support a familiarity with her."

Mark's hand closed in a fist. Cassie saw this and immediately took hold of his arm, while Robbie was already pulling Sebastian away. She hadn't realized how strong Mark truly was. His arm felt like a band of steel, rigid and unmovable. Had he wanted to strike Jameston, she would have been a very poor obstacle to keep him from his goal.

Robbie, however, seemed more than capable of handling Sebastian. He pulled the man along with him into the house, but Sebastian's eyes never left Mark.

"That man deserves to be punched in the mouth," Mark declared. He flashed an angry look at Cassie, which immediately caused her to let go of her hold and back up a step. She'd never seen him like this.

He immediately saw her confusion and fear. "I'm sorry, Cassie. I couldn't stand the implication Jameston so freely suggested. Perhaps you should leave this place."

"I cannot. I cannot leave Mrs. Jameston to fend for herself. If she passes away, I will immediately have Wills take me home. But I cannot desert her."

Mark smiled and put a finger under her chin. "My Cassie isn't afraid of anything anymore. Even Posie is no longer a threat."

Cassie laughed nervously and looked away. "I wouldn't go so far as to say that. I fear a great many things."

He shook his head. "I don't believe you."

"Everyone is afraid of something," she countered. "I would guess that even you have fears."

Frowning, Mark dropped his hold. "On occasion, I suppose I do."

Cassie felt sorry for him. He looked genuinely upset by her comment. "I didn't mean to cause you pain. What is it that you fear?"

"Losing those I love," he replied, looking deep into her eyes. "I've lost twice before—my wife and my best friend—and with the passing of those dear people, it lent me another fear."

"And what was that?" Cassie asked softly.

"The fear that God had forsaken me. That maybe He'd never been there for me at all, but rather was only there because of them."

She wasn't about to chide him for his feelings, for she'd experienced them herself when her father had died. She nodded knowingly and took hold of his arm. "It's quite a hopeless place to be." Moving toward the back gardens, Cassie was glad that Mark willingly joined her.

They said nothing for several minutes, and it wasn't until Cassie led them to the garden settee that she managed to work up her courage. "Mark, I think it only fair for you to know that I . . . Well . . . I don't know how to say this."

"Are you going to tell me that time will heal my wounds and I will magically begin to see how wondrous God is and that His love for me is real?"

Cassie was momentarily caught off guard. "Ah . . . no . . . I wasn't—"

"Please don't worry about me, Cassie. I'm sorry I got so angry. It's just that I feel like I've put you in mortal danger. If something were to happen to you, I would never forgive myself."

But something has *happened to me*, she thought. *Something I never expected and just as dangerous as anything Sebastian Jameston could do to me.* She felt such a sense of frustration. How could she explain without sounding pathetic—even desperate?

Mark drew a deep breath and blew it out slowly. "I suppose we will have to consider putting an end to our game. I can't bear being the reason Jameston would strike at you."

Cassie shook her head. "Jameston wants me for reasons that have nothing to do with you, I'm afraid. He has an idea of becoming my lord and master after the death of his mother. My biggest fear is that he will somehow advance that threat and harm his mother before her time." She paused and squared her shoulders. How could she convince Mark that the only way for her to protect Mrs. Jameston would mean putting her own safety on the line?

"We have to see him put behind bars; otherwise this will go on and on until he manages to have things his way. So you see, Mark, whether I try to overhear his conversations or not, whether you never grace the doorstep again, Sebastian Jameston will do exactly what he feels he must."

"That's what worries me," Mark said, his jaw clenching.

"Then we should do what we must."

"No matter the cost?" he asked, looking deep into her eyes.

Cassie felt the protective wall she'd tried to put between them begin to crumble. The ordeal had already cost her heart—what more could possibly be required of her?

"The price will be worth it in the long run," she told him. Now. . . if she could only convince herself.

CHAPTER 18

By the last day of June, Mrs. Jameston had improved—so much that the doctor agreed she should start to eat regularly again. Cassie was glad to hear this, for the woman was terribly pale and thin. Cassie's mother had assured her daughter that the soup was quite beneficial, but it seemed that Mrs. Jameston had lost a great deal of weight.

"It is so wonderful to see you up again," Cassie told her friend. "I have prayed long hours for your recovery."

"I have as well," Mrs. Jameston said, finishing her tea. She shook her head when Cassie offered to pour more. "I have several things I want to accomplish right away. Given that

Independence Day is Saturday, I would like to get into town before the celebration madness takes over."

"Are you certain you feel well enough?" Cassie presumed the woman had in mind to get her son the money he craved. He had barely been civil to anyone these last few days.

"I will be fine with your help."

"I suppose you want to get money for your son," Cassie said in an offhand manner.

"Yes, among other things. I've determined to speak to the lawyer about several issues. I want to drop by his office and see if we might make changes to my will."

"I see. Well, we can certainly attend to that. Mark had planned for me to take my first horseback ride off the grounds tomorrow afternoon, but I can cancel if need be."

"Nonsense. We can attend to our business in the morning. I'm delighted to hear that you will ride. I feared that my gift was of no use to you."

"I'm glad to overcome my past." Cassie paused as thoughts of that long-ago accident came to mind. "I know I cannot bring back my father by holding on to an irrational fear."

"That shows a great deal of maturity, my dear."

"Excuse me, ma'am. Silas says the meal is ready," Essie announced.

"Very good. We'll be right there," Mrs. Jameston told the young woman. Essie smiled and exited the room as quietly as she'd entered. With Sebastian out of the house for the evening, Essie was much calmer.

As they walked to the dining room, Mrs. Jameston gave Cassie a knowing look. "You've come to care a great deal for your young man, haven't you?"

Cassie knew there was no reason to lie. "Yes."

"You sound rather ashamed of that fact."

"No, not at all," Cassie admitted. "I'm just not sure he'll understand and return the feelings."

Mrs. Jameston laughed, and Cassie found her amusement somewhat startling. The older woman stopped and reached up to touch Cassie's cheek. "My dear, the man is positively smitten with you. I've seen the way he watches you—the way he attends to you. The look in his eyes is just like that of my Worther so many years ago. Your young man adores you, Cassie. I'm certain a proposal is soon to come."

Cassie considered her words for a moment. She would love nothing more than for Mark to declare he'd moved past pretense, just as she had, but Cassie had no reason to believe he had. She sighed and took her place at the dinner table, hoping Mrs. Jameston would simply drop the subject.

To Cassie's relief, Miriam entered the room with a large bouquet of flowers. "I thought you might like to have these brought in," she announced. "A sort of celebration that you are feeling better."

Mrs. Jameston smiled at the sight. "Oh, they are lovely. Put them on the table by the window. Tell me, has Wills yet hired additional workers for the yard? I'd like to speak to him on the matter before he does."

"He hasn't yet seen to that, Mrs. Jameston." Miriam came back to the table. "I'll let him know to discuss the situation with you first."

"Very good. I want to make some rather large changes. We will surely entertain more in the future, and I'd like to make a place for such gatherings."

Miriam nodded. "I'm sure Wills can accommodate exactly what you have in mind."

Cassie was surprised at this news. "I didn't know you were planning big changes to the gardens," she said as Miriam took her leave.

"Yes, well, I believe it would benefit us all to make changes. Besides, you never know when we might need to host a wedding party." The older woman gave Cassie a wink. "I think the gardens would be perfect for a beautiful autumn wedding. Don't you?"

Cassie suppressed a moan and looked away. She did think the gardens would be an ideal setting. The only problem was, she didn't have a groom.

The next morning Cassie helped Mrs. Jameston into the carriage. It had been such a long time since they'd been out together, and Cassie couldn't help but feel it was a good sign of things to come.

"I told Wills to take us to my lawyer's office first. I won't need to be there long," Mrs. Jameston told Cassie. "Afterward, we can go to the bank."

"If you start to feel overly tired," Cassie began, "let me know, and we will return home immediately. There is no sense in overdoing matters on your first day out."

"I assure you, Cassie dear, I will be quite mindful of such things. You know, I have to tell you how sorry I am about being ill. We have missed some lovely parties, and I'm certain to be too tired to attend the Fourth of July celebrations. Still, I want you to enjoy yourself. Perhaps Mr. Langford will accompany you."

"We shall see. I will speak with him about it this afternoon. But you should know, I've never been one for parties. Our life after Father's death has allowed little opportunity for such things. However, I find that I really don't miss it. I prefer quiet evenings. I can hardly wait for the cold weather to return. I love a good fire in the hearth and an equally good book in my hand."

"You remind me of myself in so many ways. I was never one for going out much when my husband was alive. I preferred to sit by his side in the evening. I would often embroider while he read to me, just as you have read to me. I'm afraid I am otherwise not a strong reader. And now my eyes grow weary if I strain them on print for long periods of time."

"Well, that is why you have me," Cassie said with a smile. The carriage came to a stop in front of a modest address. The sign by the door read *J. Daniels, Solicitor.*

"Ah, we're here. Come in with me. I want you to meet Mr. Daniels. He's English by birth but completely American now. He came to this country in 1830 and fell madly in love with a beautiful young lady. He never desired to leave after that." She smiled and gave Cassie a wink. "I'm certain the same is true of your Mr. Langford. I doubt he will stay long in Boston now that he has met you."

"We shall see." Cassie knew her voice sounded rather wistful.

They made their way to the lawyer's office but were disappointed to learn that he was unavailable. Mrs. Jameston set an appointment for the following Monday, then handed the clerk a sealed letter.

"I would like Mr. Daniels to read this before we meet."

"Very good, ma'am. I'll see to it that he has it immediately upon his return. He should be back late this evening, but I know he will come here before retiring to home."

"Thank you."

The women made their way to the carriage and instructed Wills to head to the bank. Mrs. Jameston seemed to be growing tired, but Cassie said nothing. She wanted to leave the woman with some semblance of control.

"It seems the town is all aflutter," Mrs. Jameston said as they drove down Market Street.

"Our Independence Day celebrations are always wonderful," Cassie said. "Mother and Elida love to go to the parade. And, of course, the picnics. Many of the church parishioners gather to share the celebration together, which Mother truly enjoys. It's the part she always looks forward to."

"Yes, I enjoy that as well. Being with people of like mind is always a blessing. There is no reason for deception."

The word hit Cassie hard. She thought again of telling Mrs. Jameston everything about Mark and the investigation. She hated keeping the truth from the older woman, but knew, as Mark had said, that it was to benefit her safety. The fewer people who knew of his situation, the better for everyone. But it didn't feel better to Cassie.

As they approached the bank, Mrs. Jameston patted Cassie's gloved hand. "I have been so very remiss in seeing to all of you at the house. I do hope my delay in paying you has not caused you grief."

"No, I've been fine. I believe the others have managed, also, although I cannot speak for them."

"Well, I intend to rectify the problem today. I want to assign you an account from which you can draw your salary and the salary of the household staff should I be too ill to do so."

"Mrs. Jameston, I'm honored but also fearful of the responsibility."

"Do not be afraid. You are a good woman—a considerate and honest young lady."

The declaration only served to increase Cassie's guilt. "Mrs. Jameston, truly, perhaps having Brumley see to it would be better."

Wills came to help them down. Mrs. Jameston shook her head. "No, I want you to oversee this matter. Now come, and we will make the arrangements. However, do not tell my son. Otherwise he will connive to get money out of you. I want no part in his harassing you because of this decision."

Cassie followed after the woman in frustrated silence. She felt overwhelmed with guilt and concern. How could she take on this responsibility and not tell Mrs. Jameston everything about the investigation?

They entered the bank through large, stately brass doors. Immediately inside the lobby, Cassie caught sight of a large plaque that read *"Honesty is the first chapter in the book of wisdom. —Thomas Jefferson."*

Cassie lowered her gaze lest guilt consume her. She had always held the truth dear. Lies were what evil people told. Appearing to be something you weren't was the mark of a prideful person who didn't care about those around him.

The bank manager was immediately at their side. "Oh, Mrs. Jameston. We heard that you were ill. I do hope you are much better now. Was it the fever?"

"Goodness no," she replied. "Just old age."

The man chuckled nervously. "Hardly that, madam. Please come and have a seat. I'll have my man bring refreshments while you tell me of your needs."

Cassie marveled at the attention the man lavished on Mrs. Jameston. She supposed a woman of means was the most important thing to a man of finance. By the time they finished an hour later, Cassie found herself treated with the same detailed interest.

"If we can do anything to assist you, Miss Stover, please do not hesitate to let us know," the stern-faced man declared as they headed toward the door to leave. "We will look forward to doing business with you."

"Thank you," Cassie said. The transformation of attitude was quite amazing. She thought how sad it was that money should suddenly make her acceptable to society.

"Louise?"

A matronly woman of plump stature came forward. Her burgundy walking-out dress clung snugly to her form. "I thought that was you. Goodness, but we've not seen you in church for some time."

"I've been ill," Mrs. Jameston said. "Annabelle Holiday, this is my dear friend Cassandra Stover."

Cassie curtsied and smiled. "Mrs. Holiday."

The woman looked down her nose at Cassie. "Miss Stover."

"I hope your family is well, Annabelle."

"They are fine. We're heading to the mountains for the summer. What of you?"

"Since I've been ill, Cassie and I will remain at home."

She looked disapprovingly at Cassie. "Pity."

"I'm sorry I cannot remain to chat. We need to make our way home," Mrs. Jameston said with a smile. "It was good to see you, Annabelle."

"I hope you're feeling better. I'll expect to see you Sunday in church, unless of course something else happens to interfere."

Cassie thought the woman sounded snide but said nothing until she was seated in the carriage beside Mrs. Jameston. "She certainly sounded . . . well . . . rather obnoxious."

Mrs. Jameston laughed. "Oh, Cassie, you do cheer me. Annabelle Holiday is always obnoxious. She feels it her duty to keep track of the comings and goings of everyone. It feeds her hunger for gossip."

"Well, I didn't believe her curiosity was born out of concern. I haven't seen her appearing on your doorstep to see why you've been absent from church." Cassie frowned. The sad fact was, she hadn't seen anyone making an effort to see Mrs. Jameston or learn about her absence.

"I used to have friends," Mrs. Jameston said, as if reading Cassie's thoughts. "Sebastian has done much to drive them away. His public behavior has caused many to shun me, while others feign interest only to know the details of what new fiasco Sebastian has caused. Henrietta cares and would visit, but she has been ill as well."

"I can't believe true friends would desert you because of your son's action."

"No one wants to be reminded that there but for the grace of God could be their own situation. I really do not mind. I have you now, and your mother and sister have been so sweet to check in on us."

"They have benefited greatly by our arrangement. I hope you know what that means to me," Cassie told the older woman.

"I believe I do. To know that someone you love so very much is safe and provided for . . . well, it does much to give a person peace of mind."

Cassie nodded. "It means a great deal."

Mark watched Cassie's face as she sat atop Posie. She no longer held the same expression of terror that had once registered anytime a horse came in sight, but still she was pale and looked quite uncomfortable.

"Relax," he urged. "I promise you will enjoy this outing."

Cassie looked at him as if he'd lost his mind. "I will be glad when it's behind us. I'm still not certain that this was a good idea. What if Posie gets it in her mind to just take off and go her own way?"

"Then hold on tight, and I will come after you both," Mark said.

"You'll come after us? I've seen how fast this horse can run. We might be all the way to Ohio by the time you catch up."

"You have so little faith in me," Mark said as he mounted Portland. "What must I do to win your good opinion?"

"Lose your obsession with equine activities and teach me something far less dangerous."

He laughed. "I have a feeling that most everything involving you, Miss Stover, would include some element of danger."

"You're doing very well, Miss Stover," Wills announced as he stepped from the stable. "You're a natural horsewoman."

"Indeed, she is." Mark moved his horse ahead just a few paces and encouraged Cassie. "Come along, dearest. I thought I might teach you to jump fences today."

Cassie's eyes widened, but she seemed to realize he was teasing and nodded. "I believe that would be just fine, Mr. Langford. So long as we can leave the horses home."

Roaring with laughter, Mark shook his head. "How you delight me."

After about ten minutes, Cassie seemed to relax a bit in the saddle. They kept their pace slow as they rode side by side through Mrs. Jameston's neighborhood. While he could see Cassie tense when carriages passed them, the ride went off without any major complications. She looked so irresistibly charming in her dark blue riding habit. Mark thought her the picture of social perfection as she sat atop Posie.

After half an hour, he guided them back to the Jameston mansion. Posie picked up the pace a bit, knowing the stable was in such close proximity. Mark took hold of the horse's reins and warned Cassie, "She'll try to make a run for it, knowing that home and food are so close, but you must keep a tight hold on her and show her who is boss."

"But she already knows she's in charge."

"No, you are in charge," Mark corrected. "Once she picks up a bad habit, it'll be twenty times harder to break her of it."

Cassie nodded nervously. "I suppose we're both anxious to be home."

"Why? You did wonderfully. You look like you were born for the saddle."

Her brows furrowed. "What exactly does that mean? Is that an insult or a compliment?"

He laughed. "I would never have an insult for you, my dear girl. You get only my highest regard and praise."

Wills met them at the carriage house and held Mark's horse as he dismounted, then took hold of Cassie's, as well, while Mark went to help her down.

"Should I unsaddle your mount, sir?" Wills asked.

"No. I won't be staying. I have to pack." He turned to Cassie. "I have another trip to make. I wonder if I might impose upon you for a ride to the train station tomorrow? If it's inconvenient, I can hire transportation."

"No, I'm sure Mrs. Jameston wouldn't mind," Cassie said, looking to Wills. "Do you know of any reason we couldn't take Mr. Langford to the station tomorrow?"

"None, miss. What time should we plan for?"

"If you could pick me up at ten in the morning, that would be perfect."

"Ten it is," Wills announced before handing Portland's reins back to Mark. "I'll see to your horse, Miss Stover."

He led the horse off as Cassie met Mark's gaze. "Will you be gone for long?" she asked.

"No. It's my mother's birthday. I plan only to be gone two days. She doesn't even know I'm coming. Father has taken her to New York to celebrate, and I intend to join them there."

"I'm sure she'll be pleased."

Mark couldn't help but believe she sounded disappointed at his leaving. Perhaps it was only wishful thinking. She'd said and done nothing to indicate to him that his work to charm her had altered her affections beyond their agreed-upon arrangement.

"In the morning, then," he said, tipping his hat.

Cassie nodded. "I'll be there."

By the next morning, Cassie was in a dither. The day had started off well enough, but shortly after breakfast, Mrs. Jameston had once again showed signs of feeling ill. She had taken herself to bed under Ada's care, insisting that Cassie see to Mark's needs.

Sebastian acted as though his mother's illness was nothing to be concerned about. "She's an old woman, Miss Stover. Old people get sick and die all the time."

Cassie tried not to react. Sebastian was heading out for the day. His casual attitude and comments were only issued to rile her. The less she responded, the more it seemed to perplex him into silence. Cassie would just have to remain strong and say nothing.

By a quarter of ten, Cassie allowed Wills to hand her up into the open carriage. It was a beautiful day, and the ride to the depot would prove the perfect time to make her declaration to Mark. Cassie had thought about it all night. She had to tell him of her feelings. He might think her completely silly, but at least she would be honest, and they could judge matters together from there. He might have a suggestion for putting things back on a neutral track. On the other hand, maybe he felt the same way.

Cassie practiced what she would say over and over in her head. She didn't want to sound like a babbling idiot or a schoolgirl with a crush. She thought of Mark and all of the things that she liked about him.

If I start by telling him how wonderful I think he is, then perhaps he won't be surprised when I declare my love, she reasoned. *I certainly can't just blurt it all out like I usually do.* That would truly give her the appearance of being naïve and inexperienced.

Wills stopped the carriage in front of the small two-story address that Mark had given Cassie. The boardinghouse looked quite clean and orderly—at least on the outside. Cassie smiled as Mark appeared on the doorstep with a small valise in hand.

He handed the case over to Wills and climbed into the carriage to take the seat opposite Cassie. "Good morning."

She smiled. "It looks to be a beautiful day for travel. I hope you will have a safe journey."

"I'm sure it will be quite good."

Wills put the carriage in motion, and Cassie began to clear her throat. "There's something I want to say to you."

"Has something happened? Is it Jameston?"

Cassie frowned. "Well, no. I mean, Mrs. Jameston wasn't feeling very well this morning, but that wasn't what I had in mind." She knew the distance to the station was not all that long and tried to refocus her thoughts on what she wanted to say.

Mark, however, seemed to have his own ideas. "I am worried about you and Mrs. Jameston. I've given it a great deal of thought, and I wonder if it might be possible to hire an additional man or two to work at the house in order to act as guards."

Cassie met Mark's gaze and forgot what she was going to say. "An additional man or two?"

"Yes. I know I heard Mrs. Jameston mention at one time that she often hired additional workers for the summer. I would like very much to send a couple of trustworthy men to you. You could let Mrs. Jameston know that I vouched for them and that they needed the work. Do you think that would be acceptable to her?"

"I suppose it might, but she only hires help for outdoors during the summer. From what I've been told, they don't usually live at the house, but rather come to work each day from their own homes." Just then, she remembered that Mrs. Jameston wanted to improve the garden. Cassie felt flushed at the reminder of Mrs. Jameston's suggestion for an outdoor wedding.

"Well, perhaps you could convince her to hire them to actually live on the estate. The men I have in mind will be very capable and will treat both her and you with the utmost respect."

The carriage slowed, and Cassie could see the station come into view. A feeling of desperation poured over her. "Mark, I wanted to talk to you."

"We're here already," he said, shaking his head. "I'm sorry, but I suppose our conversation will have to wait for another time. My mother's party is tonight. I will hopefully catch a late train back tomorrow. That should still allow me to be with you on the Fourth of July."

Wills stopped the carriage, and Mark immediately got out. Cassie surprised him by exiting as well. He barely realized she'd followed him in time to offer her assistance.

"You needn't see me to the train."

"But I want to," she said softly. Wills handed Mark his valise. "Would you wait for me here, Wills? I will be right back."

"Of course, Miss Stover." Wills climbed back up onto the driver's seat and smiled down at her.

Mark shrugged and offered his arm. "I feel privileged to have your attention. Even if it is for just a few minutes. The train will leave shortly, you know."

"I do know, but I felt it important to come with you. Mark, I need you to know something. It's troubled me now for a while."

He looked at her oddly. "Go on."

They moved among the other travelers to the depot platform. The warmth of the day was already making Cassie warm in her stylish plum-colored suit. She felt tongue-tied at the prospect of confessing her love for Mark.

"It's about our arrangement." She swallowed hard.

"Miss Stover, is it not?" a woman called out. She swarmed around Cassie and Mark with a brood of children and offered a smile. "My, but in that beautiful gown, I scarcely recognized you."

Cassie recognized Mrs. Blanchard and at least half a dozen of her children. "Mrs. Blanchard, how very nice to see you again."

"Are you traveling today?"

Cassie shook her head. "No. I escorted Mr. Langford. He is traveling to New York."

"Oh, how nice. We are meeting Mr. Blanchard. His train is overdue, however." She looked to Mark as if for an explanation or introduction.

"Mrs. Blanchard, this is Mr. Langford. His family is in the hotel business in Boston."

"How very nice to meet you, Mr. Langford."

"All aboard!" the conductor called.

"That's my train," Mark declared. "I suppose we will have to continue our conversation another time." He tipped his hat at the ladies. "It was nice to meet you, Mrs. Blanchard."

"And you," she said with a smiling nod.

Cassie met Mark's eyes and watched as he turned to head to the train. She couldn't let him go without explaining her heart. "Excuse me, Mrs. Blanchard. I forgot to tell Mr. Langford something important."

She pressed through the crowd, momentarily losing sight of Mark. Just as she was about to give up, she saw him on the steps of the train.

The whistle blew as the train jerked forward the tiniest bit. Cassie pushed her way past the last of the onlookers and called out, "Mark!"

He looked down and shook his head. "What's wrong?"

The train began to inch forward as the train whistle sounded again.

"I'm not pretending anymore," she called. She saw the confusion on his face.

"What?"

"I'm not pretending about how I feel. I've come to care for you." She had to walk down the platform to keep pace with Mark's car. "In fact," she added, "I love you."

She came to the end of the platform as the train pulled away. Mark's expression was one of surprise. He said nothing as the car moved away from the station. He was nearly gone from her view when a smile crossed his face. He waved, but he was too far away for her to hear the words he called back, since the train engineer chose that moment to blast the whistle one last time.

Cassie didn't know what to think. Had she offended him? Had he smiled at the silly notion of Cassie actually loving him? Or could she dare to dream he shared her affection? She watched the train disappear from view and sighed. She would find out what he thought the day after tomorrow. There was little else to do about the matter but wait. Wait and wonder if her boldness had driven away the only man she truly wanted to spend the rest of her life with.

Mark felt exhilarated as the train made its way toward New York. The hours passed by in joyous contemplation for him. Cassie's words had warmed his heart and given him hope for his future. She loved him. She loved him, and he loved her. How he wished they'd had time to discuss their feelings more thoroughly.

Despite the heat and noise of the car, the rocking of the train was making Mark drowsy. Given that he was in a car for men only, he took off his coat, as most of the men had done, and loosened his tie. He checked the timetable one more time, then tucked it along with his ticket and wallet into the coat pocket. There were still another four hours or so before he'd reach New York. He began to think of what he would do and say when he returned to Cassie. She needed to know that he felt the same way, and he knew she hadn't heard his declaration from the train steps.

He smiled and thought of how pleased his mother would be. Telling her that he planned to marry Cassandra Stover would be the best possible birthday present he could offer her.

The train suddenly lurched to the right and then to the left. Mark's eyes flew open as he looked outside to see what had happened. The entire world seemed to be rushing up to meet him, however, as the car turned sidewise and flew off the tracks.

Men cried out as they were hurled through the air. Mark tried to hold on to his seat for support, but the momentum of the train derailing was too much for him. Without warning, he felt himself thrown against the seat in front of him—hitting his head hard against the metal bracing. After that, his world went black.

CHAPTER 19

Cassie looked at the clock on the mantel and realized that yet another day was half gone without word from Mark. He'd been gone for nearly three weeks now. Three weeks and not a single word.

A million thoughts ran through her mind, and none of them were good. Mark had said he'd only be gone until the third of July, yet here it was the twentieth. Had her declaration scared him off? Had he been so baffled by her actions that he'd abandoned the investigation—perhaps given it over to someone else? Cassie opened and closed her book several times before heaving a sigh.

"I suppose your moping around has something to do with Mr. Langford's absence," Sebastian Jameston said as he stood in the doorway of the sitting room, watching her intently.

"I'm hardly moping," Cassie countered. She picked up her book and headed to the door. The last thing she wanted was an encounter with Sebastian. "Good day, Mr. Jameston." She tried to pass, but he put out his arm and held her back.

"I have only just arrived home. Surely you can spare a short time of conversation with me."

She looked into his icy blue eyes. "I'm sorry, but I need to go check on your mother."

He smiled. "Mother will wait. I'm glad Mr. Langford is gone. It gives us a chance to get to know each other better, and this would be a perfect opportunity."

"I have no desire to know you better, Mr. Jameston."

"I suppose I have been a bit overbearing at times," he said, stepping back. "But you must understand, most of the women I've known appreciate having the man take the lead. I suppose you are among those women seeking to be free of such things—even vote in public affairs and elections."

"I have no such affiliation," Cassie replied, "but I do not like to be handled or forced into any situation. I also have very little respect for someone who shows no concern for the feelings of others. Especially his own mother."

She hadn't known how Jameston would react to such a bold statement, but she was surprised when he merely crossed his arms against his chest and leaned back against the wall. "It is easy for you to suppose you know the situation, but you were not here for my upbringing. My mother mourned the death of my brothers as if she had no other child."

"I find that hard to believe," Cassie said, meeting his gaze.

"Believe it or not, but the truth is what it is."

"Even if she made mistakes," Cassie said, remembering Mrs. Jameston's confessions, "that's hardly any reason to believe she didn't care for you."

He seemed to consider her words for a moment. "Do you see her treating me with a regard that would suggest she cares?"

"She allows you to live here. She gives you practically anything you ask for."

"And that proves love to you?" He gave a shake of his head. "Tsk, tsk, Miss Stover. I would have thought you, the devoted Christian, would suggest otherwise. After all, isn't God supposed to be love? I have yet to have Him offer me a sum of money."

"God is love, Mr. Jameston. But I do not believe you to be familiar enough with that to understand it."

"Then why not explain it?" he challenged.

"You wish only to engage me in an argument. I do not suppose that your mother was a perfect woman. The pain she must have endured upon losing her children most likely did affect the manner in which she dealt with you. For that I am sorry, and you have my sympathy."

He gave a harsh laugh. "I do not want your sympathy, Miss Stover."

"No, you want her consumed by guilt. That serves you better. You speak of God being love, yet you know nothing of forgiveness or compassion. If your mother made mistakes in your upbringing, if she failed to give you the attention you felt you deserved, then why not forgive her and strike out to have an honest relationship with her now?"

"I would not give her the satisfaction," he replied. "It would serve no purpose." The mocking sarcasm in his tone was clear.

"It would offer her comfort. She spoke of your being that for her when you were younger."

"Well, it was certainly no comfort for me. But that is unimportant right now. I certainly have no desire to discuss my mother when there are other issues at hand. I've never meant to offend you. I'm simply used to having to go after what I want—to fight for it, if you will. You are a beautiful woman living right under my roof. It's only natural that I would be attracted to you."

"Well, do not feel the need to fight for me, and do not be attracted to me. I love Mr. Langford and have no interest in any other relationship. You would be wasting your time to try and convince me otherwise."

"But I can be most persuasive," he said. "And Mr. Langford is hardly here to defend his place."

The grin on his face seemed to mask something far more sinister, and Cassie couldn't help but shiver. She could only pray that he would tire of this game and leave her be. Her salvation, however, came when someone knocked on the front door. Cassie prayed it might be Mark and hurried to answer it before Brumley could even appear.

To her surprise her mother and sister stood outside. "Mother! Elida! How very nice to see you both. Come in." She turned to find Sebastian had already gone.

"We wanted to inquire as to how Mrs. Jameston was feeling. And of course to see you," Cassie's mother said, smiling.

"I want to see Posie," Elida declared. "May I please?"

"Of course. Wills is in the stable. Just run out and ask him to help you," Cassie replied. She hugged her mother. "I'm so glad to see you."

Her mother looked at her oddly. "Are you all right?"

"Yes," Cassie said with a sigh. "I was just a bit—well . . ." She looked at her mother, then lowered her voice as Brumley appeared and then quickly went about his business. "I've heard nothing from Mark. I don't know where he is or even if he's all right."

"I have been praying. Ever since you told me of your declaration to him. Do you know where his family lives in Boston? Might you send them a letter? Surely they haven't been in New York all this time."

"I don't know an address. I know of his boardinghouse here in Philadelphia; I had thought to go there and inquire."

Her mother nodded. "Perhaps that would afford you some comfort, if not information. The housekeeper might know an address in Boston."

"I know he works for"—Cassie lowered her voice before continuing—"an insurance company. I think I know the name and had considered writing to them, but I hardly know if that would be fitting. I mean, what if Mark simply wants nothing more to do with me? What if my declaration was not to his liking?"

"He hardly seemed like the kind of man who would act in such a manner," her mother said in an equally lowered voice. "Besides, even if he doesn't return your feelings, he would definitely want to see the investigation through to completion. He has a purpose here besides your courtship."

"You are right, of course. I know he wouldn't just give up on investigating his friend's death, which makes me worry even more that something has happened to him. Something very bad."

"Now open the other eye," the doctor told Mark. He held up a candle and moved it back and forth in front of Mark's face. "Follow the movement with your eyes only."

Doing as he was told, Mark completed the exam and waited for the doctor to raise the heavy green window shade that had been lowered to darken the room.

"Well?" he asked.

"The good news is that you have fully recovered from your concussion, and I see no lingering effects. The lacerations you suffered have healed nicely, and your headaches are of a less severe nature than they were even days ago. I would say you're nearly whole again."

"Then why can I not remember anything, Dr. Shoemaker? Why can I not remember my own name?"

The man offered Mark a sympathetic shake of his head. "I know this is difficult for you, Mr. Smith. No one wishes to be without their identity. But you might have been killed in that train derailment. Others died, and you were fortunate to live."

"It's hardly fortunate if I have no idea who I am or where I am supposed to be."

"But you said that images were coming back to you. What of the young woman you keep dreaming about? Could she be the one you were calling for when you were brought to us?"

"I don't know. I can't remember." He put his hands to his head. "Will I ever be able to remember?"

The doctor moved to his desk and sat down. He was a kind man who had taken Mark in after the train accident. So many people had been injured that Mark felt fortunate to have the doctor's continued care.

"I believe you will regain your memory, Mr. Smith." The doctor and his wife had chosen the surname to call Mark, but it always sounded hollow to him.

"But how long will it take?" Mark questioned. "I cannot go on indefinitely accepting your hospitality. I have a debt to pay you and no idea of how to do so."

"I am hardly worried," the man said. "God brought you to us to care for, and we will see to the task until it is complete. We have plenty of room."

Mark shook his head. "I feel hopeless."

"Son, there is no hope only where there is no God. You cannot allow the devil to get the best of you. Why don't you spend some time in prayer and the Bible? It will comfort you."

"But is there nothing else we can do to help my memory return?"

Dr. Shoemaker took up a book and considered it for a moment. "I have read all that I could on your condition. This book offers as much authority on abrupt memory loss as is available to me, but in all of my searching, I come to the same conclusions. Most situations of amnesia are reversed in time.

The swelling of the brain takes time to reduce and as the brain heals, your memory should return."

"And if it doesn't?" Mark asked bitterly. "Then what?"

"I cannot say. I suppose we shall have to simply take it one day at a time, and see to that matter when there is no other choice. You must maintain your faith."

"But I don't know that I had any to begin with," Mark said, getting to his feet. "I find the Bible comforting and familiar. I find myself feeling quite at ease with the things you have shared with me. But still, I cannot say I have a faith to fall back on. I cannot say that I was a man who put his trust in God."

"I feel confident that you were." Dr. Shoemaker put the book down and leaned forward. "Mr. Smith, you have endured a tremendous ordeal. You have suffered injury and overcome great obstacles. If you were not already a man of God prior to this event, I believe that you are one now. Surely no one can face such a brush with death and not desire to know what lies on the other side."

Mark nodded. "I know that much. I feel certain that things you've shared with me are nothing new. Even as I read the Bible, I find passages familiar. Bits and pieces of stories that come back to me."

"And all of that is good news. You simply must give your mind time to mend."

Mark sighed. "I suppose you are right. There is little else I can do." He noted the clock on the wall. "Mrs. Shoemaker will wonder what is keeping us so long."

The doctor smiled. "Supper will see us both comforted. Of that, I have no doubt."

Late that night, Mark found sleep impossible. He got up and lit a lamp, hoping to drive away the dark thoughts that tormented him. He couldn't make sense of anything in his life. Here he sat in Trenton, New Jersey, having no idea where he'd come from or where he was headed. He didn't even know what significance Trenton or New Jersey might have held for him.

He ran his hands through his hair and suppressed a desire to cry out in frustration. His isolation and loneliness were nearly more than he could bear. The doctor and his wife were kind and generous, but he didn't know them. He didn't know himself.

Mark went to the window and stared out on the darkened neighborhood. The world seemed completely quiet and at ease. It was as if he were the only man in the universe suffering such a malady.

Cassie.

The name came back to haunt him. They had said he'd called for her over and over when they'd first found him. Was she his wife? Did he have a wife? Was Cassie the woman who appeared to him in his dreams?

He closed his eyes and conjured that image. Golden brown hair pinned in gentle curls atop her head. Brown eyes that seemed to take in everything. Finely arched brows and a perky little nose that had been dotted with several freckles from days spent in the sun without her bonnet.

"Riding a horse," he whispered. He could see the image in his mind and felt certain that the woman had some connection to him through horses. He searched his memory to see if something else might come to him, but the image blurred just as the woman smiled at him.

Mark lit a lamp and sat down on the bed. He lifted the Bible Dr. Shoemaker had lent him, opening to the forty-second chapter of Isaiah. The words seemed to jump off of the page and pin themselves to his heart. He read them aloud.

"'I the Lord have called thee in righteousness, and will hold thine hand, and will keep thee, and give thee for a covenant of the people, for a light of the Gentiles; To open the blind eyes, to bring out the prisoners from the prison, and them that sit in darkness out of the prison house. I am the Lord: that is my name: and my glory will I not give to another, neither my praise to graven images. Behold, the former things are come to pass, and new things do I declare: before they spring forth I tell you of them.'"

Mark looked at the words again. He felt just like a prisoner, locked in a cage of his own inability to remember. Blind to whom he might be and where he might belong.

"I need to remember, Lord. I read these words, and I feel that I must have relied on you in the past. The comfort here is evident. The words familiar," Mark prayed, his eyes ever fixed on the Bible.

Behold, the former things are come to pass, and new things do I declare.

The words seemed to hold some sort of message for him. Could it be that God didn't want him to remember the past? Was there something so terrible there that God had blotted it from his memory so that he couldn't be hurt by it any longer?

Mark closed the Bible and began to pace. Dr. Shoemaker had told him all of the details of the accident. The train rails had separated, causing the wheels to disconnect. The first six cars, including the engine, had gone off the track and crashed into the woods that ran alongside the railroad. Dozens of people had died. Dozens more had been injured.

He wanted to remember the sights and sounds of that accident, but nothing came to him. Exhausted, he threw himself across the bed, not even bothering to turn down the lamp. Perhaps if he left it burning, he would feel less terrified of the darkness in his mind.

Cassie rose feeling restless the next morning and felt only the desire for a bath. It had been unbearably hot throughout the night and her thin gown was drenched in perspiration. Fears of disease were now rampant in the city as news came that one neighborhood or another was experiencing sickness. Cassie worried about Mrs. Jameston but knew the woman would not want to leave Philadelphia. Cassie had even mentioned the idea to her, hoping that the older woman's bouts of illness might leave her if she went to a cooler climate, but Mrs. Jameston thought it too much fuss at this late date.

Three knocks sounded on her door, followed by a pause and three more knocks. It was Ada. Cassie went to let her in and smiled at the sight of the woman.

"I have a tepid bath waiting for you," Ada told her.

"You have no idea how I long for just that. I've not even checked in on Mrs. Jameston yet."

"The night was quite warm, but Mrs. Dixon said there are signs of rain. That might cool things down a bit."

"We can only hope." Cassie reached for the door, then cast an apprehensive look over her shoulder at Ada. "Where is Mr. Jameston?"

"He's already left. He said something about needing to conduct business. He had Wills saddle his horse and told him not to expect him back before nightfall."

Cassie breathed a sigh of relief and opened the door. "That is good news. Perhaps we will have a peaceful day."

"Cassie . . . uh . . . there is something," Ada called, as if uncertain how to continue.

"What is it?" Cassie turned to catch Ada's fretful expression.

"I don't know if it's important or not, but since you haven't heard from Mr. Langford, I thought I might mention it."

"What?" Cassie asked, coming to where Ada stood. "If you know something, please tell me."

"That's just it. I do not know if it is relevant or not."

"Tell me anyway," Cassie pleaded. "As it is, I have nothing to even consider."

"Well, it's just that I was visiting my friend across town. Her husband works for the railroad and . . . well . . . she said there was a bad accident."

"An accident?" Cassie felt a sense of dread wash over her.

"Yes. A train derailed somewhere in New Jersey. It was mentioned in the paper, but since Mrs. Jameston doesn't take one, I suppose we didn't realize it."

"Could Mark have been on that train?" Cassie asked, horrific images passing through her mind.

"Well, I can't say, but it did happen on the day he left to go to New York, and the train was . . . well . . . it was known to have come through Philadelphia."

Cassie felt the wind go out from her. Her vision seemed to blur and her head began to spin. "I don't feel very well," she said as her knees gave out. The thought of Mark being dead—of lying in a grave all this time—was more than she could bear.

O God, please don't let it be so!

CHAPTER 20

Days continued to trickle by, and still there was no word from Mark. In two days it would be August. Cassie's desperate need for information caused her to write a letter to the management of the boardinghouse where Mark had stayed. She hoped they might offer her some kind of insight. When Mr. Westmoreland, the boardinghouse proprietor, showed up in person, Cassie feared the worst.

"Is he dead?" she asked without thinking.

"I don't know, actually," the stocky man told her.

Cassie had directed him to the sitting room, grateful that Mrs. Jameston was relaxing in her garden. She didn't want the woman to hear the bad news firsthand—if there was any information to be heard.

"I do know that Mr. Langford was on the train that derailed. I've been able to get that far. However, while there were many deaths from that accident, Mark's name was not listed among them."

Cassie slid into a chair, feeling her strength give way in relief. "If he's not among them, then where is he?"

Westmoreland took a seat in the red fan-backed chair and shook his head. He twisted his hat in his hands. "I don't know. Neither does his family, for I've had a telegram from them and sent one in return. They are trying to investigate from their end. They didn't know that Mr. Langford was traveling to meet up with them in New York, and therefore didn't realize that anything was amiss until I contacted them."

"People don't just disappear, even when involved in accidents of this magnitude," Cassie said, shaking her head. "Besides, surely he would have had some sort of identification with him."

"It's hard to tell. The wounded were taken to various places, so it's hard to know exactly where Mark might have gone. I've been told several of the injured were mentioned in the newspaper, but their names were given and family notified."

"I don't understand any of this. What are we to do?"

Westmoreland gave her a weak smile. "We feel—that is, Mark's family and I—that it's imperative I journey to Trenton. Apparently, that was the nearest town to the accident. They took most of the survivors there to be treated. Some of the injuries were quite serious and required hospitalization. I'm thinking perhaps I can learn more in person than by simply posting inquiries. I cannot help but believe that it's just a misunderstanding."

"Or it could be very bad. If he's unconscious and unable to tell them who he is, there would be no way of finding his family."

"I believe the hospital would have put that much information in the paper as well. I will go there, nevertheless, and investigate the matter thoroughly."

"I wish I could accompany you," Cassie said, knowing even as she spoke that such a thing would be impossible. "I cannot bear to think of him injured and alone."

"Miss Stover," Westmoreland began, then paused to look around. He lowered his voice. "I know about the game you and Mr. Langford were playing."

Cassie started at this and stiffened. "Excuse me?"

He looked around again and rubbed his chin. "I know about the investigation."

A sense of relief eased over Cassie. It was good to at least have someone else who understood the nature of their situation. "Then you must know I fear that Mr. Jameston might have done something to Mark."

"I understand your concern, but I seriously doubt it to be the case. The train accident was from pure neglect. The rails were warped, as I understand it. Jameston couldn't have done anything to cause that. Besides, he would have had no way of knowing that Mr. Langford was on that train. The trip was decided at the last minute."

"But what if Mr. Jameston took advantage of the accident?" Cassie questioned.

"How would he do that, Miss Stover?"

Cassie realized the senselessness of her suggestion. "You're right, of course. I'm grasping at straws and hoping to find answers."

"That's why I will go to Trenton. I know that if Mr. Langford is there and injured, he would want someone to notify his family. Especially if he is seriously injured and unable to give information over for himself."

Cassie nodded, but the thought of Mark in such a condition nearly drove her to tears. "Will you let me know as soon as possible?"

"I will. I'll send a telegram to you here, but don't worry if you don't hear from me right away. It may take days or even longer to track him down. I'll start with the railroad management and then the hospital. Trenton is a good-sized city, however, so it may not be a simple task."

Cassie reached into her apron pocket and brought out a handful of coins. "Take this for your trouble. It's not much, but perhaps it will help."

"No. Keep your money, miss. I told Mr. Langford's folks the same. I have no need of it." He got to his feet. "I've grown to care about Mark. I will be as quick about this as I can. In fact, I will leave immediately. Try not to worry in my absence."

She shook her head. "That would take a miracle."

He smiled. "Then a miracle is exactly what we need."

The past few days had yielded some hopeful clues for Mark. He had begun to remember little things. The faces of his parents, although he couldn't recall their names or location, had come more frequently to him. He could remember a friend named Richard and knew that the man was dead. But he couldn't remember how or why. The thought gave him great sorrow, as if he were losing the man for the very first time.

He also remembered his first name. It had come unexpectedly as he spent time reading the Bible. He was turning through the pages when his eyes fell upon the book of Mark.

"Mark."

The name had such a familiar ring to it. He coursed through the pages, devouring the entire book. By the time he finished, Mark knew without a doubt that this name was significant. This name . . . was his own.

He had shared that information with the Shoemakers, and they had rejoiced with him. The doctor had told him it was just a matter of time before he completely recovered, as the memories were pouring in with regularity.

Mark trusted that the man was right in his assessment, but it did little to comfort him. Now sitting alone, facing another night of questions, Mark knew the only hope he had was in God.

"I don't know what kind of man I was before," Mark prayed. "I long to know—I need to know. I need to regain my life, Father."

He glanced down at the Bible he held. It was open to the eighth chapter of Mark. He read, *"For what shall it profit a man, if he shall gain the whole world, and lose his own soul?"*

Mark considered the words. For days now, he had turned more and more to prayer and God. He felt a peace he'd never known, despite not knowing who he was or where he needed to be. Mark felt God's presence, and that, in and of itself, was more beneficial than all the panic and worry he'd allowed himself prior to that moment.

What if I never regain my memory? What if this is all I have? A first name and no last name? No family, but this new group of people who seem to care greatly for me? Would it be enough? He shook his head.

"Lord, you are all I have at this point. All that I can count on. I believe the words I read here in the Bible. What would it profit me if I remember everything and regain my world, but lose my soul? I do not know what condition my soul might have been in prior to this, but I pray that you would save me. Save me from myself and from this awful torment."

"You look well rested," Mrs. Shoemaker stated as Mark took his place at the breakfast table.

He took up a red-checked napkin and smiled. Mrs. Shoemaker had a passion for ginghams and had even told Mark how the fabric was from the East Indies and used to be striped rather than checked. The material graced her kitchen curtains as well as the tablecloth of blue and white upon which their meal sat. He was sure that, given time, Mrs. Shoemaker would cover her entire house with the fabric.

"I feel rested," Mark admitted. "I spent a great deal of time in prayer last night."

The older woman brought him a cup of hot coffee and beamed him a smile. "Prayer is always a haven of peace for me. I'm sure it put things to right."

"I feel it has," he replied. "I cannot say exactly how or why, but I feel confident that in time God will show me what He wants me to know."

"And if your memory doesn't return?" she asked gently.

"Then I will have to believe that God has something better in store for me." And for the first time Mark had a peace about that thought. He could give it over to God and trust that things would be kept in His hand. He felt completely renewed. Perhaps this was what it was all about. Leaning on God when life made no sense, as well as when the answers seemed clear.

"There's ham on the stove should you want something more," Mrs. Shoemaker said as she placed a plate in front of him and pulled off her apron.

Mark looked at the generous portion already stacked on his plate. "No, I believe this is fine."

"I'll be outside in the garden. I promised the neighbor across the street some of my flowers for her dinner table. She's having a party tonight, and since I have an abundance of roses, I told her I would cut her a nice bouquet."

"Mrs. Jameston had some of the loveliest roses I've ever seen," Mark said after taking a sip of coffee. "But I believe yours would rival hers."

Mrs. Shoemaker stopped at the door and looked at Mark with a smile. "Who is Mrs. Jameston?"

Mark didn't even stop to think about it. "She's the woman who employs Cassie." He startled and looked up. There was no true memory or picture of the woman in his mind, but he knew the words to be true. "I don't remember anything else."

The woman chuckled. "You didn't remember that much yesterday. I'd say we're making progress."

Mark nodded slowly and returned his gaze to his plate. "Yes. I believe you're right."

For the remainder of the day, Mark felt a mixture of peace and anxiety. He knew peace in his soul—feeling for the first time since the accident that everything would be set right in time. He knew anxiety because having his mind back in order couldn't happen quickly enough. Not only that, he couldn't shake the feeling that something wasn't quite right. There was something he was supposed to be doing. Something important.

Throughout the day, flashes of memory came back to Mark. He began to see images and numbers, towns and names in his mind. He remembered Ruth and knew that they'd been married. She was dead, of that much he was certain. He couldn't remember how long ago this had happened, but the pain was not as intense as it had been in remembering Richard. This gave Mark reason to believe that Ruth must have died quite some time ago.

And always there was Cassie. She seemed to remain with him through the best and worst of it. He had taught her to ride a horse, but she was afraid. He couldn't remember why, but he knew that she had trusted him to help her. More than this, however, Mark felt certain that he loved Cassie—that she loved him. Were they married? Were they engaged?

The next day brought a few more answers. Mark was reading the newspaper, trying hard to find anything that seemed familiar, when he scanned an article about a policeman who was shot in the leg trying to stop a thief. Mark's head immediately filled with images. There was a large man with curly hair and another man with shoulder-length brown hair and icy blue eyes. The two images were mixed together for several minutes before separating to reveal the man with the cold, harsh blue eyes to have a leg wound like the police officer he'd just read about.

Mark put the paper down and closed his eyes to focus in on the man and his injury. His memories remained muddled, but Mark felt certain that man was trouble. The other image, however, bore a little more clarity. Mark remembered the man was named Wesley or Wester or something along those lines. He knew the man was his landlord, but he had no understanding of where he knew him from otherwise.

Dr. Shoemaker came home for a short time and found Mark pacing in the living room. "You'll hardly do yourself any good this way."

"But I want so much to remember," Mark said. "The peace I had earlier is gone now. I suppose it's because as some memories come back to me, it goads me into wanting more and more."

"And in time it will all come back," the doctor told him. "At least for the most part. There will most likely be things you don't remember. Those associated with the accident for instance."

"I don't care so much about remembering the accident." Mark sat down and took the newspaper in hand. "I've read enough about it and heard you discuss the matter. I don't feel at a loss in not being able to remember something so horrendous."

"You know, I did have a thought," Dr. Shoemaker said, nodding toward the newspaper. "What if we were to put a notice in the papers for the towns along the railroad's path? We could find out where the train originated and then post an announcement in the major cities."

"What kind of announcement?"

Dr. Shoemaker rubbed his chin. "Well, we could describe your features and explain that you had been injured in the railroad accident and had no memory. We could ask for anyone who might be missing a loved one fitting your description to contact us here."

Mark felt a surge of excitement. "That might very well work."

"When I return home this evening, we can figure out what to say." The doctor got to his feet. "Whatever else, do not lose hope. You've already come so far."

Mark knew the doctor was right, but he couldn't help turning his attention back to the newspaper in hand. The article had triggered memories. Who was to say that other articles might not do the same?

The hours ticked by in frustration. Mark tried to concentrate on the printed pages for so long that he gave himself a fierce headache and decided to lie down for a short rest. He had no sooner dozed off, however, than new pieces of the puzzle began to fill in. He dreamed of kissing Cassie and of her telling him at the train station that she was no longer pretending—that she really loved him. He struggled to see the name on the depot wall but couldn't make out the letters.

The scene faded, much to his frustration, and in its place came a petite older woman who smiled and handed him a dapple gray. "You must teach our Cassie to ride," she said. A little girl danced around him and chanted, "Teach me, too, Mr. Langford. Teach me about horses because Mama and Cassie are afraid."

He woke with a start and called out the girl's name. "Elida Stover!"

Mark sat up and pressed his hand to his temple. The little girl was Cassie's sister. Cassie Stover. Cassandra Stover.

His eyes widened as a flood of memories returned. "I'm Marcus Langford. I live in Boston." He shook his head. "No. I've been living in Philadelphia."

More memories inundated his mind. He fell back against the pillows laughing. "I'm Marcus Langford!" he cried out.

Mrs. Shoemaker knocked on his door. "Are you all right, Mark?"

"Come in! Come in!" He jumped to his feet. "I'm Marcus Langford. I live in Philadelphia!" He grabbed up the older woman and lifted her in a fierce embrace. Laughing, he set her back down and took hold of her shoulders. "I remember now. I remember."

Her eyes welled with tears. "Oh, the Lord is good. He has answered our prayers."

Mark suddenly stopped and remembered that part of his life as well. God had taken him from a place where his faith was based on the relationship he had with others. God had taken him to a place where Mark had to meet his heavenly Father face-to-face—all on his own. No parent to guide him. No wife to encourage him. No friend to bring him, kicking and protesting.

"He has answered our prayers indeed, Mrs. Shoemaker." He smiled and took hold of her again and hugged her tight. "In more ways than you could even begin to imagine."

CHAPTER 21

Memories were still filling in the emptiness of the last few weeks the next morning as Mark made plans to head back to Philadelphia. First on the agenda, he wired his parents in Boston. They would be frantic with worry about his well-being. Cassie would be worried, as well, but with only three hours separating them, Mark preferred to go to her in person—especially now that he remembered her declaration of love.

He smiled and hummed to himself as he thought of seeing her again. He would make his own declaration and ask Cassie to be his wife. The thought filled him with a feeling of completion such as he had not known since Ruth's death.

Still, he couldn't say there weren't some regrets in leaving Trenton. After borrowing some money from the doctor, Mark found himself at a loss as to how to say good-bye. The doctor and his wife had been his lifeline since the accident. Their care had seen Mark recovered, and their patience and tenderness had kept him calm as he waited for his mind to come right. He cared a great deal for the Shoemakers.

"You are like family to me now," Mark told the older man and his wife. "I cannot find the words to tell you how much it means to me that you would take a stranger into your home and care for him like a son."

"It was what the Lord would have us do," the doctor replied. "We've always been in the business of lending aid whenever we could."

"I will not forget it," Mark declared. "And I'm certain my mother and father will not. I know my mother will wish to correspond with you and offer her personal thanks."

"That is hardly necessary," Mrs. Shoemaker said. "We were happy to help." She came and embraced Mark as if he were her own. "God go with you, Mark."

Mark held her tightly for a moment, then released her and turned to the doctor. "Thank you." He shook the man's hand and met his gaze. "Thank you for the physical help, but also for the spiritual guidance. I feel whole for the first time in a long, long while."

"I'm glad," the man answered with a hearty smile. "God knew what He was doing when He put us all together."

A knock sounded, drawing their attention. Mark let out a yell when Mrs. Shoemaker opened the door.

"Westmoreland!" He shook the man's hand vigorously. "I am so glad to see you again."

"As am I to finally find you. We have been quite worried. Your folks, Miss Stover . . ."

Mark laughed. "I can well imagine. I've had no memory of anyone until yesterday. Well, there were bits and pieces for some time, but it all came clear for me just yesterday. I've wired my parents but thought to simply get on a train and head back to Cassie. I thought it might be easier to explain in person."

"I promised her that I would telegraph when I found you."

"Well, we could, but I happen to know that the train will leave for Philadelphia in twenty minutes. I cannot be late, even to send a telegram."

Westmoreland nodded. "Perhaps it would be best to simply arrive. After all, this will allow you to get there before nightfall."

Mark turned back to the doctor and his wife. "I feel terribly remiss. This is a good friend, Mr. Westmoreland. August, these are the Shoemakers. Dr. Shoemaker and his wife cared for me after the accident."

"How do you do?" the man said, tipping his hat.

"Very well," Mrs. Shoemaker declared. "Especially now that our Mark has been reunited with a friend. We will not feel so bad about sending him off with a companion."

"Mr. Westmoreland, it is indeed a pleasure to meet you," the doctor added, "but I fear I am overdue to visit a patient. Mark, I will bid you farewell and God's blessing."

"Thank you, sir. I feel that the latter has already been bestowed."

Cassie stirred the boiling oats and hummed to herself. It hadn't been easy to get Silas to allow her to fix the concoction in his kitchen, but she had finally won out. She wanted to prepare a special treat to share with Mrs. Jameston for lunch. The woman had been feeling poorly again and thought oatmeal might settle her stomach. Cassie wasn't at all sure it would, but she hoped that she might make an appealing surprise with cinnamon and sugar, knowing that the older woman had a sweet tooth. Meanwhile, Silas was in the pantry taking inventory and sulking.

Unable to find the cinnamon, Cassie wondered if she dared to ask Silas. He was a sweet old man, but he was highly possessive of his role in the Jameston kitchen.

"Silas?" she called as she made her way to the back pantry.

He pretended not to hear her, or so Cassie surmised, as he studied a list in his hands. He made an unintelligible grunt as he wrote something down.

"Silas?"

He turned and raised a bushy white eyebrow. "Yes."

Cassie smiled. "I wondered if you might show me where the cinnamon is. I want to add it to the oats while they're boiling."

He gave her a disapproving look. "Very well. I'll show you."

He walked from the pantry into the kitchen with Cassie close on his heels. She was so close in fact that when Silas stopped short, she nearly ran into his back.

"See, this is exactly what I feared would happen. You let one person come into your kitchen and then everyone thinks they have to join in."

Cassie peered around to find Sebastian Jameston stirring the oats. "Now, now, Silas, you know you don't mind my being in here. Besides, the oats were boiling over," he said with a shrug. "I didn't want you to have a mess on your hands."

His demeanor suggested something else, however. He gave Cassie a leering smile before dropping his hold on the spoon. "I suppose you are making this for my mother? I heard her say something about oatmeal for lunch. Seems like a rather strange request."

"Not when you're sick," Cassie countered.

Silas brought her some ground cinnamon. "If you want more than this, you'll have to grind your own."

"Thank you, Silas. I know it will mean so much to Mrs. Jameston."

He muttered something and stomped off to the pantry, but Cassie could see in his expression that he wasn't really all that mad anymore.

She went to the pot of oats and started to sprinkle the cinnamon into the mixture. Spying something at the edge of the pan that looked like a white powder, she nearly said something but held back. For some time now, she'd worried that Sebastian was doing something to cause his mother's illness.

A shiver went over her. Had Sebastian poisoned the oats? She had to remain calm. She forced her hand to steady and prayed that God would give her the strength to pretend just a little longer. Cassie couldn't allow Jameston to suspect that she thought him planning his mother's murder.

Stirring the cereal, Cassie wondered what he'd put into the mixture. She put the cinnamon aside and dropped the spoon back on its holder. Sebastian watched her with great intensity. She could feel his gaze on her even before she turned to find him watching her.

"What do you want, Sebastian?"

"I want what I've always wanted: you. I'm trying to figure out how much longer you intend to play this game with me."

Cassie felt the wind go out from her. Did he know what she was up to? "I don't know what you're talking about."

"I'm speaking of us. Of living day in and day out, under the same roof. I'm speaking of Langford being gone now for a month. I believe he has deserted you. At least I hope that's the case, for, Cassie, I still desire to see us together."

"I used to desire to be a princess," Cassie said rather flatly. "But alas, there are few royal family members living in Philadelphia."

He laughed. "I will treat you like a queen."

"And how will you do that? You have to beg your mother for money," Cassie said, a plan forming in her mind. Jameston was always talking about how he would be lord of the manor once his mother was dead. No doubt he was seeking to hurry that matter along.

As if reading her mind, he sneered. "I won't have to beg anyone for anything after she dies."

"And how do you figure that, Mr. Jameston?"

"I don't understand." He seemed genuinely puzzled.

Cassie rolled her eyes and moved to retrieve the sugar. "I fail to understand how you will benefit from her death, now that she has changed her will."

She didn't dare look at Jameston for fear he would recognize her trepidation. Mrs. Jameston had decided to make changes in her will, but she hadn't told Cassie what those changes amounted to. Cassie personally hoped that the older woman had disinherited her horrible son, but she had no proof of that. Still, if Jameston thought he'd been stripped of his future fortune, perhaps he'd stop trying to kill his mother long enough for Cassie to ensure her safety.

For several minutes the kitchen held a deadly silence. Cassie knew she would have to face Jameston. She drew a deep breath and turned to find him standing not a foot away.

"What did you say?" he questioned through clenched teeth.

Cassie clutched the sugar bowl even more tightly to keep Jameston from seeing that her hands were shaking. She could see the rage in his blue eyes. What was normally a handsome face had now contorted into something that looked rather demonic.

"I said," Cassie began, trying hard to breathe evenly, "that you won't benefit from your mother's death, as she has changed her will."

Sebastian remained calm. He backed away with closed fists at his sides and paced the length of the kitchen. "Are you certain of this? She's said nothing to me. Surely if she were that angry with me, she would have threatened me or told me."

"And why should she? You've done nothing but threaten her and treat her abominably since you arrived here with your leg injury. You even implied that you would burn the house down around us. Why should any mother tolerate such things, much less reward them?"

Jameston stopped and looked at her hard. "This is your doing. You caused this."

"I had nothing to do with it. I did accompany her to the lawyer's office, but I didn't even meet Mr. Daniels." She hoped the name reference would add credence to her story.

Apparently it did the trick, because Sebastian paled and began to pace again. Cassie decided enough time had been spent in explanation. She went to the stove with the sugar and poured a small amount into the mixture. There was no possibility that this would be served to anyone, save perhaps rats in the cellar, but she had to make it appear that all was well.

"What are you doing?" Sebastian asked, coming to the stove.

"I'm finishing the preparations for the oatmeal I promised your mother." She put aside the sugar bowl and went to the cupboard for a bowl. "Now I plan to dish it up and take some to her."

Sebastian seemed to panic. Cassie paid no attention. She hoped that he was notably upset and concerned about what would happen next. He'd already caused so much trouble, and if Cassie was right and he'd been poisoning his mother all along, she couldn't imagine what lengths he might go to in order to finish the job. However, if she'd convinced him about the will, he couldn't possibly want to carry on. At least not until he assured himself that Cassie was wrong or that the will was changed back to his favor.

"I'll carry it to the table for you," he announced, eyeing the pot on the stove.

Cassie wondered what he planned to do, but it was only another moment before she knew, as he pretended to trip and sent the pot and all of the oatmeal flying across the floor.

"Oh, look what you've done. Now I shall have to make another batch," Cassie said, pretending to be upset.

"I suppose you will," he said, straightening. "Now if you'll excuse me, I have an appointment in town."

"But what of the mess you've made?" Cassie questioned, not at all sorry to see him go.

"Get one of the servants to see to it." He hurried from the kitchen and disappeared.

Cassie met Silas's disapproving glare as he came to see what had caused the commotion. She shrugged.

"Silas, it seems I've made a bit of a mess."

As soon as the oatmeal was cleaned up, Cassie knew that she would have to tell Mrs. Jameston the truth about everything. It would break the woman's heart to know her own child had been responsible for her months of illness. Of course, Cassie couldn't know for sure that all of her sickness had come at the hands of Sebastian, but it seemed awfully coincidental that she hadn't really taken a turn for the worse until after he'd appeared in the house.

She couldn't imagine what went through the mind of someone like Sebastian Jameston. How could he want to end the life of the woman who'd given life to him? Mrs. Jameston had done nothing but indulge her son, and he hated her for it. How ironic.

The thought of Jameston returning to somehow force a confrontation between him and his mother caused Cassie to feel a sense of panic. What if he returned with a gun and forced his mother to accompany him to the lawyer's office?

Oh, Mark, where are you? Why are you not here? Cassie fought back the urge to cry as she made her way up the grand staircase. They were in such danger now. Cassie could feel it. Once Sebastian found out the truth, one way or another, she and Mrs. Jameston would be in for more trouble.

"We need to get out of here," she told herself as she paused at the top of the stairs. "We must leave. But where should we go?"

She looked down the long hall and considered her dilemma. No matter where she took Mrs. Jameston, once they left, it would leave no doubt in Sebastian's mind that she perceived him as a grave threat.

"O Father, help me. Help me to know what to do."

A thought came to mind. She didn't know if it would work or even be safe, but Jameston didn't know where her family lived. He could probably find out eventually, but it would take a little time. She could take Mrs. Jameston to her mother's house. From there, she and her mother could figure something else out. Once the old woman knew the details of what was happening, perhaps she could even advise Cassie as to where they might go for safety.

She looked back at the door to her employer's bedchambers and sighed. There was no time to waste and no easy way to deliver such bad news.

CHAPTER 22

Mrs. Jameston sat in a chair before the fireplace and listened as Cassie explained the details of what had transpired.

"I feel quite certain that this is the reason you have been sick," Cassie told her. "I hate to be the one to bear such unimaginable news, but your son's actions seem to affirm my suspicions."

The older woman had tears in her eyes as she nodded. "I've no doubt it is true. I have wondered as much myself. Sebastian has come several times with tea for me, as well as sliced fruit, which he knows I love." She drew a ragged breath and faced Cassie. "I wish I had died rather than come to the place in life where my own child was trying to kill me."

Cassie reached out and took hold of her hand. "It is a terrible thing, but I will see you safe. I will not allow him to hurt you any longer."

"He wasn't always like this," she said, gazing into the empty hearth. "I should have given more of myself to him. It is because of my misery and pain that he is this way. I tried to make it up to him, but I did a poor job of it. I'm afraid I gave of my possessions but not of my heart. Now it is too late . . . and the damage is done."

"The damage might well be done, but healing is always possible as long as we draw breath. We make our own choices as we grow up. Even if you had neglected him, and later overindulged him, Sebastian knew right from wrong. Which brings me, sadly, to another aspect of this situation."

Mrs. Jameston cocked her head to one side. "There is more?"

"I'm afraid so. I don't know quite how to explain, but you must know the truth. Mark is an investigator for an insurance company that Sebastian has been defrauding. Mark's dear friend Richard was investigating the matter first, but unfortunately your son . . . he . . ." Cassie dropped her hold on Mrs. Jameston and looked away. "Mark believes that Sebastian killed Richard."

"Oh no." Mrs. Jameston shook her head. "Oh, this is terrible news. I cannot even begin to bear the thought." She put her hand to her chest, and Cassie feared the worst. "To ply his hatred against me is one thing, but to wrong others . . . oh . . . I can scarcely bear it."

"I'm sorry. I probably shouldn't have told you. But there is a reason for my declaration." She patted the woman's arm. "Are you in pain?"

"My heart is broken," Mrs. Jameston admitted. "The pain, however, is not physical." She began to cry and drew her lace-edged handkerchief to her face. "Oh, Cassie, I cannot even begin to understand my son's actions."

"I know. Mark approached me to help him get enough information and evidence on Sebastian that he could put him in jail for good. I feel horrible for not having told you sooner. Mark and I have only been pretending to care for each other so that he could get closer to Sebastian. Please, please forgive me."

Mrs. Jameston dried her eyes and looked at Cassie. She gripped the younger woman's wrist and shook her head. "There is nothing to forgive. You did the right thing. I would not lie to protect my son. I would not wish for anyone to let a murderer go unpunished. Oh, my dear Cassie, what you must have suffered. I am so very sorry."

"No. I am fine. You are the one who has endured more than you should have had to."

"But I am his mother." She released Cassie's arm and looked away again. "I should have seen him jailed long ago. After he attacked Essie and after so many other inappropriate incidents, I shouldn't have fought to keep him from his punishment—but I felt so responsible. I thought if I interceded on his behalf he would be grateful and change his ways. How could he so completely abandon the truth he was taught?" She met Cassie's gaze. "What are we to do now?"

"I have a thought—a plan, really—and I want very much for you to agree to my terms."

Mrs. Jameston eyed her curiously. "Go on."

"I feel certain that your son will only be stirred by his hatred. I fear he will return and pose an even bigger threat. Therefore, I would like to take you away immediately. I don't think your son knows where my family lives, and while he could eventually find out, it will give us time to better plan our situation. We might find it necessary to go elsewhere. If you have thoughts on that, I would certainly be willing to entertain them."

"Dr. Riley had suggested a place in New York where the mineral waters have curative powers. I suppose we could lead Sebastian to believe I have gone there," Mrs. Jameston reasoned.

"That's a good idea. We can discuss the details at my mother's. Right now, we need to pack our things and leave before Sebastian returns."

"I'm certain you are right," Mrs. Jameston said.

Her sorrow was so evident that Cassie could not help but lean over to hug the woman close. "God will see us through this. I'm convinced He even gave me aid with the oatmeal. The reason Sebastian pretended to drop the concoction was because I told him you had cut him from your will. I realize it was a falsehood, but it was the only thing I could think of to delay his actions. I felt certain the poison was in the oats, and I couldn't allow him to know that I suspected such a thing."

"It wasn't a lie," Mrs. Jameston said softly. "I did have Sebastian removed from my will. His threats and temper made me realize that he was not to be trusted. I couldn't see giving any more money to such a person." She sighed and looked at the far wall. "I suspected him to be involved in illegal happenings long ago. I had hoped that by giving him enough money to sustain his needs he would avoid such entanglements in the future. Instead, I suppose I merely funded his desires."

"There is nothing to be done about that now," Cassie said, drawing a deep breath. "He may well have gone to check into the specifics of the will himself. He will seek you out to berate you for your actions." She got up and went to the servants' bell. "I'll ring for Mr. Brumley. We'll have the servants gather here, if you don't mind. I'll explain the situation, and they can help us. We need to leave immediately."

"I suppose you are right, but there is something else I want you to know," Mrs. Jameston said, getting to her feet. "I didn't only remove my son from the will, I included someone. Someone who will take his place as my heir."

"That seems reasonable." She gave the pull a yank, knowing that it would quickly bring Brumley to the room. She opened the door and waited for him to appear.

"I added you, Cassandra."

The words seemed to hang on the air. Cassie turned and peered at Mrs. Jameston's face. Surely she was jesting. One glance, however, at the older woman's expression proved otherwise.

"What? But . . . why? You shouldn't have done that."

"You are the only one besides my staff to have ever shown me any real concern or care. You offered to come here and be my friend without any kind of recompense."

"But that is because I care about you," Cassie said, still baffled. "I have come to love you as my own family member."

"I know this. You came for the love of your mother and sister as well. Even when you were forced into uncomfortable, threatening situations by my son, your focus was on me and your family. Your sacrifice was the determining factor in my decision. That is why you seemed the logical one to leave my estate to." Mrs. Jameston came to where Cassie stood and reached out to touch her face. "You have proven yourself to be pure of heart. Your motives have been to see to my welfare and that of your own family. I hadn't realized how much I missed a companion until you came into my life."

"But, Mrs. Jameston, I would not have you believe I've done these things in order to inherit your money." Cassie felt a sense of guilt course through her. What had ever given the woman such an idea?

"I never believed that of you, my dear. I simply wanted to reward you for your kindness and mercy to an old woman who had no one else. As I've told you before, I have made provision for my staff, and while I care dearly for them, I felt after much prayer that you were the one who should receive the bulk of my fortune. I want you to have this house and all of its furnishings. I hope you might even keep the staff in place. There will be more than enough money, and the house is big enough to bring your mother and sister to live with you—and your husband."

Cassie shook her head. "As I said, Mark and I have only been pretending."

"Bah," the older woman said with a laugh. "You might have started out that way, but I know better. I'm seventy years old. I recognize true love when I see it. Tell me that you do not love him."

"I cannot. I even told him I was no longer pretending, and he's not returned since. I doubt he cares for me or he would have come back to speak of the matter."

"He loves you, Cassie. Of this I am certain. There has probably been some circumstance to keep him from you, but when that obstacle is cleared, he will come back."

"I hope so." Cassie didn't want to add to the woman's burden by sharing her fears that Mark had been seriously wounded in the train derailment . . . and might even now be dead or dying.

Brumley appeared in the doorway. "You rang for me, ma'am?"

"Actually, I did," Cassie said. "Brumley, we have a most serious problem. I need you to gather all of the staff members here to Mrs. Jameston's chambers. We must act fast, or I fear for her life."

His eyes widened ever so slightly. "I will get them immediately." He didn't even wait for Mrs. Jameston to confirm the situation before darting off down the hall. For an older man, he could certainly move quickly when needed, Cassie thought.

It was only a matter of minutes before the staff was collected. They came en masse and seemed anxious to hear what had to be said. Mrs. Jameston was already seated, leaving Cassie to take charge of the situation.

Cassie explained the danger. "It seems that Sebastian has been poisoning his mother's food and drink for some time. I caught him earlier today having put something in the oatmeal that I was preparing for Mrs. Jameston." She gave details of the incident and saw the shock pass over each person's face. It seemed Silas was more affected than the others.

"Are you certain?" he asked, meeting Cassie's eyes.

"I can only tell you what happened and what I saw. When Mrs. Jameston ate nothing but the soup my mother prepared, she was fine. Do you recall times when Sebastian might have been in the kitchen while food was being prepared for his mother? Perhaps when you were setting up a tray for her, or tea?"

Silas's countenance fell. "The young master was often there." He shook his head. "I didn't know that he meant to cause you harm, madam."

"Of course you didn't."

"I've always loved him as a son. You know that to be true."

"I do know that," Mrs. Jameston said. "You and your wife were good to see to Sebastian's needs when I was unable to do so. You cared for him as I should have."

Silas appeared decidedly upset. "If he has done what you say, he should hang."

The declaration startled Cassie. The look on Silas's face suggested a combination of betrayal and anger. She guessed he had only just come to see Sebastian for the monster he'd become. Mrs. Dixon put her arm around Silas's shoulder in support but said nothing.

Cassie realized the time was getting away from them and continued. "Sebastian left earlier, but he'll be back. He was quite upset, and I fear what he might do. We must, therefore, get Mrs. Jameston from this house."

"Where will she go?" Mrs. Dixon asked, her eyes welling with tears.

"I would like to take her to my mother's house. At least temporarily. It would allow for a momentary solution while we determine what the next step is to be."

"However," Mrs. Jameston added, "we will tell him I've gone to New York to take the cure. I will pen him a letter that suggests as much. Without actually lying, I will explain that the doctor suggested the journey, which he has. We hope this will throw him off the trail and give us even more time to decide what must be done."

"What of contacting the police?" Wills asked.

"We have no proof," Cassie told him. "There is nothing I can present to anyone to prove my case. Mr. Langford can possibly help in that matter, but . . ." She stopped, a lump forming in her throat. "Should he return, you can, of course, tell him where we've gone. He can be trusted with our lives."

"We will do as you say," Brumley replied.

Cassie could hear the anger in his voice. He cared very much for his employer and wasn't about to let anything happen to her . . . or to Cassie.

"We need to pack Mrs. Jameston's clothes and leave immediately. Wills, can you arrange the carriage in the back alleyway? That way if Jameston comes home before we leave, he won't see us."

"I'll do it now," Wills declared. "We can leave when you are ready."

Cassie nodded. "Mr. Brumley, I would like for you and Mrs. Dixon to aid Mrs. Jameston to the carriage. The sooner the better. We need to get her out of the house and at least to the safety of the carriage before Sebastian returns."

"Of course," Brumley answered for them both as Mrs. Dixon went to help Mrs. Jameston from her chair.

"Ada and Essie, we will pack as quickly as possible."

"Please remember my Bible," Mrs. Jameston called as she moved to the door with Mrs. Dixon. "Oh, and my shawl." She pointed to the end of the bed, and Brumley hurried to retrieve it.

"What should I do?" Silas asked. He seemed desperate to prove his loyalty.

Cassie smiled. "Keep a lookout at the top of the stairs. If Sebastian returns before we get out of the house, make a pretense of needing to show him something in the front of the house or in the front yard."

"We've had a few rodents burrowing in the cellar," Miriam suggested. "You could suggest he come with you and view the damage."

"I will do whatever is necessary," Silas said.

"I will help you pack, Cassie," Miriam declared as she moved to the younger woman's bedroom.

Cassie nodded. "We must hurry. Mr. Jameston will not show us any mercy if he returns to find us getting ready to leave."

"We can take care of ourselves, Miss Cassie," Ada said, squaring her shoulders. "You don't worry about us. We've had many years of dealing with Mr. Jameston."

"That's right," Miriam said. "We can handle the likes of him—especially now that we know exactly what he is capable of. God will give us strength."

"And wisdom," Ada added.

Cassie felt encouraged by the resolve in their voices. These women were her allies in a grave affair that would mean the difference between life and death. God would indeed guide them and give direction. After all, it was only too clear that He had done so all along.

CHAPTER 23

Mark left Westmoreland in the hired carriage and ran for the Jamestons' front door. He had been unable to stop worrying about Cassie and whether Sebastian Jameston had caused her harm. He thought of poor Mrs. Jameston and her constant illnesses and feared the worst for her as well.

It was hard to know what to expect. His absence might well have prompted Jameston to take advantage of the women, and if that were the case, Mark didn't know how he'd respond. Then, too, Cassie might hate him for having left her without explanation. Of course, she was the type of woman who would listen and forgive—of that he was confident. Still, having a month of his life taken from him had left him anxious about a great many things.

He knocked loudly and waited for Brumley to open the door. When he did, the older man seemed completely shocked to find Mark on the other side. He seemed to size up Mark for a moment, then stepped back.

"Good afternoon, sir. You've been long away from us."

"Indeed I have. I wonder if you would call Miss Stover to come down."

"I'm sorry, but she isn't here." Brumley glanced over his shoulder and lowered his voice. "She has fled with Mrs. Jameston."

"Fled? When did that happen? What has happened to cause this?"

"Mr. Sebastian. He isn't here at the moment." Brumley seemed more than a little nervous about the entire matter. "Miss Cassie discovered he was trying to poison his mother. She then thought it best to get Mrs. Jameston from the house."

"Where did they go?" Mark questioned. He was glad that Cassie had proven so capable and so sensible, yet he felt a surging guilt for not having been there to aid her.

Brumley stepped closer. "Miss Cassie took her home. To the Stover residence."

"I see." Mark considered the words for a few moments, then nodded. "I will find her there, then."

He turned to go, but Brumley put out his hand. "Sir, if you would wait but a few minutes, Miss Ada is heading over there as well. She's packing her own things at the moment, and Wills was set to drive her."

Mark nodded. "I'll let Mr. Westmoreland know. He's still in the carriage. Tell Ada to wait for me, and I'll accompany her. I'll meet her at the carriage house."

"Very good, sir."

Mark went to the carriage and opened the door. "Cassie's not here. She's felt a direct threat from Mr. Jameston and has taken his mother to stay with her family. I will go with one of the servants and see what else is to be done. I'll meet you at the boardinghouse later to discuss what our next step will be to ensure their safety."

"I'll be there," Westmoreland assured. "And Mark . . . be careful." The concern on his face was evident. No doubt he worried that Mark had already been through a great deal. Perhaps he even thought Mark wasn't up to the challenge, but that was not the case. Mark was stirred and strengthened by his desire to see justice and truth win out. He was driven by his love for Cassie and his hope that they might share a future.

He informed the driver, then made his way back to the carriage house as fast as he could. Wills was loading the last of Ada's things into the carriage when Mark arrived.

"Good to have you back, sir. We've been worried about you," Wills said in greeting. "Ada should be here directly, and then we can leave for Miss Stover's house."

"Is there anything I can do to help?" Mark asked, noting the time. "When is Mr. Jameston expected back?"

"I don't know, but we've tried to be quick about this. We moved Miss Cassie and Mrs. Jameston earlier this afternoon, but Ada wasn't able to gather her own things at the time. I came back for her as soon as I got the ladies settled in."

"So both of them are . . . uh . . . well?"

"Yes, sir. Mrs. Jameston had been quite ill, but we're hopeful she'll soon mend. Oh good. Here comes Ada now. She can probably tell you more."

Mark looked up the walkway to find the maid hurrying toward them. She smiled when she saw Mark. "I'm so glad you've returned to us. Miss Cassie was beside herself with worry."

"I've been worried for her as well." Mark helped Ada into the carriage and nodded to Wills. "Let's leave quickly."

Wills set the carriage in motion even as Mark took his seat. The sense of desperation was heavy in the air. Ada kept looking from window to window and twisting her gloved hands nervously.

"I believe we'll be just fine now, Ada. Try not to worry. Mr. Jameston will cause you no harm while I'm here."

"He tried to kill his own mother, Mr. Langford." Her words were whispered, but Mark heard them clearly. "Cassie found out the truth this morning. He tried to put poison in the food she was preparing."

"How did she handle the situation?" Mark asked.

Ada smiled. "Our Cassie is a smart one. She appealed to the only thing that she knew for sure mattered to Mr. Jameston. Money. He kept telling Cassie how rich he would be once his mother was dead. Cassie told him this wasn't true because she knew he'd been written out of Mrs. Jameston's will. Strangely enough, Cassie thought she was making up the entire thing, but Mrs. Jameston truly had written Sebastian out of the will. In fact, she had named Cassie her main beneficiary."

The news took Mark by surprise. Mrs. Jameston was vastly wealthy. "And what did Jameston do when he found out that he'd been written out of the will?"

"That was the amazing part. That confirmed what Cassie had suspected. She had been making oatmeal for Mrs. Jameston and herself. When she stepped away she came back to find Sebastian stirring the concoction. He told her it was about to boil over, but Cassie saw white powder on the edge of the pan and knew that something wasn't right. She pretended, however, that everything was fine."

Mark thought of all the games of pretense they'd played, and knew that this one had been Cassie's most deadly. "What happened then?"

"When Cassie told Sebastian that he was out of the will, he apparently realized he couldn't let her serve his mother the oatmeal. Cassie thinks there must surely have been a lethal dose, because he took up the pot on the grounds of taking it to the table for her and dropped it instead—spilling it everywhere."

"Smart man. Who could become suspicious of a mere accident?"

"Well, Cassie said he was very upset but held his calm. He left quickly, and once he was gone, Cassie went to work. She called all of us together and explained everything. Of course, I got to hear more of it while she and I packed for her and Mrs. Jameston to leave." Ada looked at Mark in earnest. "I'm so glad you've returned. I'm very afraid. Not so much for myself, but for Mrs. Jameston and Cassie. I believe Sebastian means to harm them both—especially now that Cassie will inherit his fortune."

"Please try not to fret. I will do what I can to see this situation dealt with so that no one is hurt."

"Cassie said that God would look after us—that He would not allow Mr. Jameston's evil nature to prevail—but I've seen bad men do horrible things to good people." She bit at her lower lip, as if trying to decide whether to continue or not. "Mr. Jameston is dangerous. He's not to be trusted under any circumstance."

"I completely understand, Ada. Try not to worry. It is my hope and plan to see him soon behind bars."

The carriage came to a stop in front of the house that Mark knew the Stover family occupied. Light shone from nearly every window, both downstairs and up. He imagined Cassie pacing the floors and refusing to rest until she knew that Ada was safe.

"You go ahead to her," Ada said with a smile. "She's missed you terribly."

"And I have missed her," Mark replied. He stepped down and reached back to help Ada.

"Don't worry about me. Wills will see to me. You go ahead. I know this is what she's prayed for." Ada motioned him away.

Mark bounded up the front walk and knocked on the door. It seemed an eternity before anyone came, but when the door opened it was Cassie who looked back at him in wonder.

"Sorry I'm late," he said with a grin. "I was a bit detained."

Her mouth dropped open, and without warning she wrapped her arms around his neck and plied his face with kisses. "Oh, you're safe! You're alive. Oh, thank God!" she declared in between bestowing her affection.

Mark was surprised by the welcome but tightened his hold on her. "I'm so sorry you had to wonder about me. I was injured—the train derailed."

"I know—at least we figured as much," she said, pulling back to gaze into his eyes. "I feared . . . I mean . . . I worried that perhaps I'd . . ." She looked away, embarrassed.

Understanding dawned on Mark almost immediately. She thought she'd driven him away with her declaration of love. He started to reply but found himself interrupted.

"Ada!" Cassie dropped her hold as the maid approached. "I'm so glad you've returned. Was he there? Did you have any trouble?"

"No," Ada replied. "Mr. Jameston hadn't yet shown up at the house. I was greatly relieved to hear it too. Miriam and Essie helped me collect my things, and Wills kept the carriage ready."

Mark stepped aside to usher the ladies into the house. "Let us get inside, lest we're observed," he suggested. Wills came up with the luggage, and Mark helped him inside as Cassie led the way.

The house was cozy and simple. Mark remembered it well from when he'd come for Elida's birthday. In some ways, it reminded him of the Shoemakers' home. There was a sense of family here, just as there had been in Trenton with the doctor and his wife.

"Mr. Langford!" Mrs. Jameston declared as Mark stepped into the sitting room. "I am so happy to see you. Cassie has told me everything."

Mark looked rather apprehensive and glanced at Cassie. "Everything?"

"I had to," she explained. "I thought it only fair. Earlier, when Sebastian tried to poison her food— Oh goodness, but you don't know about that, do you?"

"Yes. Yes, I do. Mr. Brumley and Ada have informed me of what took place."

Cassie looked to Ada and smiled. "Thank you. It's just been so strange. Everything has happened all at once. I felt that I had to explain to Mrs. Jameston about our little game and what you were really trying to do."

Mark went to Mrs. Jameston and knelt beside her chair. "I am so sorry. I know that my actions must grieve you."

"Not nearly so much as the actions of my son," she replied. "You are upholding the law and seeking justice for your friend. I cannot fault you for that. Sebastian has . . . well . . . dug his own grave, I suppose." Tears came to her eyes. "He's my child and I love him so much, but I do not know this stranger he's become."

Cassie came to her and put her hands on Mrs. Jameston's shoulders. "No matter what happens, we will see you through this." She looked to Mark as if for confirmation.

"She's right," he agreed. "What plans have been made up until now?"

"Very few, actually," Cassie admitted.

"Mr. Langford!" Elida fairly squealed as she dashed into the room. "I cannot believe you are here. I thought you had gone away forever." Her mother followed in behind her and offered Mark a beaming smile.

He smiled at the ten-year-old. "I was in a terrible train accident and I lost my memory for what felt like a very long time."

"Were you hurt very badly?" she asked in awe.

Mark caught Cassie's worried expression. "I was hurt, to be sure. But a kindly doctor and his wife took me in. It wasn't until yesterday that my memories fully returned. Even now, little things sometimes stump me for a moment."

"We're so glad you were able to recover," Dora Stover said. "We have been quite beside ourselves for news."

He stood and smiled. "I am sorry for the worry it caused."

Dora nodded and looked at her daughter. "God has a way of setting things right."

"Indeed He does," Mark replied.

"Mrs. Jameston, I'll show you where everything is," Dora Stover instructed. "Come along, Elida. You can help."

The room emptied quickly, leaving Cassie and Mark to stand, looking at each other. Mark thought he'd never seen anyone more beautiful in all of his life. Cassie's words came back to him, and he shook his head.

"Why did you say those things at the train station that day?"

Cassie drew a deep breath and twisted her hands together. "You know me and my big mouth—always speaking my mind. I guess I thought maybe you'd forgotten about it."

He grinned. "It's hard to forget something as shocking as that."

"Shocking? Why shocking?"

He folded his arms. "I suppose because we had an agreement to pretend."

"Yes, well, I thought I was rather good at such things, but I find that apparently I am not," Cassie said, her words spilling out at a quickening pace. "I felt it was important to let you know the truth. I certainly didn't want to deceive you. I also didn't wish to upset you, and I do apologize if I did. When you didn't return immediately as planned, I thought my blurting out such declarations may have been more than you could deal with."

He laughed. "Ah, Cassie, you have no idea."

She looked at him oddly. "I didn't mean for it to happen. I didn't set out to fall in love with you. It's just that every time you came to see me, I found myself more and more excited to share your company. I cannot help speaking the truth. You have always known that my mouth seems to have a mind of its own." She stopped her pacing and raised her hands as she shrugged. "I suppose I have ruined a perfectly good friendship."

"Well, it may well have altered that friendship," he said seriously.

She sighed. "I knew I should have kept quiet."

"But how did you know it was love? You told me that you'd never been in love before."

Cassie began to pace again, her face contorting. She seemed to ponder the answer for several seconds. "I hadn't been in love before, and perhaps that is why I knew it to be love now. The absence of something is often just as revealing as the presence of a thing."

"That is true." He stepped before her, halting her progression. "You'll put a hole in your mother's carpet if you don't stop pacing."

"I cannot help it. I feel so mortified."

He laughed. "Then put your mind at ease. I am not offended by your declaration. In fact, you were all that I could think of the entire time I was gone. I called for you even in my unconscious state—or so they told me. I didn't know who you were, but your image haunted me day and night."

Touching her cheek, he gazed with deep longing into her eyes. "I prayed to find you. I prayed to know my mind again, simply that I might know you. It's no longer a game for me either. It hasn't been for some time. I just didn't know what to do about it."

Cassie's eyes were wide with wonder. "What are we to do about it?" She barely breathed the words.

He smiled and dropped to one knee. "I suppose we should marry. That is, if you will have me."

Her mouth formed a silent O. He wanted to laugh out loud at the expression of shock on her face. For once, she was stunned into silence.

"Will you marry me, Cassandra Stover?"

"I . . . uh . . . you truly . . ." She couldn't form a coherent sentence.

This only made Mark laugh all the more. "I've never seen you so speechless in all the time I've known you."

"I've never been asked such a question before," she said. "Are you sure this isn't just part of your game?"

He stood so quickly she nearly toppled backward. Taking her in his arms, he kissed her passionately, bending her backward until she was helpless to move from his arms without fear of falling. "What do you think?"

She grinned. "No more games of pretense?"

"No," he said, shaking his head ever so slowly.

"No more secret desires and hidden emotions?"

"Absolutely none."

Cassie giggled. "What about clandestine meetings?"

He gave her a wicked grin as he arched a single brow. "Perhaps we can still arrange those. But only if you say yes to my proposal."

"Then consider this to be my yes. I will marry you, Marcus Langford. I happily consent to be your wife."

CHAPTER 24

Sebastian returned to his mother's house, bringing with him a driving rage and desire for revenge. Through his own connections he'd learned the truth of his mother's changes to the will. Cassie had been right. His mother had disinherited him, but what Cassie hadn't bothered to tell him was that she had been put in the will to replace him.

Nothing enraged Sebastian more than to have his plans disrupted. Since returning to his mother's house back in April, he'd known that the time had come to eliminate her from the picture. His plans for the future were such that he felt certain he could triple his money if he could only manage to set up his business the way he wanted. Insurance companies were springing up everywhere and insuring most everything. A person could now insure not only ships and cargoes but houses, livestock, and lives. The entire business stirred his imagination. If a man worked things right, he could easily insure a variety of things and make a tidy profit by arranging to have those things disappear, killed, or stolen.

How very creative, he thought, *to have articles taken by your own people and sold elsewhere so that you might capitalize on the situation twice.* As he had done with several ship cargoes, Sebastian had managed to make a tidy sum for himself and his men. Of course, the expenses involved were also steep. That was why he needed to expand his business in such a way that he could have several jobs going on at the same time.

Cassandra Stover, however, had become a thorn in his side. Where he might have previously been able to talk his mother out of large sums of money, now his mother had been persuaded to cut him completely from her will. He seethed at the thought of Cassie convincing his own mother that he no longer deserved his rightful inheritance.

"Well, she won't have an opportunity to cause me further harm," he muttered. "If Miss Stover is dead, she can hardly inherit."

The plan was fixed in his mind. He would force his mother to write a new will. If she balked, he would threaten to kill Cassie on the spot. Once the will was written, he would kill her anyway. He would kill them both. He already had a plan in mind.

The schemes energized Sebastian and made him smile as he entered the house for what he thought might be the last time. With any luck at all, he would find Cassie and his mother together reading or chatting. It was just past breakfast time, so he didn't anticipate finding them still at the dining table. No, they would be casually gathered some place more intimate, where he could easily confront them.

The house was strangely quiet. Sebastian called for Brumley and then for Mrs. Dixon, but neither servant came. *Odd.* Usually Brumley guarded the front door as though he were a warden of an asylum.

"Brumley! Where are you, man?"

The words echoed back at Sebastian. The upper floors proved to be deserted. There was no one to be found on the second floor—not even in his mother's room. It was possible they might have gone for a carriage ride or into town on some sort of business.

Still, it seemed strange that the entire house should be vacated. Where were the servants? Sebastian walked slowly through the downstairs rooms and finally found Silas baking bread in the kitchen.

"Where is everyone?"

Silas looked up and his expression registered surprise, then what appeared to be disgust. "Busy at their jobs, sir."

"Where's my mother?" Sebastian asked, noting that Silas seemed nervous.

"I couldn't say, sir. She rarely checks in with me."

The impudent response caused Sebastian to narrow his eyes. "Where is Brumley?" The butler would know every detail of his mother's comings and goings just as he always had.

"I believe he's gone to town for a few supplies. Mrs. Dixon was to have gone with him, but I suppose that could have changed."

Well, at least that explained their absence. Sebastian crossed his arms. "I suppose my mother and Miss Stover are out on some errand as well?"

"I believe that is quite possible," Silas replied, focusing on his bread dough. "Will you be with us for dinner?"

Sebastian shrugged. "Who can say? I suppose it will depend on what I'm able to accomplish this morning. I'm going upstairs to change my clothes. If my mother returns in the meantime, please tell her that I'm looking for her."

"Yes, sir. I will do just that."

Sebastian bounded upstairs, anxious to change into fresh attire. He'd spent the previous night with his mistress and still reeked of her perfume. Tossing his coat to the bed, Sebastian worked the buttons of his vest. While doing so, however, he spied a letter left for him on his side table.

He left off with his clothes and took up the missive. It was clearly his mother's script. Glancing through the letter, Sebastian felt his jaw tighten. She wrote that the doctor had advised her to go away for a time to regain her health. The man wished for her to go to a spa somewhere in New York, but she didn't say where exactly. *"I apologize for not being able to give you this information face-to-face,"* he read. *"I do not expect to be gone long—surely no more than a month."*

Sebastian crumpled the letter and threw it across the room.

"No more than a month!" That would ruin his plans completely. He tore at the vest and threw it off as soon as the buttons were unfastened. "How could she do this to me?"

He thought of Cassie and knew she'd no doubt played a role in the decision. His only recourse would be to go to the doctor and learn where they had gone. Reason came back to him in tiny bits, replacing the rage that threatened to blind him. Perhaps this would work to his advantage. After all, accidents happened all the time. It might prove to be the case with his mother and Cassandra. They could have a carriage accident on the way to or from the spa. Or they could meet with some calamity while his mother took the cure. There were numerous choices to consider.

Sebastian dressed quickly and headed out as soon as he had finished. Wills was working in the stable when he came for his horse. The man seemed to avoid him, but Sebastian knew it was possible he already knew the location of his employer.

"Wills, do you know where my mother is?"

The man looked up from where he was tidying up one of the stalls. "At this moment, I couldn't really say." He looked at Sebastian for a moment. "Would you be wanting your horse saddled?"

"Yes. I need to go out again." Sebastian watched the man. "My mother left a letter saying that the doctor wanted her to go to a spa. You wouldn't know the location of that place, would you?"

Wills shook his head. "No, sir. I've not been informed."

Wills put aside his pitchfork and went to the stall where Sebastian's dark gelding waited. He quickly saddled the horse and led him out, never once offering a comment. Sebastian thought it strange. The man was usually quite talkative. Things were definitely not as they should be.

Sebastian headed to Dr. Riley's office first thing. No matter what else happened, he would have to confirm the location of the facility where his mother had gone. After that, he would visit with Robbie and see what plans seemed best.

Dr. Riley was busy with an elderly woman when Sebastian showed up. There was nothing to do but wait for the man to complete his task. Sebastian sat in the tiny waiting area, thinking of all that the future might hold for him once he squared things away with the will. Robbie had already managed to get a positive reaction from men in Charleston, Baltimore, and several other towns. Now what they really needed was the money.

"Mr. Jameston," Dr. Riley announced from the doorway. "What can I do for you?"

"I had hoped you might tell me where you've sent my mother. I had to be away from the house for a time, and when I returned, she had already left."

The man's expression changed to one of confusion. "I'm not certain I understand."

"My mother told me that you wished for her to regain her health at a spa in New York. I wondered where I might locate that spa, and in turn find my mother."

The doctor shook his head. "I made no arrangements for your mother. She told me that she didn't wish to leave Philadelphia."

Sebastian looked at the man hard. "Do you mean to tell me that she didn't go to the spa as you suggested?"

"That's exactly what I mean. She said she would think on it, but that's as far as things went. Now if you don't mind, I need to return to my patient."

Sebastian nodded. He thought of the letter his mother had left. What could it mean? She had lied to him—that much was evident. But where would she and Cassie have gone if not to the spa?

He climbed atop his horse and considered the matter for a moment. Because of his earlier investigation, he knew where Cassie's mother and sister lived. Perhaps that was the answer to his concerns at the moment. If his mother had gone away with Cassie, then surely Miss Stover's mother would know her daughter's whereabouts. He would simply go there and let her know that something terrible had happened at the house and that he needed to immediately contact his mother.

Smiling, he urged the horse in the direction of Cassie's home. His sense of anticipation began to build. As soon as he learned where the twosome had gone off to, he would set out to take control of the situation once again.

Sebastian urged the gelding into a trot, weaving in and out of traffic as best he could. All of Philadelphia seemed congregated on Market Street as Sebastian made his way north. Most of the people appeared to be the working classes. They weren't all that well dressed but seemed intent on their duties. The wealthy of Philadelphia had departed for the summer to avoid yellow fever, cholera, and other epidemics, but the poorer residents had no choice. They would stay and face the brunt of whatever came their way. Sebastian had spent too much time among their number, recruiting men to work for him, not to know their desperation.

Leaving the frenzy behind him, Sebastian headed down Fourth Street to the east and approached Cassie's neighborhood. He had checked out the residence on another occasion, so he wasn't unfamiliar with the area. However, Sebastian knew that getting information from Cassie's mother might prove difficult. Cassie might have warned her against saying anything to him. Her mother might even be in on the plan to help Cassie steal away his fortune. Perhaps if he could catch her little sister alone, he might be able to learn more. Still, he had no way of knowing whether Elida was ever left to fend for herself.

Just then movement down the street caught his eye. To Sebastian's surprise, he saw Cassie. She was strolling with Mr. Langford as if the entire world belonged to her. She laughed and gazed up at the man with the same look of adoration she'd given him for months.

Sebastian halted his horse and held back. What was she doing there? What was going on? If she hadn't gone away, then that would most likely mean his mother hadn't either. Yet, if Mother hadn't gone elsewhere, then where was she? It didn't make sense, but Sebastian intended to find out the truth of the matter.

You think you can outwit me, Miss Stover, but you do not realize with whom you are dealing.

"Mother is quite delighted that you have proposed. Mrs. Jameston is, as well, but then, she constantly suggested that a proposal would be forthcoming any day now," Cassie said. She looked up at Mark with a smile. "She always said you were a wonderful young man with 'great potential.'"

Mark laughed. "Great potential, eh? Well, I suppose that is yet to be seen." He sobered. "She may think differently about me once everything is said and done with regard to her son."

"I know her heart is broken by the sins he's committed, but she is not one of those mothers to excuse her child's behavior. We had a long talk about it, and while she regrets what might happen to him, she knows he's brought it upon himself. She doesn't blame you or me."

Mark patted her arm as she held on to him. "I'm glad. I would hate for a rift to come between the two of you—especially on my account." They approached the door to Cassie's house, and he paused. "I cannot tell you how happy I am. I never thought to love again. I was certain there could never be another woman to take Ruth's place."

"And there isn't," Cassie said, shaking her head. "I have no desire to take her place. I simply want to take my own place at your side."

He touched her face. "I know, and that is what makes you so special. I cannot imagine any other woman speaking in such a way. Ruth will never come between us. I will not hold you up to her or her to you. It's important that you know I have no expectation of your being the same kind of wife she was."

Cassie laughed and it made him smile. "I should hope not," she said softly, "for I would be sure to disappoint. I'm done with pretense. I can only be Cassandra Stover."

"Langford," he said, gently kissing her nose. "Cassandra Langford."

After supper that evening, Mark had arranged to discuss the situation at hand with all involved. "I have a great deal of information that links Mr. Jameston to the fraudulent insurance claims," he told the women as they found seats in the parlor. "However, I have less proof where the death of Richard is concerned. I would like to have had more, but I'm hopeful that in time, as arrests are made with Jameston's men, perhaps someone will be willing to trade information and proof for a lighter sentence."

"What of his attempt to kill his mother?" Cassie asked. "I saw that firsthand."

"It would hardly be proof enough in court. You saw something in the oatmeal that made you suspicious. You cannot prove it was poison."

"True," Cassie replied, "but his actions suggest it must have been."

"Yes. I understand that, but you wouldn't get far on that as evidence. Even if the doctor testified to the fact that her symptoms were very much in keeping with being poisoned, it wouldn't be enough."

Cassie's face grew red. "I won't allow him to go unpunished. He tried to kill his mother. He killed your friend."

Mark frowned. He knew her frustration. Would he ever be happy just to see Sebastian Jameston behind bars, yet not held responsible for Richard's murder?

Mrs. Jameston patted Cassie's hand. "There, there, my dear. Do not grieve so. The Lord knows the truth, and the truth will win out. Sebastian will not go unpunished." She smiled sadly, and Mark felt as though it might be time to change the subject.

"I know you long to return home. I'd like to find a way to make that happen sooner than later. If we can push through to have Sebastian arrested for the insurance fraud, you will be free to go home."

"I've thought about that. I've thought about you and Cassie as well. Now that you plan to marry, have you given any thought as to where you will live?"

"I suppose we haven't," Mark said, glancing at Cassie. He could see her look of confusion. It was as if the question were only just now dawning on her.

"I know you make your home in Boston," Mrs. Jameston continued, "but I wish to suggest something. I would very much like to invite you both to live with me after you wed. I have an entire floor that can be made over in any way that pleases you. I have a wing of rooms on the same floor as mine that could easily serve you. There are many possibilities."

"That offer is most generous," Mark replied. "I'm sure we would be pleased to consider it. I have to say, though, that the real concern I have will be my employment. I need to keep in mind that the insurance company is located in Boston. If I am to remain with them, I might well have to return there. On the other hand, there may be opportunity to open an office here. And there is always that idea of starting up a new Langford hotel."

He could see that Cassie hadn't even heard his words. She was deep in thought, and he knew she was troubled by the topic. The complication of the matter had never really occurred to him. He only knew that he loved her and wanted to marry her. Where they would live hadn't really seemed an obstacle until just now.

"Well, I am afraid that Elida and I have a full day ahead of us tomorrow," Mrs. Stover announced. "I do hope you will forgive us if we retire. Mark, you mentioned bringing your friend here. I hope you will invite him to join us tomorrow for supper. We can perhaps further discuss your plans."

"The hour is pressing upon me as well," Mrs. Jameston admitted. She got to her feet, as did Mrs. Stover. Mark stood in acknowledgment. "No, do not stand," Mrs. Jameston said, waving him back to his seat.

"And do not feel that you must rush off," Mrs. Stover added. "Stay and visit with Cassie. You have my complete trust."

Her words warmed Mark's heart. He already loved Cassie's mother and sister. It would be easy to be a part of their family. "Thank you. I will remain for a little while."

After they had gone, he retook his seat and looked at Cassie. Her mood hadn't changed. She still looked quite worried about something.

"What's going on inside that pretty head of yours?" he asked.

Cassie looked at him and frowned. "I hadn't thought about where we would live. Mark, I cannot leave Philadelphia. At least not if it means leaving my mother and sister behind. They need me."

He smiled and leaned forward to grasp her hands. "And do you suppose I am such a wretched man that I would suggest such a thing? I know you love them. I know they need you. I would not seek to separate you. In fact, I like the idea of remaining here in Philadelphia. I even mentioned as much to my mother on my last trip to Boston."

"You talked of staying here when you were last in Boston? But that was before . . ." She fell silent and looked away.

"Before you all but proposed marriage at the train station?"

Her eyes snapped up to fix on him. "I wasn't that bold."

"But very nearly. To answer your question, however, yes. I spoke with my mother and told her about our game of pretense and how I wished it might be something more."

"Truly?" Cassie seemed dumbfounded.

"Truly. Did you suppose you were the only one losing your heart?" He got up and came to help her from her chair. "Cassie, I believe that we might very well have had a case of love at first sight. When I saw you there on the ground, passed out from fear of poor Portland . . . well . . . you totally won my heart."

She laughed and let him draw her into his arms. "Did I ever tell you," she asked, gazing deep into his eyes, "that when I first woke up after that hideous attack I thought you were God?"

Mark saw that she was quite serious and began to chuckle. "No, I don't believe you ever mentioned that before now. What convinced you that I wasn't?"

"The hard cobblestone on my backside," Cassie said, then bit her lip.

Mark only laughed all the harder. "Did you not suppose that heaven had hard streets as well?"

"I suppose I didn't," she said, cocking her head to one side. "But I do remember thinking how very dashing God was." She put her arms around his neck and sighed. "But then I realized you weren't God—you were simply His servant, come to rescue me."

"And you seemed like an angel to me—until you regained consciousness, of course."

"Of all the things to say!" She tried to pull away, but Mark would have none of that.

"My sweet Cassie, you are infinitely better than any angel." She relaxed in his arms. "You are so very sweet in nature. So giving and loving. Fear not for your mother and sister. They are my family now as well. I would never allow anything to happen that would jeopardize their happiness. Just as I will never allow anything to jeopardize ours."

CHAPTER 25

Cassie ushered Mark and Mr. Westmoreland into the house the next evening. "I'm glad you could join us." Both men were dressed in dark suits and starched white shirts. Mr. Westmoreland looked rather uncomfortable in such attire, but the fashion seemed exactly perfect for Mark's tall stature.

"We have much to discuss," Mark announced. "We've come up with several ideas that might help us to see Jameston pay for Richard's murder, as well as his attempts on his mother's life. August has given me some additional insight."

Cassie smiled and took their hats. "Perhaps after dinner we can—"

"August? Is that you?" Dora Stover exclaimed as she entered the room.

"Dora." Westmoreland shook his head as if seeing a ghost. "I . . . well . . . I can scarcely believe it's you."

Cassie watched as her mother crossed the room to take hold of the stocky man's hands. She smiled up at him. "I know exactly how you feel. I haven't seen you in over twenty-five years."

"You hardly look a day older," he said in reply.

Her mother seemed to light up in a way that Cassie had not seen since her father had been alive. It was obvious they knew each other from their youth, but also just as obvious that the reunion met with both parties' approval.

"Who is that man?" Elida asked, coming to stand beside her sister.

Their mother turned. "Girls, this is Mr. Westmoreland. We grew up together. We were neighbors and dear friends. How is your sister?" she questioned, turning back to the man.

"She's widowed now. We both are. She lives with me at the boardinghouse I run. I know she'll be pleased to see you again."

"Oh, I shall very much look forward to that."

He glanced around. "So this is your house?"

"Yes," Mother said, smiling. "My husband passed on ten years ago. Elida was just a few weeks old when he was killed in an accident. Since then, we've worked at running a laundry service."

"And I help her," Elida said as she came to stand beside her mother.

"You must be Elida," Mr. Westmoreland said with a wink.

Elida's face broke into a smile. "I am."

"You are just as lovely as your mother," the man said. "She and I were good friends when she wasn't much older than you are now. I thought her the prettiest girl in all of Philadelphia."

Cassie's mother appeared flustered. "I . . . uh . . . supper is nearly on the table. I'm so happy you could join us." She gave the man's hands a squeeze before dropping her hold. "Why don't you all take a seat at the table? Elida, come help get the last of the meal on."

"I'll help you too," Cassie said.

They hurried into the kitchen, where Mother handed a large bowl of potatoes to Elida. "Now put these on the table and then take your seat. Cassie and I will bring the rest."

Cassie waited until Elida was out of earshot before turning to her mother. She could see the sparkle in the woman's eyes. "Care to tell me about our visitor?" she asked.

"I don't know what you mean," her mother replied and offered her a bowl of green beans.

Laughing, Cassie took the offering and pressed again. "There is something between you and Mr. Westmoreland. You both look at each other as if . . . well . . . as if there were something more than merely having been old neighbors."

Her mother laughed and handed her a bowl of stewed okra. "He was my first love. We were passionate about each other. At least as passionate as children can be."

Cassie looked in disbelief at her mother. "I always thought Father was your first love."

"I was just a girl of fourteen when I fell in love with August. He was a few years older, and his father was determined he make something of himself. He sent August away to get a better education. Shortly after that, my family moved. We lost track of each other. I later heard he had married, but nothing more. I thought it was just as well, and when your father came into my life, I completely lost my heart to him."

"And now Mr. Westmoreland is back in your life, and he's a widower." Cassie couldn't help but raise a brow as if silently suggesting the possibilities.

Her mother's face reddened. "Oh, how you do go on. Just because you're hearing love's golden bells doesn't mean anyone else is." She laughed and turned to lift a platter of roast.

Cassie giggled. "You're blushing, Mother. I think there may be more bells ringing than you give credit."

"Oh, go on with you now." But Cassie thought there was something lackluster in her protest. Perhaps she should ask Mark more about this Mr. Westmoreland.

After the meal concluded and they'd all retired to the sitting room, Cassie was further amazed at the way Elida took to Mr. Westmoreland. She watched in delight as the man took a piece of string, tied the ends together, and then began to weave it between his fingers to make various shapes. Elida cheered loudly at the man's creative game.

"Teach me how to do that," she begged.

He only laughed. "If I teach you, then I won't be so interesting anymore."

They all laughed at this. When the clock on the mantel chimed eight, however, Cassie's mother directed Elida to bed. Her sister protested, but gave in when Mark promised to take her horseback riding in a few days.

"I never get to stay up and hear the really interesting things," she said as she moved toward the hallway stairs.

"I promise to tell you anything important that pertains to you," Cassie told her sister.

Elida pressed out her lower lip in a pout. "But that's just the trouble. None of it will pertain to me." The adults chuckled at this, but Elida ignored them. Once she was gone, the conversation turned much more serious in nature.

"August and I have been discussing the situation with Jameston. We figure there is one chance to get a confession from him regarding Richard. It won't be easy, and it involves some risk on your part." He looked at Mrs. Jameston and then to Cassie.

"What do you have in mind?" Mrs. Jameston asked.

"August is retired from the police force here in Philadelphia. He has good friends—honest men who also work for the department. He proposes you and Cassie return to your home. When your son is out of the house, we will come and position some of those men near your room. Since Cassie's room adjoins yours, it would be a reasonable place to listen in without being detected.

"Our hope is that you might coax a confession from Sebastian while witnesses overhear the entire conversation. Anything would help. You could tell him that you'd heard rumors of his being involved in the murder of an insurance investigator. You could say most anything that you think might motivate him to open up about what happened."

"I see." The older woman looked quite thoughtful.

"What about getting him to confess to trying to kill his mother?" Cassie threw out. "If he's angry enough, especially with me, then he might very well blurt out the truth."

"He might. He also might become very dangerous if you stir him to anger," Mark countered.

"He's going to be angry no matter what," his mother said. "I suppose it is the only thing to be done. I could take to my room on the pretense of feeling ill again. Of course, given the subject at hand, I'm certain that won't be too hard to accomplish. If he wants to see me about anything, he will have to come to me. And if he doesn't voluntarily come, I could send for him."

"It seems our best course of action," Mark offered rather apologetically.

Cassie's mother weighed in on the subject. "Must they return to the house? Couldn't this be accomplished somewhere less difficult to offer them protection?"

"The house is a reasonable place, given Mr. Jameston will be more at ease. He won't suspect that we've planted officers to watch his every move," Westmoreland explained.

"But why must Cassie endanger herself?"

Putting her hand atop her mother's, Cassie met her fearful gaze. "If I fail to return with Mrs. Jameston, her son might believe something has happened to scare me away. We must pretend that everything is just as it always has been. He will feel at ease that way, and there will be no question of whether anything is amiss."

"She's right," Mark said. "But I promise you, Mrs. Stover, I will not allow anything bad to happen to our Cassie."

"Nor will I," Westmoreland assured.

And so the plan was settled. On the following day, Cassie and Mrs. Jameston would return home as if they'd only been on a holiday of sorts. It was a risky scheme at best, but Cassie felt better knowing there would be men around whose sole intent was their protection.

"Is everything set?" Sebastian asked Robbie one final time.

The man nodded. "Aye. I have the men ready to move at your instruction."

"Then we'll go tonight. It appears the only way to drive my mother back into my grasp is to force the issue." Sebastian straightened and stretched. The time was fast approaching midnight.

"What if they fail to wake up?" Robbie asked.

Sebastian shook his head. "Make enough noise. Otherwise, if something does happen, we will merely get the documents forged, and with Cassie dead as well as my mother, the courts will have no choice but to award the estate to me."

Robbie leaned back in the chair and seemed to consider the plan for a moment. "What if they escape only to decide to go elsewhere? Your mother is quite capable of leaving the country or just heading to a hotel instead of her home."

"That's true, but I do not believe that will be her choice. I think she'll readily come here, and Miss Stover will be on her heels."

"What of Miss Stover's mother and sister?"

"What of them? If they come along, they will become pawns in my game. Stop worrying about the details, Robbie. I've thought this through."

Knowing that Mark and Mr. Westmoreland would be with her when they returned to the Jameston house didn't help Cassie sleep any better that night. She tossed and turned restlessly, not managing to drift off to sleep until well after midnight.

Even in her sleep, she dreamed of dangerous situations with Sebastian Jameston exacting his revenge. He was not the kind of man who would take well to being bested. There would be no room for error. This, Cassie knew quite well.

She awoke with a start sometime in the night. Something had made a noise downstairs. In fact, it rather sounded like pans being dropped. She strained to listen. The house was now quiet, and even Elida seemed to be in a deep sleep across the room.

"I'm just being silly." Cassie closed her eyes and tried to relax.

She drew a deep breath and folded and unfolded her arms from across her waist, but it did little to help. Cassie tried to pray, knowing that God had a plan in all of this. Still, she worried about whether doing such a thing was putting God to a foolish test.

Thoughts of her mother and Mr. Westmoreland came to mind. She smiled at the memory of her mother's cheerful spirit. She had seemed years younger from the moment Westmoreland entered their house. Could there be a future for them?

"Would I want a future for them?" she murmured aloud. The thought of her mother remarrying had never really entered her mind. It would be strange to have another man in the life of her mother and sister.

"Elida seemed to like him well enough," Cassie mused. "Of course, string tricks performed by a dinner guest are one thing. Instruction and rebuke by a new father are quite another."

She looked at her sleeping sister. Cassie felt sad for the girl. She had no memories of a father's love. Every time a man came into her life, she seemed starved for the affection he offered. Hadn't Cassie seen that with Mark? Elida was always dogging their heels if the opportunity presented itself. She would sit and hang on Mark's every word and drink up the slightest bit of attention he offered.

A father might be exactly what Elida needed. A strong, godly man would make her feel safe and protected. He would do the same for her mother. Mr. Westmoreland at least shared a past with her mother. That familiarity would give them something upon which to build a relationship.

"They both have lost their mates," Cassie reasoned. "They understand marriage and what compromises are required." She laughed at herself and silently chided her thoughts. After all, she'd never been married and the knowledge of such a relationship was truly only something she had witnessed secondhand.

She thought of Mark and what it would be like to be his wife. Could she make him a good wife? Could she compromise when necessary? What if she failed to please him? She wasn't a very good cook. The poor man might well starve to death if they weren't wealthy enough to hire help.

Cassie closed her eyes, willing her mind to calm. Tomorrow would come soon enough, and the issues of the day would press her in every direction. She would need her rest.

It seemed she'd only just dozed off, however, when something woke Cassie again. She yawned and struggled to come completely awake. Getting up, she went to the open window and gazed out. Nothing seemed amiss.

She yawned yet again and made her way back to bed. It was then that she caught the tiniest whiff of smoke. She craned her neck and breathed deeply. As far as she knew, no one had lit a fire in the house. It was much too warm. Of course, Mrs. Jameston was given to chills.

Cassie pulled a shawl around her nightgown. She would go check on the older woman and see if there was a problem. If Mrs. Jameston had started a fire in her hearth, she might have forgotten to open the flue.

Elida moaned and rolled over in bed as Cassie opened the door. Smoke billowed into the room, stinging Cassie's eyes and choking her. Immediately Cassie slammed the door closed. Panic coursed through her. There was a fire in the house!

She quickly woke up her sister. Elida protested the rude awakening and sat up, pushing Cassie back. "What's happening? Why did you shake me?"

"The house is on fire," Cassie said as calmly as she could. "We must get out."

The words caused Elida to immediately jump up from the bed. "Fire? Where's Mama?"

"I must help the others. I have no idea if the stairs are on fire or where exactly the danger is."

"Don't leave me," Elida said, clinging to Cassie's side.

"I won't. Come with me. We'll see if we can find the easiest way out. I'll need to wake up the others. We haven't much time. Pull the sheet from the bed."

Elida did as instructed while Cassie went to the pitcher of water on their nightstand. She doused the material as soon as Elida brought it to her. "We will use this to help against the smoke and . . . flames."

"I'm scared," Elida said, her voice cracking.

"We must be brave. Pray and ask God for strength." Cassie pulled Elida with her and wrapped the wet sheet around them both. "Get down low. The smoke isn't as bad near the floor."

"Are we going to die?"

Cassie felt a surge of protective power come over her. She tightened her grip on Elida. "No. I won't let that happen. Come on!"

CHAPTER 26

Cassie stood across the street with her family and watched as the flames danced high in the night sky. Minute by minute, a lifetime of memories was rendered to ashes and soot.

The fire department battled to see the blaze put out, but there was little hope of saving much. Neighbors had come outside to offer what help they could. Having escaped with only the clothes on their backs, the women had need of nearly everything.

Mrs. Jameston had been taken inside by the Radissons while Cassie's mother accepted a dressing gown from someone and remained outside. Elida clung to her even now, the wet sheet still wrapped around her body. Tears streamed down their faces as the dawn of new day revealed the destruction in full light.

Suspicion raged in Cassie's mind like a maelstrom. It pulled in every rational thought and refused to calm even for a moment. Sebastian Jameston was behind this fire. Cassie was certain of it. Only her anger served to keep her from collapsing into sobs.

Twenty minutes had passed since Cassie had sent a man to notify Mark. She had no doubt that he would arrive as soon as possible. They would need a carriage in order to transport Mrs. Jameston, and she had issued the suggestion that Mark might ride his horse to the Jameston house and awaken Wills in the carriage house. Cassie had never felt so alone.

"Such a terrible ordeal," Mrs. Radisson said, coming to stand behind Cassie. "Here, I thought you could use this." She handed Cassie a man's robe.

"Thank you." The words didn't sound like they were her own. They certainly lacked the emotion that threatened to rage out at any moment.

Cassie pulled on the robe, finding it several sizes larger than her frame. She tied it securely, all while searching the street for some sign of Mark. The entire area seemed alive with people and noise. The activity had brought the entire neighborhood to life much earlier than most mornings. There was a great deal of conversation and speculation about what had happened and why the fire had started, but Cassie held her tongue. The image of Sebastian Jameston haunted her. She would make him pay for this. She would make him pay for taking away her mother's security.

"There's Mr. Langford," Elida called out and pointed down the cobblestone street.

Cassie looked and found Mark pressing through the crowd on Portland. She left her mother's side and went to meet him.

"Cassie! Did everyone get out?" Mark called as he dismounted.

She rushed into his arms and then her own tears could not stop flowing. "Yes, everyone is safe. Oh, Mark. I'm so glad you came."

He held her close, whispering comfort in her ear as she sobbed. "It will be all right. I promise you. I'm here now. It will be all right."

Cassie pulled away. "He did this. I know he did." She had no need to explain. Mark's expression immediately registered understanding.

"Are you certain?"

"What else could have done such a thing?"

"Fires do happen, Cassie. Besides, Jameston had no way of knowing that you were here. Mrs. Jameston's letter would have led him elsewhere."

She shook her head. "It would have led him to Dr. Riley, who would in turn have told him that his mother had refused to go to the spa. It may sound ridiculous, but I know it was him. I feel it. Remember—he once threatened to burn the house down around his mother and me."

Mark's features darkened. "If that's the case, we need to rethink our plans. You certainly can't go back to that house—not so long as he is there."

"He's tried to kill us. He won't stop now. No matter where we go. Mark, we have to trap him now. We cannot allow him to strike again."

"How are your mother and the others?" Mark stroked her cheek, wiping at the wetness there.

"Shaken. Mrs. Jameston is resting inside our neighbor's house. Ada is with her. Elida and Mother are just over there. Mother wouldn't leave the scene. She's watched the fire ever since we escaped."

"August is on his way. He'll be able to offer her some assistance. In the meantime, we need to get you all inside. If Jameston did do this with the intent of killing you, then he now knows that you aren't dead. He wouldn't leave it to chance. He'd have men watching, or he'd be watching himself."

Cassie nodded. "I'm sure you're right. I hadn't thought about it."

Mark led her to where her mother and sister stood. Portland walked behind them and, to Cassie's surprise, gave her a feeling of protection rather than fear.

"The fire is out for the most part," Cassie's mother told them as they rejoined her. "Everything is gone."

"August is on his way with a carriage. He said to tell you that you could come and stay at the boardinghouse. Nancy is preparing rooms for you now."

"Oh, I'm so sorry about this," Cassie said, hugging her mother close. "This is all my fault."

"Nonsense. It's a fire," her mother said, shaking her head.

Cassie looked at Mark. He shook his head as if to warn her from speaking. "Look," he said, "here comes August now."

Cassie turned to find the stout man driving a team of blacks. He maneuvered the carriage through the people who were by now starting to thin out and head back to their own homes. When Westmoreland reached them, he threw on the brake and jumped from the driver's seat in one fluid motion.

"Dora, are you all right?" He went to Cassie's mother and took hold of her shoulders.

Cassie thought her mother looked so small against the man's barrel chest. So small and helpless. Jameston could have killed her, taken her and Elida from Cassie forever. Her mother fell against Mr. Westmoreland in tears.

Cassie clenched her jaw and squeezed her hands into fists. "I want him to pay. If Sebastian Jameston did this, I want him to pay."

Mark took hold of her arm. "He will, Cassie. Believe me."

Mark observed Cassie as she sat across from her mother at Mrs. Jameston's breakfast table. It had been the older woman's idea that they all return to her home. They would act as if nothing had ever been amiss with their hasty retreat from the mansion. They would also mention having stayed at the Stover house and then share details of the horrible fire. If Sebastian thought they would play into his game of fear, Mrs. Jameston declared, he could just think again.

"So you believe as Cassie does—that your son had something to do with the fire?" Dora Stover asked her hostess.

"I do. It's exactly in keeping with his previous threat. I mean to expose him." Her tone made no question of her disgust. She appeared stronger than Mark could ever remember seeing her.

"How do you hope to accomplish that?" Mark asked. He had accompanied the ladies to the mansion, fearing that Sebastian Jameston would be there to harm them. However, upon their arrival, Brumley announced that Mr. Jameston had been gone from the house since the previous afternoon.

"If I know my son, he will make the announcement without much prodding. He's no doubt proud of his accomplishment, and once he hears us talking about it as if it were nothing more than an accident, he will have to set the record straight and take the glory for his work."

Mark nodded. It sounded reasonable, given the type of person Jameston had proven himself to be. "But once he does that, the danger will be greater than ever. You will have to get him to confess to his role in your poisoning and the death of Richard. Westmoreland is on his way even now with his friends. Once they are in place and Sebastian confesses, they will take him into custody. It might prove to be very dangerous, Mrs. Jameston."

"I understand. However, it cannot be more dangerous than what we've already faced. Cassie and her family might have been killed because of me. I intend to put an end to this once and for all."

"I'm glad Elida fell back to sleep," Cassie's mother said, shaking her head. "I would hate for her to hear any of this. She's so upset about losing her beloved dolls."

"She doesn't need to know the details," Cassie assured. "And the dolls can be replaced."

"Oh goodness, yes," Mrs. Jameston declared. "I intend to replace the house and everything in it. It was because of me that the fire was set."

"I cannot let you take that responsibility," Cassie's mother countered.

"Look, all of this can be dealt with at another time," Mark interjected. "The important thing is to get the information needed and resolve this problem once and for all."

"I'd still feel better if Mother and Elida were able to stay elsewhere. Mr. Jameston isn't going to have any compunction about hurting them. He's proven that."

"I agree." Mark took in Cassie's worried face and smiled. "Mr. Westmoreland and I discussed it. We will have them driven back to his boardinghouse. They can stay there with his sister and the other boarders."

"But what about Cassie?" her mother asked. "She'll be in danger as well."

Mark nodded. "She'll be under my watch the entire time. You needn't worry. She will have less to concern herself with if she knows you and Elida are safe."

Cassie squared her shoulders and gave a slight nod. "It's true. I'll be able to completely concentrate on helping Mrs. Jameston."

"Excuse me," Brumley interrupted. "Mr. Westmoreland and his friends have arrived. They are being taken upstairs."

Mark reached out to squeeze Cassie's hand. "And so it begins."

There was scarcely time to get Elida and her mother from the house before Sebastian came waltzing in as though everything were right with the world. He found the ladies in his mother's bedroom. The women had hurried there only moments before, after Miriam had come running in from the garden to announce his return, but they looked for all intents and purposes to have been there for hours.

It did little to comfort Cassie to know that Mark, Mr. Westmoreland, and two of his friends occupied her bedroom. She knew it would be difficult to act as though the house fire were nothing more than an accident. It would be her finest performance to date, if she was able to pull it off.

"So you have returned," Sebastian said, eyeing the women as they sat calmly in front of the hearth.

"Yes," Mrs. Jameston said. "There was a horrible fire, and we found ourselves with little choice."

"A fire? At the spa?" Sebastian asked in mock surprise.

"No. We were with Mrs. Stover. Given the wondrous results from her soup, I wanted to put myself into her care for a few days," Mrs. Jameston replied easily.

"I see. Why did you not notify me? It would have been good to have known where you were."

Mrs. Jameston met her son's icy gaze. "I felt confident that you could find me if needed. You were always very good at such things."

Sebastian leaned casually against the fireplace mantel. "I see. Well, tell me of this fire. Was anyone harmed?"

"No, the good Lord kept us safely in His care. Such accidents are fearful things, however. It made us all very mindful of the frailty of life."

"Accident? How did the fire start?"

Cassie looked away at the ball of yarn she pretended to roll. If she wasn't careful, she would give it all away. She had to be strong. She had to be calm. Drawing a deep breath, she heard Mrs. Jameston reply.

"It's difficult to say. Most likely a candle was carelessly left burning."

A knock came on the bedroom door, and Cassie nearly jumped out of the chair. She looked at Sebastian, then quickly looked away. He laughed.

"You certainly are jumpy." He went to the door and opened it. "Yes, Brumley?" Cassie heard him question. She didn't dare turn around.

"Mr. McLaughlin has arrived. He says it's urgent you join him immediately."

Sebastian muttered something, then left without another word. Cassie leaned back in the chair, feeling as though she could barely draw breath. Much more of this intrigue and she'd pass out cold. The women sat in silence for several minutes before Cassie got to her feet.

"I'm going to my room for a moment."

But before she could leave, Ada appeared at Mrs. Jameston's door. She entered quickly and crossed to where the women were. "Mr. Brumley said to tell you that Mr. Jameston has left the house. He mentioned his intention to be back by supper."

Mark came in from Cassie's room. It was evident he'd heard everything. "Did he say where he was going?"

"No," Ada replied. "He seemed in a hurry, but otherwise there was no mention of where he was off to."

Mark nodded. "I suppose there is nothing to be done about it. We will simply have to wait him out."

Cassie hated the idea of facing Sebastian again. Mark seemed to understand. He came to her and took hold of her shoulders.

"You did just fine. I know it was hard."

"I'm not entirely sure I can sit through that again. It took all of my self-control not to attack him. When I think of what could have happened . . . what did happen . . . My father built that house for my mother—it was all she had left of him."

"No. That's not true. She has you and Elida. You're both safe, and that means far more. Ask her, and see if I'm not speaking the truth."

Cassie felt her shoulders slump forward. "I know you're right, but I cannot help the feelings I have."

"Give it time, my darling." He leaned forward and kissed her forehead. "So many times in my life, I have felt overwhelmed by my own anger. Anger that God would allow my wife to die and leave me behind. Anger that God would allow a monster to kill my best friend. Such ire serves no purpose, however. The anger will merely burn inside until it destroys the good things and leaves ashes and bitterness in its place. Just as the fire destroyed your home, anger will destroy your heart. And I couldn't bear for that to happen."

His words were comforting, but also difficult to hear. Cassie knew the importance of letting her anger go—of letting God control her heart—but it was so hard.

"I love you, Cassie. Think on that rather than the hatred and ugliness of Sebastian Jameston." Mark smiled and pulled her close. "Think of the future—not the past."

CHAPTER 27

Sebastian looked at the bruised and bloodied man now crumpled on the floor. The sight of the man groveling there on the ground, pleading for his life, gave Sebastian a kind of exhilarated energy.

"If you enjoy this pain as much as I do," Sebastian said in a snide, assured tone, "then, by all means, continue to avoid giving me the truth."

"I . . . agh . . ." The man moaned and rolled away from Sebastian as if to guard from further attack.

"Stand him up," Jameston ordered.

Robbie and another man quickly lifted the victim. He sagged between them, apparently lifeless, but Sebastian knew there was a great deal of life left in the man. Life that he could squeeze out a little at a time until the wretch confessed everything he knew.

"I want to know who you work for, and why."

The man's head rolled from side to side in exhausted defiance. Sebastian had to admire his strength. But his admiration went only so far. "Get the pliers."

"No!" the man half moaned, half screamed.

"Then give me the name."

The man remained silent for another few moments and finally nodded. "Westmoreland. He hired me to help in an investigation."

"What investigation?" Sebastian narrowed his eyes. "Tell me now." He forced the man's head back so that he had no choice but to look at him—if the swollen and bloody eyes were able to see anything at all.

"He's helping another man . . . with the missing cargoes . . . and the death . . . of his friend."

"What is the man's name?" His informant was losing consciousness so Sebastian put his hands around the man's throat and shook him. "Tell me his name!"

"Langford. Marcus Langford."

Sebastian dropped his hold as if the man had suddenly grown red-hot. Langford? Miss Stover's Mr. Langford? He growled out a string of expletives, wondering just how much of his operation had been jeopardized.

"How could I have missed it?" He turned to walk away then stopped and looked back over his shoulder. "Kill him. Let it be a lesson to any other traitor in our midst."

Ada had just arrived in Mrs. Jameston's bedroom with afternoon tea when Sebastian returned to the house. "Your son is back," she whispered. "Mr. Westmoreland is here as well. He barely made it up the servants' stairs ahead of me." She knew the other two police officers and Mark were in place behind the adjoining bedroom door.

"Then hopefully this affair can be concluded," Mrs. Jameston said. "You'd best run along now, Ada. I do not want you in harm's way." The maid started to say something, then thought better of it and hurried from the room.

Cassie poured a cup for herself and for Mrs. Jameston, and tried to bolster her courage. She could hear Jameston booming out orders to Brumley—something about Robbie returning by supper and to see that he was included.

They had purposefully left Mrs. Jameston's door open to the hall in order to better hear when her son came home, but Cassie seriously doubted that it was necessary. The man seemed quite satisfied to yell at the top of his lungs.

"I hope this will be over soon," Cassie said, taking her seat. She looked at the small table between them and noted that Ada had included some cookies. "Would you care for something to eat?"

Mrs. Jameston shook her head. "No. I'm just as anxious as you are. I'm afraid food would only serve to further upset my already-roiling digestion."

Cassie nodded. She could hear pounding footsteps on the stairs and knew that Sebastian was on his way. Looking to Mrs. Jameston, who appeared far calmer than she suggested, Cassie took a deep breath. "Oh, Father . . . help us."

"So you are still holed up here. An entire mansion is yours to roam at will, and yet you sit here," Jameston said as he entered the room without as much as a knock. "What a very dull life you lead."

"We had quite enough excitement last night," his mother replied. "Will you join us for tea?"

"No." He turned his icy eyes on Cassie. "I've come for something much more important. We need to discuss several matters, including your last will and testament, Mother."

Mrs. Jameston looked up with a blank expression. "Whyever would we need to do that? I've already seen my lawyer, and he assures me that everything is in order."

"Yes, well, I might have agreed with him, prior to your recent changes to give my fortune away."

Mrs. Jameston pointed at a chair in the corner. "Oh, do sit down. I refuse to discuss anything with you towering over me in such a rude fashion."

Sebastian grimaced and seemed to weigh the matter momentarily. He pulled some papers from his pocket and slapped them down on the table beside the tea tray. "I have no need for a chair. I've merely come to see you sign these papers. Miss Stover can stand as witness."

"And what papers are these?" Mrs. Jameston asked, not bothering to even glance at them.

"I've had your will rewritten." He looked at her as if daring her to challenge him. When she said nothing, he continued. "You were quite heartless to reject me in such a fashion. Especially when you added insult to injury by making Miss Stover your beneficiary." He smiled. "Or did you think I wouldn't find out about that?"

"I did not concern myself with it one way or the other," his mother admitted. She took a long sip of her tea. "I hardly believe it to be your business."

"It *is* my business. My father built that fortune with the intention that it would one day fall to me."

"He also assumed that you would be an upstanding citizen who would put the needs of others before your own. Your father had a great many dreams where you were concerned, and you disappointed him in every one."

Sebastian's jaw clenched, and his face went rather pale. Cassie felt a growing unease. It was clear the man was enraged, and while she knew that goading him into confessions was a necessary evil, she feared the outcome. What if Mark couldn't get to them quickly enough? What if Jameston had plans that none of them could counter?

Mrs. Jameston put her cup and saucer aside. "Sebastian, you were such a joy to me at one time. I am sorry that I wasn't a better mother to you. I blame myself for overindulging your whims, but I blame you for not only refusing to do what was right but also yielding yourself over to evil."

He laughed. "And what is that supposed to mean?"

"You tried to kill me. To poison me," his mother said flatly.

Cassie forced herself not to react. She kept her focus on the tea in her cup and prayed that her rapid breathing wouldn't betray her desperate fear. She waited for what seemed like an eternity for Sebastian to reply.

When he finally spoke, he acted as though he were discussing nothing more heavy-hearted than the weather. "Yes, well, it was necessary. You simply have outlived your usefulness."

Cassie's eyes shot up at this. She met Sebastian's cool expression and shook her head. "You are a complete monster. How could you speak in such a manner? She has loved you more dearly than life."

"Then she'll have no regret in giving it up. After all, if she loves me as you say, then she'll desire that I be happy."

"And killing your mother is the only way you can be happy?" Cassie slammed her cup and saucer onto the table. "You are without any conscience whatsoever."

"What good would a conscience do me?" He came to her side, and Cassie couldn't help but shudder as he reached out and touched her cheek. She jerked away, but to her surprise he grabbed her and buried his hands deep in her hair. Forcing her head back to meet his eyes, he grinned in a leering fashion. "A conscience would not allow me the plans I have for you. And I do have plans for you, my sweet Cassie. Plans that start with a better understanding of who your fiancé is and why he is threatening my livelihood."

Cassie stiffened. How could he know about Mark? She tried to twist away.

"Enough of this nonsense. Unhand her, Sebastian," his mother ordered.

Sebastian looked at the older woman but never loosened his hold on Cassie. "You are hardly in a position to order me around. You have slipped around together, conspiring against me. You sought out your lawyer to change your will, then hid away so you wouldn't have to face me with what you'd done."

"The only reason I left my home was for fear of my life," his mother replied.

"Yes, well that proved to be a rather poor decision. Didn't it?" He stared hard at her for a moment, then returned his attention to Cassie. "Pity about your mother's house."

She narrowed her eyes. "It wasn't an accident, was it?"

He laughed heartily and released her with a shove. Cassie fell back against the chair, but immediately righted herself. She needed him to confess. She had to get him to admit what he had done.

"Why did you set fire to our home?" Cassie demanded to know.

"Well, I suppose the answer is quite simple. I needed my mother here where I could better control the situation."

"But you could have killed us all. My mother and sister," Cassie began. "They have never done anything to you, yet you would have seen them burned alive."

"Or dead," he said snidely. "I really didn't care and cannot pretend that I did. That would simply be cruel."

"Everything you do is cruel," Cassie countered. She started to get up from her chair, but he pushed her back.

"Stay where you are. Until my mother signs these papers, neither of you is going anywhere."

"I will not sign," his mother said softly. She looked at him with such an expression of disappointment that Cassie felt overwhelming sorrow for the woman. He was her only remaining child, and he had so completely rejected her love that he now stood ready to end her life.

"Do you honestly think to defy me? You could not bear to refuse me when I was a child—what foolishness causes you to think you could do so now?"

"When you were a child . . . oh, I had such hopes." Mrs. Jameston closed her eyes. "I loved you so dearly. Your father did as well. We delighted in you—in your brilliance and loving nature." She opened her eyes and looked to Cassie. "He wasn't always like this. You must understand."

"I do," Cassie whispered. She was unable to imagine Sebastian Jameston in the same way that his mother remembered him, but she wanted to encourage the older woman.

"Reminiscing isn't going to help you." Sebastian took up the papers and thrust them into his mother's hands. "Read this and sign it. Better yet, just sign it."

Mrs. Jameston glanced at the papers in her hands before looking back up at her son. "No. You may kill me as you have planned all along, but I will not aid your cause by yielding this to you."

Without warning, Jameston grabbed Cassie by the hair once again. This time he pulled her to her feet. "Sign it or you both die. Cassie will go first, however, and you will have to watch her suffer." He pulled a gun from his pocket. "It's horrible to watch someone die a little bit at a time."

"No!" Mrs. Jameston cried. "Let her go."

Cassie clutched at her skirt to keep from fighting Sebastian in her own strength. She prayed the men might storm the room and take him captive, but supposed they delayed for fear of the risk to her life. She tried to think of what she should do—what she could do to benefit herself. She forced herself to remain calm.

He still hasn't confessed to killing Mark's friend, she thought rather irrationally. *He's mentioned Mark's interference, but nothing more. I have to get him to confess.* As if such a thing mattered at this moment. She very nearly laughed out loud at her own foolish thinking. Here Sebastian was about to kill them both, and she was worried about justice for Mark.

"If the money is all that you want, I will go to the bank with you at this moment and get it for you," his mother said in a pleading tone. "You needn't involve or blame Cassie for what I've done. She is quite innocent."

"She's hardly that, Mother." He pressed his lips to her cheek. "She doesn't even smell innocent. She smells like fear." His eyes widened in excitement as he pulled away just enough for Cassie to see his face. "I like having you afraid. I like it very much."

His comment angered Cassie in a way she couldn't begin to explain. She fought against him, but he only pulled her closer and tightened his grip.

"Besides, Cassie and I need to have another talk—one that doesn't involve you, Mother. Cassie needs to explain to me about her Mr. Langford. Apparently, he has been investigating my business affairs."

"Let her go, Sebastian, and I will accompany you to the bank. I will turn everything over to you." Mrs. Jameston fixed a stern gaze on her son. "You have caused enough harm—enough death and destruction. Let us resolve this in a manner that doesn't require bloodshed."

He seemed to consider her suggestion for a moment. Cassie could see that for just a minute, the idea held merit for him. Then just as quickly the moment passed. "I happen to like bloodshed. Sign the papers, and I will have what I want anyway. You cannot win, Mother. I have bested you, as I always have."

CHAPTER 28

Mark moved in the direction of the door, but Westmoreland reached out to stop him. He pulled Mark back across the room, then whispered against his ear, "He hasn't yet confessed to killing your friend."

At that moment, Mark didn't care. He could now see how his selfish desire to exact revenge on Richard's behalf had only served to endanger Cassie.

"He'll kill her."

"I know it looks grim, but if you charge into the room, he'll kill her for certain."

Mark put his hands to his head and rubbed his temples. "Maybe we can distract him. Have someone go to the hallway entrance and knock. Maybe that will cause him to rethink the situation and give us a little time. It doesn't matter anymore if he confesses to Richard's death—not if it means losing Cassie."

One of the officers near the adjoining door motioned the men to return. Mark pushed past Westmoreland and went as quietly as he could to where the man crouched down beside the barely open portal. The man touched his ear, then pointed to Mrs. Jameston's room. Mark strained to hear. Cassie was speaking. She sounded frightened but resolved.

"Bullying women around is hardly a difficult task. Especially with a gun." Her words took on a sarcastic tone. "I suppose you need a weapon to make yourself feel more like a man."

"Miss Stover, you seem not to care a great deal for your life."

"And why should I? God has my life in His hands."

"Hardly. I would say God is absent at the moment. I'm the one with the gun," Sebastian replied with cold indifference. "Now do as I say, Mother, and sign the papers. I want to end this now. Cassie and I still have much to discuss."

"I have nothing to say to you," she countered.

"You will. I intend to hear what plots and plans your Mr. Langford has in mind for me. Apparently, you two have been playing quite a game at my expense."

"Hardly. I came here to care for your mother. You weren't even in residence when I arrived. You showed up with that silly story about getting shot by accident, when we all knew you were wounded on purpose. You're the one truly playing games."

"Why, you . . ."

Mark heard Cassie give a yelp of pain but couldn't see what was going on. He reached for the door handle, but the man beside him interceded.

"Tell me what you know," Sebastian demanded. His voice raised in volume. "Tell me now."

"Why don't you tell me?" Cassie suggested. "You seem so confident that I have some intimate knowledge of your actions."

"Could it really be that you don't know?" Jameston questioned in disbelief. Mark desperately wished he could see into the room to know exactly what was happening. "Your Mr. Langford is not all that he appears to be. He is here on purposes other than panting after your skirts."

Cassie laughed, and it completely took Mark off guard. What was she doing? Didn't she realize how easily provoked Jameston could be? He would be far less rational if she pushed him too far.

"I would venture to say that, with the exception of your mother, none of us here is exactly what we appear to be. Especially you."

"And what is that supposed to mean?"

"I think you've played everyone here false. I don't believe you are an investor or a businessman. I believe," Cassie said boldly, "that you are nothing more than a common gambler. You lost your money in a bet—probably got yourself shot the same way."

"The man who shot me lies dead now. Perhaps you would care to join him? I used this very gun. It would be rather ironic, don't you think, for two of Mr. Langford's friends to die in the same manner, by the same hand?"

"You killed one of Mark's friends?" Cassie asked, sounding shocked. "I don't believe you."

For a long moment, there was only silence. Mark straightened and glanced at Westmoreland, who was whispering to one of the police officers. They were up to something, but Mark was hesitant to leave his post. This was the quickest means to Cassie, and if need be, he would sacrifice himself for her. He would draw Jameston's attention away from Cassie and do whatever was necessary to save her.

Cassie looked hard at Sebastian. He seemed to be wrestling with his thoughts, almost as if her comment caused him some kind of dilemma.

"Perhaps you are as innocent as you seem," Sebastian began finally. "It really doesn't matter. But your Mr. Langford isn't without guilt. Perhaps he's been using you to get to me, but it isn't important at this point. I'll deal with him in time—just as I dealt with his friend."

"What do you mean?" Cassie asked, allowing fear to edge her words.

"I mean that I'll kill him when the opportunity presents itself."

"Just as you killed his friend?" Cassie asked.

Sebastian laughed. "Exactly. And just as I plan to eliminate you . . . unless, of course, you change your mind about cooperating with me."

"But why kill him? Mark has done nothing to you." Cassie hoped that the confession he had already given was enough. Sebastian hadn't provided any names, however. "And who is this friend you speak of? Mark is from Boston—he had no friends here in Philadelphia."

"Your Mr. Langford and his friend Mr. Adkins both worked for an insurance company that meant to see me destroyed. I've dealt with Mr. Adkins by putting a bullet in his heart. And after I finish here, I will deal with Mr. Langford." Sebastian turned away from Cassie. "Mother, sign the papers. Sign them now."

Cassie could see the resignation on Mrs. Jameston's face. The older woman got to her feet. "I will sign them, but first you will hear me out, because what I have to say is very important."

Jameston shrugged. "Say what you will, but be quick about it. I've wasted enough time on explanations."

Cassie knew that so long as Sebastian had a gun trained on her, Mark and the others would be hesitant to come into the room. She had to do something. She glanced down, noting the table. The hot pot of tea sat there—the handle very nearly close enough to touch.

"I am sorry," Mrs. Jameston began, "that you felt my love for you was somewhat conditional. I suppose it is hard for a child to understand a parent's sorrow in losing their offspring. When Plymouth drowned, it brought back all the pain of losing Bristol as well. It was a dark period in my life, and you were so very young."

"I was old enough," Sebastian replied. "Old enough to know that I didn't matter as much to you as they did. I was packed off so you could console yourself. I was given to the care of Silas and his wife, while you and Father shared your grief. Even as the years went by and you included me more—it was a relationship always based on sorrow."

His mother looked at him oddly. "I suppose it was. I suppose it was yet another thing I did wrong by you and cannot take back. As you grew older, I always knew there was a great deal of anger and hostility in your heart, but I never fully understood until now. I tried to spoil you and pamper you—give you everything possible—but it was never enough."

Sebastian laughed harshly. "You still fail to understand. Just sign the papers and let's put an end to this."

Cassie knew the time had come to act. She reached her hand slowly around the handle of the teapot and grasped it tightly. The pot was still hot and would serve her purpose quite nicely. When Sebastian shifted the gun from one hand to another, she drew a deep breath and brought the china up, smashing it hard against the man's face. Hot tea splashed out on her hand, burning her skin, but Cassie didn't care. She felt the pot shatter into pieces even as Sebastian screamed in pain.

Behind her, she heard the door burst open, but she couldn't turn away from Jameston's contorted face. She had caused his pain, and it mattered little that he would have caused her that much and more had he the opportunity. He would have killed her, there was no doubting that. Still, it didn't console her.

Cassie went to Mrs. Jameston as Mark and Westmoreland aided the two police officers in restraining Sebastian. Tears coursed down the weathered old face as she watched her son.

Putting her arm around the older woman, Cassie tried to offer what comfort she could. "I'm so very sorry. Why don't you sit over here and rest?"

Mrs. Jameston allowed Cassie to lead her to the bed. Sitting on the edge of the mattress, the woman watched as the officers dragged her son into the hall.

"You'll all pay for this," Sebastian cried out. "I have friends, and they'll see you pay."

Cassie shook her head and sat down beside Mrs. Jameston. "Don't listen to him. He cannot hurt you anymore."

The older woman met Cassie's gaze. "He will always hurt me, so long as he allows evil to rule over him. I cannot stop caring about him. I cannot stop loving him, and because of that I will never stop hurting for him—with him."

"Of course not" came a male voice.

Cassie looked up to find Mark standing only a few feet away. He had heard Mrs. Jameston's confession and now looked at the woman with great compassion.

"Are you both all right?"

"As well as we can be," Cassie replied. "We are uninjured."

Ada appeared just then. "Oh, Mrs. Jameston, I was so worried."

"I believe I would like to lie down for a time," the older woman told her.

"I'll see to it," Ada told Cassie. "You go ahead." She nodded toward Mark.

Cassie got to her feet. "I won't be far if you need me."

"You deserve to rest as well, my dear," Mrs. Jameston said. "You saved my life—probably more than once. I am in your debt."

Cassie touched the woman's cheek. "No. You are in my heart, just as I know I am in yours. We have become family."

Mark gently touched Cassie's arm as she turned. The love he held for her was evident in his expression, but it seemed mingled with something else. Oddly enough, it seemed like regret.

He led her downstairs, and without asking, Cassie knew he was taking her to the garden. They walked to the privacy of the settee and chairs, neither one speaking a word. She liked the feel of his hand on the small of her back as Mark directed her to sit. Reaching up, she took hold of his hand and smiled.

"Sit here with me." She waited until he sat beside her on the settee before releasing him. "Tell me what is troubling you."

Mark looked at her rather puzzled. "I'm surprised you can even ask such a thing—after all that's just happened."

"But it's over with now. Sebastian confessed to your friend's killing, as well as to trying to poison his mother and burning down my home. He will no doubt be sufficiently punished."

"You could have been killed. I was so foolish to ever suggest this game," Mark said, shaking his head. "I was blinded by my desires for revenge and justice. I knew there were dangers, but I didn't account for Jameston's irrational behavior. I expected him, for some reason, to conduct himself in a civil manner. It was foolish, I know. After all, the man had tried to poison his mother. He'd shot my friend. Why would he not threaten to kill you as well?"

Cassie patted his arm. "It's over now."

"But so much could have gone wrong." He looked at her with tears in his eyes. "You could have died right in front of me, and all because you were trying to help me."

She smiled. "But I didn't die. Mark, you must account for the good as well as the bad. We are safe. Mrs. Jameston is resting upstairs, and Sebastian has been taken away where he can do no further harm. The game is over, and we have won the hand."

Mark nodded and pulled her into his arms. "And we will never play again."

She shook her head. "No. No more games for us."

CHAPTER 29

The cooling temperatures of late September put everyone in a better spirit. Mrs. Jameston's full health had returned, although she told Cassie her age caused her to tire more easily. Cassie couldn't help but think it had much to do with all that the older woman had been through as well. Sebastian now awaited trial, and from the sounds of it, things did not look to bode well for him in any aspect.

Due to the work Mark and Mr. Westmoreland had accomplished, most of Sebastian's men, including Robbie, had also been taken into custody and now faced their own comeuppance.

"I suppose I shall never fully understand what causes a person to go bad," Mrs. Jameston said, gazing out across the garden. "Even knowing how angry he was at me, I cannot hope to know what makes a man take the life of another."

"Greed seems to be at the root of this plot," Cassie said, hoping she'd not spoken out of line.

"All of this might have been his one day," Mrs. Jameston said, "but apparently, even that was not enough. Then when I saw what he'd become—when I heard the hatred in his voice—well, it was more than I could bear. All I ever wanted for him was a good life and to know God's plan. Despite my efforts, I believe Sebastian hates God more than he hates me."

"You cannot force a person to love God."

Mrs. Jameston considered this for a moment. "You are right about that. My Worther and I raised Sebastian to fear the Lord, but apparently he decided this was unimportant. I wish I could go back in time and do things differently."

"But perhaps if that were the case, we'd only make new mistakes and suffer other kinds of sorrow," Cassie offered. "I think we're probably better off putting our focus and efforts forward."

"I'm sure you're right." She sighed. "I must fight against the regret that would see me defeated. I cannot change what has happened, but it needn't separate me from a happy future." Mrs. Jameston motioned. "I see your mother has returned from her walk."

Cassie smiled as her mother crossed the garden lawn to join them for tea. Dora Stover looked years younger, despite having lost her home and all of her belongings. A certain August Westmoreland no doubt had much to do with the joyful expression.

"What a beautiful day," Cassie's mother declared. "The heavy heat of summer is behind us, and autumn promises to be quite lovely. The leaves are already changing, and they're oh so colorful."

"Cassie and I were just mentioning the other day that we might like to travel during the summer next year."

"What fun that would be," her mother said, nodding.

Cassie didn't want to talk about trips or the summer to come. She wanted very much to know more about her family's future. "So while the men and Elida are still off riding in the park, come tell us what's been happening between you and Mr. Westmoreland," Cassie said, patting the settee seat beside her.

Mrs. Jameston smiled. "Would you care for tea, Dora?"

"Yes, please," Cassie's mother replied as she took a seat beside her daughter. "I have great news to share. At least, I hope you will believe it to be great news." She looked at Cassie as if searching her face for some sign.

"Well, tell us," Cassie urged as Mrs. Jameston poured tea. "Has this news to do with your new home?" For the last week, Mrs. Jameston had talked about little except the house she wanted to have built for Cassie's mother and sister.

"In a sense, it does relate to where I will live." Her mother blushed and took the tea. "August has asked me to marry him."

"Marry him?" Cassie's surprise was evident in her voice. "But you've only just renewed your friendship."

Her mother sobered. "I know this must seem shocking, but you have to understand. We know each other's past, and have now caught up on most of the time spent apart. We care very much for each other."

"But does he love you?"

Her mother smiled. "Yes. I believe he does."

Cassie shifted uncomfortably as she tried to get used to the idea of August Westmoreland becoming her stepfather. "And do you love him?"

Her mother laughed lightly. "I've always loved him. Just as I will always love your father."

"You seem very happy, Dora," Mrs. Jameston said between sips of tea. "When will you wed? I would love to have you marry here in the garden."

Cassie's mother put her cup and saucer aside and reached for her daughter's hand. "We plan to have a simple ceremony at the boardinghouse. But first, I wanted to make sure that Cassie didn't object."

"I could hardly object to something that has made you so happy," Cassie replied, knowing that she would do anything to see her mother able to rest and enjoy life.

Just then the men returned with Elida. Cassie could hear her sister babbling on and on and laughing.

"Does Elida know?" Cassie asked softly.

Her sister came bounding across the yard, running in a most unladylike manner. "I simply love to ride horses!" she declared.

Cassie's mother laughed. "Why don't you ask her?"

Elida came to where Cassie sat, Mark and Mr. Westmoreland following. The men were deep in conversation, and Cassie couldn't help but look at Westmoreland as if seeing him for the first time. This man was about to become a part of her family. How strange it seemed!

"Oh, I simply had the best time. I'm completely overjoyed." Elida plopped into the seat beside Mrs. Jameston and smoothed out her riding habit. The ladies laughed at her enthusiasm.

Mark chuckled as well. "Your daughters are becoming quite the horsewomen."

"Thanks to you," Cassie's mother said with a smile.

"So what were you ladies so deep in discussion about when we arrived?" Mr. Westmoreland questioned. "You looked quite serious."

Cassie looked away, rather embarrassed, while her mother answered. "Cassie was just asking how Elida felt about our marrying."

Westmoreland let out a roar of laughter. "Did you tell her it was Elida who proposed?"

Cassie looked at her little sister and shook her head. "You proposed marriage for Mama and Mr. Westmoreland?"

Elida nodded, looking pleased with herself. "I decided it was time Mama found someone to love her. After all, you had plans to marry Mark. It seemed only fair that if we were to lose you, we might gain someone else."

Mrs. Jameston reached over to pat Elida's leg. "A wise thought indeed. But I hope you will remember that you always have me. I intend to be here for your wedding as well."

Elida frowned. "Well, Daniel Radisson did ask me, but I told him we were too young and that I had too much to do before I settled down. Besides, he never takes a bath and smells like old boots."

Cassie nearly choked on her tea at this.

"Those Stover women definitely know how to speak their minds," Mark said with a wink at Cassie.

"Well, for your information," Cassie began, pretending to be deeply offended, "I have learned to keep my mouth shut."

"I can hardly believe that," Mark countered.

Cassie got to her feet. "I can well prove it. Had I not learned to remain silent on many matters of interest, I might well have told you how unhappy I am that we have not already arranged our wedding day."

Mark ribbed Westmoreland. "See what I told you? Pushy women. Always instigating things."

"I . . . I . . . beg your pardon!" Cassie sputtered.

"Why, the first time I met her, she threw herself at me," Mark teased.

Cassie saw the amusement in his expression and countered his game. "He tried to kill me with that beast of an animal he calls Portland. I didn't throw myself at him. I fell to the ground in fear of my life."

Mark pulled her into his arms, laughing. "She pretended to faint."

"I did no such thing!" Cassie tried to wiggle out of his hold, but Mark held her fast. "Your abominable beast attacked me, and you merely pretended not to notice. Then you forced me to meet the unruly monster and then—"

She was silenced as Mark kissed her boldly in front of everyone. Cassie could scarcely think as he pulled away, smiling.

"And then?" he asked softly.

Cassie put her arms around his neck and sighed. "And then I fell hopelessly in love with you, but you only wanted to pretend."

"I'm not pretending anymore," he said, kissing her again.

The others laughed, causing Cassie and Mark to turn and face their audience. Westmoreland came to slap Mark on the shoulder.

"It seems you have found at least one way to silence these bold Stover women."

Cassie looked at the man and shook her head. "And you are to become my new father. I can see we are in for quite a time of it, Mother."

"So long as you love each other," Elida piped up, "the rest will work itself out. Mama told me that long ago."

Cassie met her mother's happy gaze and nodded. "And Mama was right." She nestled her head against Mark's shoulder. "The rest will work itself out just fine."

More Historical Adventures from Tracie Peterson

Follow Mia, Catherine, and Cassie as they defy the social norms of 1800s Philadelphia, taking unusual careers for the time. But as each woman finds herself in over her head, she risks losing her family's goodwill, her true love, and even her life.

LADIES OF LIBERTY by Tracie Peterson

A Lady of High Regard, A Lady of Hidden Intent, A Lady of Secret Devotion

Weaving together romance, faith, and history, the HEIRS OF MONTANA series follows Dianne and Cole Selby as they try to survive life, loss, and love in an unforgiving land. The rich, rugged landscape of the 1860s prairie frontier presents a dangerous beauty that only the boldest can tame.

HEIRS OF MONTANA by Tracie Peterson

Land of My Heart, The Coming Storm, To Dream Anew, The Hope Within

From Tracie Peterson and Judith Miller

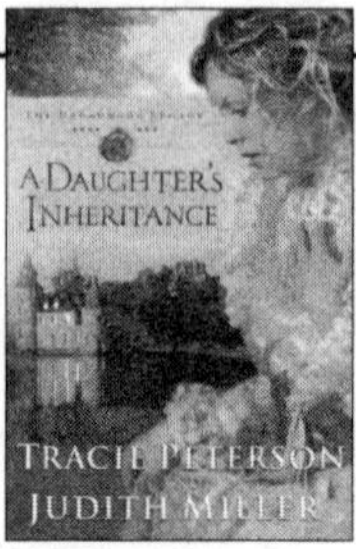

A sudden, large inheritance leaves seventeen-year-old Fanny Broadmoor surrounded by opulence, wealth…and hidden motives. And her secret love only complicates matters. In a society where money equals power, whom does she dare trust?

***A Daughter's Inheritance* by Tracie Peterson and Judith Miller**

THE BROADMOOR LEGACY #1